alis

alis

NAOMI RICH

VIKING

VIKING
Published by Penguin Group
Penguin Group (USA) Inc., 345 Hudson Street, New York, New York 10014, U.S.A.
Penguin Group (Canada), 90 Eglinton Avenue East, Suite 700, Toronto, Ontario, Canada M4P 2Y3
(a division of Pearson Penguin Canada Inc.)
Penguin Books Ltd, 80 Strand, London WC2R 0RL, England
Penguin Ireland, 25 St Stephen's Green, Dublin 2, Ireland (a division of Penguin Books Ltd)
Penguin Group (Australia), 250 Camberwell Road, Camberwell, Victoria 3124, Australia
(a division of Pearson Australia Group Pty Ltd)
Penguin Books India Pvt Ltd, 11 Community Centre, Panchsheel Park, New Delhi – 110 017, India
Penguin Group (NZ), 67 Apollo Drive, Rosedale, North Shore 0632, New Zealand
(a division of Pearson New Zealand Ltd)
Penguin Books (South Africa) (Pty) Ltd, 24 Sturdee Avenue, Rosebank, Johannesburg 2196, South Africa

Penguin Books Ltd, Registered Offices: 80 Strand, London WC2R 0RL, England

First published in the U.S.A. by Viking, a member of Penguin Group (USA) Inc., 2009

1 3 5 7 9 10 8 6 4 2

LIBRARY OF CONGRESS CATALOGING-IN-PUBLICATION DATA
Rich, Naomi.
Alis / by Naomi Rich.
p. cm.
Summary: Raised within the strict religious confines of the Community of the Book,
Alis flees from an arranged marriage to the much older Minister of her town and
her life takes a series of unexpected twists before she returns to accept her fate.
ISBN 978-0-670-01125-4 (hardcover)
[1. Arranged marriage—Fiction. 2. Runaways—Fiction. 3. Religion—Fiction.
4. Assertiveness (Psychology)—Fiction.] I. Title.
PZ7.R376Al 2009
[Fic]—dc22
2008023234

Printed in U.S.A.
Set in Minion
Book design by Sam Kim

For Eric

alis

I

Alis stood nervously in the doorway. She wondered why she was wanted. Her parents had been much troubled of late, and several times she had caught her father gazing at her unhappily. She did not think she had done anything wrong, but it was easy enough to sin without knowing it, and the Minister was there with her parents.

Of course, Minister Galin came very often to discuss Community matters with her mother, who was the Senior Elder of their Community, but these days Alis tried to be busy elsewhere. More than once, lately, he had suggested that it was time Alis behaved more soberly, or hinted that she was too much inclined to question, when she should simply obey.

The shutters were closed against the winter afternoon. An oil lamp, burning steadily on the table, cast shadows on whitewashed walls and struck gleams from the polished wood of the bookcase where the precious volumes were kept. A small fire struggled in the hearth. In black lettering above the door lintel ran the words *Praised be the Maker who created us all and in whom we trust.*

Her parents sat at opposite ends of the bare table, her mother's face pale above the gray of her dress. The Minister, in his usual dark coat and breeches, was standing with his back to the window, beyond which, Alis knew, snow was falling.

"Sit down, Alis."

It was the Minister who spoke. Puzzled, she saw her mother's eyes close briefly as if in distress. She sat down on one of the hard wooden chairs. The Minister was examining her, as if seeing her for the first time. He had a pale, rather melancholy face with dark eyes.

"You will be fifteen soon, will you not?" His dry voice gave nothing away.

"In five months, Minister Galin, at the start of summer."

He nodded slowly. Was he going to rebuke her for giggling with Elzbet when they were taking their turn to clean the prayer house? She knew he had heard, for she had seen him watching them. Perhaps it would be as well to ask his pardon.

"Minister Galin, if I did wrong by laughing yesterday . . ."

He frowned, puzzled. "Yesterday?" Then his expression cleared. "Oh, no." He smiled his wintry smile. "It is not a sin to laugh, even in the prayer house." The smile faded and he hesitated. "Alis, your parents have something to tell you that concerns us both."

Alis looked at her mother, but to her amazement she saw that Hannah had turned toward her husband, as if he were the one who must speak. He cleared his throat twice and then said huskily, "Well, Alis?"

In the silence, Alis became aware that her father, a master carpenter, was not dressed for work: he had on the clothes of stiff, dark material he wore only when there had been a death, as was the custom among them. Forgetting that in front of Minister Galin it was better not to speak until spoken to, Alis said, "Has someone died? Is it Aunt—?"

Her father interrupted her hurriedly. "No, no, child. No one has died. This is something . . . quite different." He gave his wife an anguished look and went on. "Minister Galin has done us . . . has done you . . . a great honor."

Alis stiffened. Surely her parents would not send her to work as a servant in the Minister's house. That was for other girls. She could read and write better than anyone: she wanted to be a powerful woman in the Community like her mother, not a drudge whom the Minister could punish at will and whose life would be one long round of dreary duties.

"Are you sending me to serve him, Mother?" she asked fearfully. But once more, though Hannah usually took the lead in matters of importance, it was Alis's father who spoke.

"No, daughter, no indeed. We would not want you to be a servant." Again he hesitated. "My dear, you are to be . . . a wife."

A *wife*? In horror she stared at the Minister. A *wife*? *His* wife! She turned first to her mother, then to her father. Her mother's expression was stony; her father looked away. They had agreed!

Minister Galin departed awkwardly, leaving Alis to her parents.

"But he is old!" she cried, aghast. "I cannot marry him."

"It is not for you to say what you will and will not do," Hannah said stiffly. "A child's part is to obey."

"But you always said there would be plenty of time. And when Master Zachary would have married Kezia to her cousin and she did not wish it, the Elders forbade it."

Her mother frowned. "That was different. The boy was not ready for marriage."

As always, her mother had an answer. Though she would usually listen, it was rarely of any use to argue if she had decided a thing. Desperately Alis said, "I do not understand. Why does Minister Galin want me for a wife? I am nothing to him."

"You will understand when you are older." Her mother's face was tense. "It is the will of the Maker."

"But it is frowned on—when the man is so much older. I have heard you say so. How can it be the Maker's will?" She knew it was not wise to persist but she was sick with panic.

Hannah's expression darkened. "Be silent, Alis. You know nothing."

But Alis would not yield. Never before had she defied her mother in this way. Her voice rose. "It is because I know nothing that I will *not* be silent. How is it that I am to be married against my will and against my understanding? It is my right to know."

Hannah was tight-lipped but she had herself in check. "You are a daughter of the Book. It is your right to be ruled. It is your right to obey. That is all."

Desperately Alis turned to her father. "Tell me it is not so. You cannot wish it, even if my mother does."

He looked at her with his gentle eyes, shaking his head sorrowfully at her.

"Now, Alis, we are all bound to submit to the Maker's will, as you know. And you must not blame your mother. She does what she must, not what she wishes."

Alis switched her gaze to her mother's face. For a moment, she thought she saw there a look of utter despair, but in an instant it was gone and Hannah's expression was stony again.

"Mother," she said pleadingly, "you are the Senior Elder. The Minister will surely listen to you, if you tell him that you have changed your mind."

Hannah said quietly, "But I have not changed my mind. Nor will I. No, Alis! Listen"—for Alis had opened her mouth to protest—"it is hard for you to understand, I know. You are very young, and you think that we are to please ourselves in this life. But it is the Maker we must please—as the Book tells us—and sometimes his ways are dark to us. You must be patient. Now come to me like a good child and tell me that you repent of your willfulness."

The gentler tone might have tempted Alis, but this was no ordinary matter. She could not say she was sorry and be forgiven, as if she had merely forgotten to feed the hens.

Holding back tears of fright, she said furiously, "But I am not a good child. I am not a child at all if I am to marry the Minister. He is old enough to be *your* husband."

Hannah went very still, and in the silence Alis could hear her own heart thudding. For a long moment, nothing happened. At last her mother said harshly, "You are a willful, disobedient girl. Now go to your bed. And pray to the Maker to give you a more humble spirit, lest you be flung into darkness at the last."

◈　◈　◈

In her tiny room under the eaves, Alis lay sleepless, full of terror. Who could she turn to if her own mother was against her? She could not marry the Minister! How could her mother think it? He was not a boy, to be thought of as a husband in a few years' time. He was the Minister whom she must fear and obey.

She had been taught to read the Book in times of trouble, but its rules and commandments were no use to her now. Where was she to find help in this most terrible affliction? In her mind's eye she saw the settlement: a circle of houses round the green, all dominated by the stone prayer house; dirt-track lanes with cottages scattered along them. And beyond, the farms and orchards. The houses would all be dark at this time, shuttered against the winter cold while their occupants slept. She had friends among the girls—Betsy the weaver's daughter, Susannah whose father was the cobbler, and Elzbet of course, the dearest of them all. But what could Elzbet do?

The marriage was not to be announced yet, to give her time to become accustomed to the idea, her mother had said: the summer would be soon enough. Alis longed to believe that something would happen before then to save her: her parents would relent; the Minister would say that it was a mistake. But she knew it would not be so: such a decision had not been taken lightly. Her feelings counted for nothing.

Between bouts of nightmares, into which she would fall as suddenly as she might slip on wet stones, Alis struggled to see a way out. Her brother Joel might have helped her perhaps, but he had run away seven years ago—to the city, it was thought. They never spoke of him.

She remembered him—sun-browned and bright-eyed, his fair hair cropped as was the custom. Long ago he had teased her and played with her, and she had loved him. Could she, somehow, escape from Freeborne and find him again?

When Alis rose the next morning, her mind was made up: she would seek her brother. However fearful the journey, it could not be worse than marrying the Minister. She had heard that the city was a terrible place. Adults frowned when they spoke of it. The nearer Communities traded with the city dwellers but hers was too far away for direct contact—weeks and weeks away, even if she went by wagon on the main highway, which she would surely not be able to do. Well, she did not care! She would get there somehow. The decision gave her hope and calmed the terror that had engulfed her the night before. In the meantime she knew she must not give any hint of her intention. Her mother must think that she repented of her rebelliousness, or a watch would be kept on her. She might even be locked up if it was thought she meant to run away. Miserably she realized she could not even tell her closest friend. Elzbet would never deliberately betray a secret, but she would find it impossible to behave as usual and pretend that she knew nothing. She hated lying, too, and turned scarlet when questioned even if she had nothing to hide. If Alis did get away, Elzbet would surely be interrogated.

When she went down the stairs and into the kitchen, Hannah looked at her and said in a kindly tone, "Alis, I am going to tend to Master Joseph this morning, for he is near ninety and he does not manage at all now that his wife is gone. But this once, you may remain at home, for you have had a shock I know, and I am sorry for it."

It was rare that Hannah gave her a choice: such tasks had to be done, and that was all. Alis said quietly, "He is too heavy for you to move on your own. You know the bed linens will need changing, and he must be washed, too. I will come and help you."

Hannah smiled at her daughter and said gently, "That would be good, Alis, and what I would prefer. Thank you."

With an effort, Alis smiled back.

So it went on. She attended prayer meetings, performed her house-hold tasks, and helped her mother in tending the sick and frail. Only now, when she read a portion of the Book, as she was bound to do every day, she avoided the sections where the rules for living were laid down, and returned to the stories of the first days when the Maker created men and women out of the dust, and gave them the world for their dwelling place.

For three months she waited, behaving so dutifully that even her mother was fooled. It was hard, for she did not dare speak openly to anyone. Elzbet, guessing that something terrible had happened, could not understand why Alis would not confide in her, and retreated baffled and hurt. So Alis had to bear her lot alone, but at last her patience was rewarded.

Mistress Leah's young husband had disappeared, leaving her with three small children, and her sister, Mistress Sarah, had come to Free-borne to visit her. Unlike Leah, with her lustrous, dark hair and vivid coloring, Sarah was fair-haired and pale, with huge blue eyes that seemed always on the verge of spilling tears. As the time approached for her return home, she fell ill, though the Healers could find no bodily cause for her decline. Hannah sent Alis to keep her company, and it seemed to raise her spirits a little.

Sitting wrapped in her shawl in the rocking chair by the hearth, Sarah looked anxiously at Alis out of swimming eyes. "How I wish that I might stay longer. It does me so much good to be here, and you have been a kind companion to me, Alis. But it is of no use to wish, for here is a letter from my husband in which he urges me to return. And it was sent more than two weeks ago."

"Can you not remain a little longer, and write to tell him that you will do so?" Alis asked.

Sarah clutched her hands together and swallowed convulsively. "Oh, no. I could not do that. He would be . . . he wishes me to come home. He says so quite plainly."

"Shall you not be glad to be at home again?" Alis asked curiously.

"Oh, yes indeed. It is only that . . . that I was ill before I came and . . . I do not feel quite well again. Of course, it is nothing, I know. But I . . . miss my sister so much, and now I must part with you, too."

Alis clasped her hands in her lap to conceal their sudden trembling. Very carefully she said, "It is a pity that I cannot accompany you, Mistress Sarah. I should so like to see Two Rivers; I have never visited another Community."

Sarah stared at her, a faint red mounting in her pale cheeks.

"But, oh, it would be wonderful if you could. Do you think your parents would permit it?"

"They might think that I imposed on you, Mistress Sarah. They would not wish me to do that."

Watching Sarah ponder this, Alis bit her lip, dreading to see her give up in despair.

"If I were to invite you—"

Too quickly Alis said, "That would be a kindness indeed, Mistress Sarah. You are very good."

But Sarah's face had fallen. "No, that will not do, for I must write first to my husband, and there is not time."

Alis's dismay must have shown in her face, for Sarah said unhappily, "There, now I have disappointed you. But I do not see how it can be managed. Oh dear, how difficult everything is."

The tears began to roll down her cheeks.

Unable to comfort Sarah, Alis went home in low spirits. She did not see how she was ever to get away from Freeborne. She could not simply leave—she had never been farther than her uncle's farm. If she merely set out on the road, she would be pursued and brought back again.

But Leah knew how to manage the matter. She sent for the Healers, and by the next day Sarah was provided with a letter stating that it would be well for Mistress Sarah's health if she had Alis as her companion on the journey home. Hannah gave her consent and after hearing Alis's account, said to her, "Do you truly wish to stay awhile with Mistress Sarah, Alis? You will have to curb your tongue and do as you are bid without contention there, for you will find Two Rivers a very different place from Freeborne."

Alis concealed her eagerness as best she could. "I should like to go,

Mother, if you will permit it. It is a chance that may not come again before I am married, and then, most likely, such an absence will not be possible."

Hannah gave her daughter a searching look and Alis met her gaze steadily. At length her mother said, "Well, you are a good girl and shall have your wish. You will find it a stern place, but that is to be welcomed, for it will make you grateful that your home is here in Freeborne. I will write a letter also."

And so it was arranged.

2

The wagon that took Alis and Sarah southward was a lumbering thing and not the most comfortable for a two-week journey, but Alis did not care. As it rocked past the outlying farmhouses and toward the Two Rivers Community, her heart beat faster. Here she was, many miles away from Minister Galin, many miles nearer the city. Perhaps the Maker was on her side after all.

They were entering a cobbled square surrounded by stone houses. At its center was a high wooden platform and surmounting it, a tall post. Alis wondered what it was but Sarah had sunk into silence as they neared their destination, huddling against the cushions as if she would disappear into them. It was useless to question her.

The wagon swayed to a halt outside the prayer house—a larger building than the rest, with the great circle of the Maker carved into the stone above the doorway, as in Freeborne. The wagon driver jumped down and came round to help them. Timidly Alis reached out a hand to her companion.

"I think we are arrived, Mistress Sarah."

Sarah nodded. She was pale, but she smiled tremulously and took the proffered hand.

The sunlight in the square fell upon gray stone and weathered wood. There were few people about—a couple of women in dark gowns and shawls, a man carrying a length of wood, a long-legged boy swinging a mason's hammer from his right hand. No one took any notice of them. Alis shivered a little in the chill wind. With their bundles at their feet, she and her companion said good-bye to the driver, who heaved himself up onto his seat again and clicked his tongue at the patient horses. The wagon creaked away, leaving silence behind.

Sarah seemed at a loss, so after a moment Alis said carefully, "What must we do now, Mistress Sarah? Will someone meet us perhaps or ..."

She broke off, for coming across the square toward them was a man. He was dressed in black, his dark hair cut very short. Sarah gasped and stiffened. As he came up to them, Alis saw that he was smiling to himself as if at some private joke. It was not a pleasant smile.

"Well, Wife"—the tone was light, almost friendly—"so you have come back to me at last. I almost thought you were gone forever." He took Sarah's hand and she winced.

"No, of course not. How foolish of you, Thomas. Where would I ... I mean ... marriage is a sacred state, is it not?"

"Where would you go indeed, my dear? Not to your sister's certainly, from where I should surely come to fetch you and bring you back to your *sacred* duty as a wife."

He had released Sarah's hand, and the flesh was white where he had gripped it. He was still smiling, his eyebrows raised mockingly. He was a handsome man to be sure, Alis thought, but not one it would be wise to cross. Now he was turning to her.

"And who is this? I did not know that we were to have a visitor. I have made no preparation."

Sarah began to stammer a reply, but he waved her aside.

"Your young companion can account for herself, I doubt not. If she is from your sister's Community, she will be more used to speech than silence. The women there are as free as the men with their words, I hear."

The challenge was unmistakable, but Alis was on her guard. She must do nothing to offend here or she might be sent home and lose her chance of reaching the city. So she said in her most submissive tone, "My name is Alis, Master Thomas. I am the daughter of Mistress Hannah and Master Reuben. My mother is the Senior Elder of our Community, and Minister Galin is my pastor. I have a letter for you from my mother, who hopes that I might stay here awhile and keep Mistress Sarah company, if you will give your permission."

He raised his eyebrows again but said in a milder tone, "A well-taught girl. You have good manners. Well, I daresay we can find a bed for you, and it will be a change to have a female about the place who is not always ailing and weeping."

He threw his wife a contemptuous glance and began to collect the heaviest of the bundles.

The house was narrow and tall, squeezed into a corner of the square. Inside, there was a long, dark passageway to the kitchen and a cramped staircase leading to the upper floors. Thomas summoned a servant girl, a scrawny rag of a creature with lank brown hair and a sallow, bitter face. Without a word she took the first bundle and disappeared up the stairs. Thomas motioned his wife and Alis to follow her.

On the first floor there were two rooms—one for study and prayer, and a place for dining. Above were two bedchambers, and still higher, an attic room. The door to this opened to reveal a dark space under the steeply sloping roof, with two narrow beds and a washstand. Here, Alis understood, she was to sleep, sharing the space with the servant girl, Lilith. Judging by her expression, Lilith was not pleased at this, but she said nothing and disappeared, leaving Alis alone to unpack her clothes.

In the study below, Master Thomas had seated himself at the table with his arms folded. When Alis appeared at the doorway, wondering what she should do, he beckoned her in.

"Come in, girl. My wife, I am sure, would welcome your presence. It will dilute for her the effects of my own."

Sarah was sitting in the rocking chair by the empty fireplace. There were traces of tears on her cheeks and she was twisting her fingers nervously.

"I do not wish to intrude, Master Thomas." Alis spoke carefully. It would not do to appear other than dutiful with this man but neither did she intend to show fear of him.

"There is nothing here to intrude on. My wife is unable to tell me what she has been doing these four months, though surely she must have found something worthy of report among her sister's people. Perhaps you can enlighten me."

Alis wondered what he wanted to know. Surely news of Leah's children and the daily gossip could be of no interest to him.

"What is it you would like to hear of, Master Thomas? I will certainly tell you what I can."

He smiled his grim smile and nodded to his wife. "You see, my dear, it is simple. Merely a matter of opening your mouth without bursting into tears. Even this child can do it."

Sarah stifled a sob and made to get up out of her seat. At once he was on his feet and standing over her.

"Stay where you are! Do you think I will tolerate your retreating to bed this first evening, after an absence of four months? Besides, we have a guest." And seating himself again, he turned once more to Alis.

"You may tell me first about my wife's sister. A fine woman, if a little overeager to be bedded. Does she thrive? Is there word of that idiot boy, her husband?"

"There is no news that I know of, Master Thomas. I do not think Leah expects to hear from him again."

"You mean *Mistress* Leah, do you not?" His voice was icy and Alis realized that she had already made a mistake.

"Yes indeed, Mistress Leah, of course. I beg your pardon, Master Thomas. My mother . . . sometimes speaks of her by name only and . . ."

He seemed satisfied. "Continue."

Treading carefully, Alis told him what she could of Leah and the children. He wanted to know whether the little ones were well governed, and she hesitated. The boy, Peter, was full of mischief, always up to something—tumbling out of trees and falling into streams; pestering the older boys to take him fishing, then getting in the way and spoiling their sport.

Instinct told her that Thomas would disapprove of all this so she merely said, "The children are lively but good at heart, and very loving to their mother." Then she turned quickly to other subjects— the farmer Ahab's accident and the fire at an outlying grain store. She could not see why these things should interest him but he listened attentively. When she paused, at a loss for further tales to tell, he said, "And what about your good Minister? Is he not married yet? The Great Council has said that all Ministers must marry."

Alis felt herself flushing and hoped he would not notice, but she said as calmly as she could, "He is not married yet, Master Thomas. And if it is to be, there is no word of it that I have heard, but I am not yet fifteen and not like to hear of such great doings until they are announced to everyone."

"You say your mother is the senior Elder. You must hear a good deal unless she is more discreet than most of her sex."

Alis bit back a sharp reply. He meant to provoke her, and she would not give him that satisfaction.

"My mother does not speak of such matters before me, Master Thomas, I assure you."

Even as she spoke, she felt herself reddening again. Who knew better than she about Minister Galin's marriage? She was to be his wife, was she not? And perhaps he would turn out to be like this man who sat before her with his jeering look, while his wife stifled her sobs in the corner. But she would not marry Galin. By the

Maker's good grace she had escaped this far. Surely she would make it to the city.

She hoped her blushing would not prompt Thomas to question her further on the subject of marriage; she was not used to lying. Fortunately, he was turning his attention to more immediate matters.

"Go, Sarah, and see that Lilith is preparing the supper. It is time that we should eat, and I am sure that Alis has an appetite after so long a journey, even if you are too sickly to swallow so much as a mouthful."

As his wife scuttled from the room, grateful to escape her husband's presence for a few minutes, Alis wondered why he spoke so harshly to Sarah. To be sure, her feebleness could be very provoking. If only she would not cry so often and so much! Surely if she showed a little more spirit, her husband might be less inclined to crush her?

Sarah, however, seemed more crushed than ever over the meal. She barely spoke and only picked at her food, so that Thomas complained of the waste. Lilith served them in silence, scowling when her master spoke to her sharply for some carelessness.

When the eating was done and the prayer of thanks to the Maker spoken, Thomas dismissed his wife to bed. As Alis moved to follow her out of the room, however, he said in a tone more courteous than she would have thought possible, "Pray you, Alis, sit up with me a little while if you are not too weary after your journey. There is more I would hear of your Community and its doings."

In the doorway Sarah turned her head at his words and made as if to speak, giving him a frightened look, but a glance at her husband's face silenced her, and she disappeared, leaving Alis alone with him.

He asked her first about her own occupations. Did she assist her mother in the Community? Did she read the Book every day? What other learning did she have? Did she wish to be an Elder like her mother? This she thought unwise to admit, but she saw no harm in telling him of her hope that she might be one day be a midwife, helping to bring young ones into the world. His lips curled in what might have been a smile.

"And has a husband been proposed to you that you have set your heart on this? You must be a married woman to be a midwife, must you not?"

Once more Alis felt herself flush. "No husband has yet been suggested, Master Thomas, although I know that my parents are beginning to give it thought." Her heart beat with anger at the memory of how much thought they had given it and where it had led.

He was watching her closely. "Perhaps you have ideas of your own on the subject? There is some young man of your Community who has won you with kindness and soft words."

She shook her head, wishing he would change the subject, but it clearly interested him.

"You are content for your parents to choose for you? You wish to have no say in the matter?"

"I have not given it much thought. My mother"—she broke off, momentarily choked with rage at the lie she must tell—"my mother says that there is plenty of time and that she will not hurry me."

Her mother had indeed said that . . . once. She would never, never forgive her.

Thomas was not done with the subject yet. How she wished he would let her go to bed.

"You are fourteen, I think you said."

"Yes, Master Thomas. I will be fifteen in two months."

"And you would like to have children of your own?"

"I think so, in good time. Do not all women wish it when they are married?"

"If they are worthy daughters of the Book they do. Not all women are so."

She wondered if he was talking of his own wife. There was no sign of children in the house. Abruptly changing the subject he said, "Your Minister has a name for mildness among the Communities. They say he would rather pity sin than punish it. Is it true?"

She was startled by this. Minister Galin had always seemed to her a strict man: insistent on the rules, sparing of praise, and not much given to smiling. She would not have called him mild.

"He is . . ."

She did not know what to say. How could she talk naturally about the man from whom she had fled? She must answer Thomas's questions, but it was like putting her finger in fire to speak of Galin. With an effort she said, "The people say he is hard but just. And with us . . . the young ones, I mean . . . he always seems to know when we have done wrong, as if he can see us even when we think we are hidden."

As she spoke she shuddered, wondering if indeed Galin knew what she was about, and would send after her to bring her home before she could make her escape.

"You do not like him?" Thomas spoke softly.

She looked at him. Was he trying to trap her so that he could rebuke her for her lack of respect? Nervously she said, "He is my pastor. I am under his judgment. It is not for me . . ."

He laughed at this and his laugh, like his smile, was not a pleasant one.

"Well, Alis, I thank you for your company, but it grows late and you are in need of your bed, I doubt not. We will converse more on these matters, if you will do me that kindness."

She smiled her agreement, flinching inwardly from the mockery of his tone. If she would do him that kindness! What choice did she have?

In the tiny attic chamber, Lilith was already snoring. Alis put out the candle Thomas had given her—no doubt he would be displeased if she wasted it—but sleep did not come for many hours.

3

Two Rivers was a good deal larger than Freeborne, and Alis soon found that her mother had been right about it. The Minister was a gentle old man, and his wife, Mistress Elizabeth, welcomed Alis warmly when Thomas introduced her. For the most part, however, the people seemed to have forgotten how to smile. They scurried about their business, looking anxiously over their shoulders and avoiding each other's eyes. At every prayer meeting, some shame-faced man or woman was singled out for public rebuke and obliged to declare penitence for sins that in Freeborne would have been dealt with privately. She remembered Minister Galin saying it was no sin to laugh, but here no one seemed to laugh. Even the children were like little adults, stiff and nervous in their tidy clothes.

The household was gloomy, too. Sarah's misery hung in the air, infecting everything. She would hardly talk to Alis, and when she did venture a remark she seemed terrified that her husband would hear her and disapprove. She had few visitors, and those who did come were quickly defeated by her unresponsiveness. She and Alis spent their time in sewing, in silent reading of the Book, and in such of the domestic work as was not done by Lilith, who rebuffed all Alis's attempts to be friendly. She had managed to avoid offending Thomas, who made a point of talking to her, but she saw that this was intended to distress his wife and knew he was not to be trusted. Not only was it a wearisome life, but Alis could not see that she was any nearer to finding her way to the city and her brother. If anything, she was worse off. How was she to get away from Two Rivers where she had less freedom than was allowed her at home?

One morning, she had gone to the kitchen to fetch the crock of butter that Lilith had forgotten to put on the table. As she reentered the dining room, she heard Sarah say, "Please, Thomas, I beg you. Do not make me watch. I cannot bear it."

Her voice was low and desperate. Thomas's face was red with anger.

"You must watch. This punishment is not one man's will; it is ordained by the whole Community in the persons of the Elders. The whole Community must bear witness."

"But everyone else will be there. No one will miss me. They look only for you."

"You are a fool, Sarah, or worse, a liar. You know very well that to stay away is to show dissent. I cannot have it said that my wife does not support my view, when you know with what difficulty we have established a wholesome discipline in these matters."

The early-spring sunlight fell on Sarah's pale features as she sat before her uneaten breakfast. Behind her, on the wall, was a piece of tapestry showing the great circle of the Maker embroidered in two intertwining threads, red and green. Within the circle were two figures, a male and a female, one in each color. A marriage gift no doubt, stitched in love and hope by Sarah's mother or Thomas's. It was a common practice.

In the cool early-morning light Sarah's skin seemed transparent, the veins blue under the surface, and the bones of cheek and jaw painfully prominent. She had grown even thinner in the weeks since her return home. It was not that she did not eat—sometimes, at least—for Thomas would not stand for that. But once, passing the privy, Alis had heard her retching and coughing. Sometimes, too, there was the sour smell of vomit. This morning she had not touched her food.

"I know, Thomas, how hard you have worked and that . . . that the man Samuel deserves his punishment, but can you not say I am ill? I was not brought up to this severity as you were. I am not used to it."

Thomas's fingers whitened around the tankard he was holding. "And you are not likely to become used to it if I allow you to hide yourself at home, instead of making you do your duty like a good wife of the Book."

Sarah's eyes filled with tears. "Please, Thomas. It will be of no credit to you if I faint. Better that you should say that I am sick. Indeed, it would be no lie, for I do not feel well at all."

Thomas's expression grew darker still.

"Sick! People will think that you would have the man excused and left to his filthy ways. No matter that he corrupts our young and defies our discipline. They will think that you have returned from your sister's to preach the doctrine of Master Galin and his kind."

Alis had been sitting quietly, hoping that Thomas's anger would not be turned on her for her presence at this disagreement. At the mention of her pastor's name she looked up, startled. The venom in Thomas's voice was unmistakable.

Sarah's tears were spilling over now and Thomas looked thunderous. An idea came to Alis. "Master Thomas . . ."

The room went still. He turned to look at her and her heart beat with sudden terror. What had she done? His face was a stone mask. When he spoke, his lips scarcely moved and the low voice hissed between them. "Do you dare to interrupt? A daughter of mine would taste the whip for less."

Sarah gasped and cried out, "Thomas, no! Have a care."

For a long moment he held Alis in his stare. She could not wrench her gaze from his face. At last his expression changed, the familiar sneer lifting his lip.

"You need have no fear, my dear Alis. I have no authority to punish you. What was it you wished to say?"

She was trembling. "Forgive me, Master Thomas. I should not have spoken."

"Answer my question, if you please."

She could think of nothing to tell him but the truth, though surely it would serve only to reignite his wrath. "I . . . I wondered if . . . if I might accompany you?"

She did not dare complete what she had intended to say. What folly it seemed now. He was looking at her still, as if he knew she had not said all. When she did not continue he said, "You are offering to come with us? To support my wife in her distress at seeing a sinner punished as he deserves?"

Alis nodded, hoping he would not press her further. She had intended to offer herself in Sarah's place. How could she have been so presumptuous?

"Or perhaps"—he spoke softly—"you were thinking of yourself as her substitute." It was not a question. He knew.

There was a long silence. Sarah was watching her husband with a scared expression on her face. At length he said coldly his wife, "I will say that you are sick. Let them think you are with child again."

Sarah flinched and two patches of red stood out on her pale cheeks. "Do not be so hard on me, Thomas. It is not my fault that our babes do not live. I long to be a mother. It is my dearest wish."

He stood up suddenly, pushing back his chair so violently that it clattered to the floor.

"Not your fault? *Not your fault?* My children wither in your womb and you say that it is not your fault! What sin have you committed that the Maker punishes you thus?"

Sarah was on her feet now, crying out in a wild voice, "Why should it not be *your* sin? Why must it be mine? You are cruel, Thomas, cruel and unjust."

At once he was standing over her, his fingers in her hair, wrenching her head back so that her eyes bulged and she choked. He was hissing again.

"My sin! Mine? The children are conceived, are they not? It is in *your* belly that they shrivel and die. And you dare to accuse *me!*"

He let her go so suddenly that she almost fell.

"Get out! Take to your bed! Be grateful that I do not insist on your presence at my side today. But know this. The time will come, and soon, when such disobedience will not be endured, when a man's authority in his own house will be absolute, and then you will not be able to trust to such indulgence."

Clutching at her throat, her hair coming loose from its pins, Sarah stumbled from the room.

Alis sat motionless with horror. Thomas was still standing, white-faced with fury, his fists clenching and unclenching at his sides. At last he seated himself again at the table and looked at her.

When he spoke, it was in a voice held steady by effort. "I must join the others. If you will accompany me, fetch your shawl."

Submissively, for she could hardly refuse now, she said, "I will, Master Thomas."

Clouds had already hidden the sun as they crossed the empty square to the prayer house where the Elders were to gather. The air felt cold. The wooden platform with its great post dominated the scene. Alis had no need, now, to ask what it was for. Around the sides of the square, the shuttered houses were silent. The people had been told to remain indoors until the prayer-house bell was rung, and no one, it seemed, was inclined to disobey.

Leaving Alis in the vestibule of the prayer house to wait for him, Thomas disappeared within. In ones and twos the Elders arrived. There were some women among them but not, Alis noticed, nearly as many as in her own Community. It had come as a shock to her to find that Thomas was an Elder. Surely the people here knew how he treated his wife. Sarah's tearful disposition was no longer a mystery; Alis was afraid of him herself, especially when she thought of what he might do if he knew she planned to defy her parents and Minister to run away to the city. And yet he hated Galin. For a moment she longed to be back at home with her mother and father, before that dreadful day when her world had changed forever, before she had lost faith in her parents' love for her. The tears rose in her eyes, but she wiped them away hurriedly. It was no good wishing for the past. She must face the future as well as she could. The world was a harder place than she had known, and she must harden herself to deal with it.

The Elders were emerging now through the double doors from the meeting hall into the vestibule. Among them was the Minister—an old man, tall but a little bent, with a mild face and white hair thin on top and long behind. It was a style Alis had not seen among the other men, most of whom wore their hair short like Thomas or even cropped. He was looking at her with his rather faded blue eyes.

"Thomas"—the voice had lost its firmness as old men's sometimes do—"surely it is not needful for your young guest to be here today."

Thomas, a little behind him, raised his eyebrows at this but he said courteously enough, "Alis herself offered her presence in place of my wife who is sick."

The Minister looked distressed. "Ah, my dear Thomas, the women do not like this business. They do not like it at all. And neither do I, if truth be told. I wish we might do things in the old way. My wife refuses to be there. She calls it barbarism. Your Sarah thinks the same, I daresay."

Alis held her breath as Thomas's lips tightened ominously, but he only said, "My wife is of my view in all things, Minister, but as I say she is much sick of late. And you know that we have debated these matters and are agreed that the man must be punished. He denies the Maker. He has tried to spread his poison among our young. And the half-witted woman who became his servant is with child by him."

"As to that, Thomas"—the old man looked keenly at him—"whether the child is his or not, he would have married the woman if you had not angered him with your sermonizing, that is certain."

Thomas opened his mouth to speak again, but suddenly the great bell began to ring, and the Elders moved in a group into the square to take up positions beside the platform. From the houses around the square, and from the streets and lanes leading to it, the people came, some speaking in low voices, some grimly silent. Soon the whole Community was assembled, from the bent and aged leaning on sticks to children as young as eight. Because she was with Thomas, Alis found herself right at the front.

Suddenly the murmur of the crowd ceased. From the north corner of the square, four black-clad men approached, enclosing as they walked, a fifth figure in something white. The people parted to let them through. As they came closer, Alis could see that the prisoner's hands were behind his back, tied presumably, and that two of his captors held him firmly by the arms. He was a large man with golden-reddish hair that hung down in tangles. A blue-eyed man, not handsome with his large fleshy nose and pouchy cheeks, but appealing. Alis thought his was a face made for laughter, though he was not laughing now. He was unshaven, too. He had on a pair of corduroy farm breeches and a loose white smock. Among the black-clothed, crop-haired men of the Community he looked wild. He passed so close to Alis that she could have touched him; she smelled the heat of his body and knew he was afraid.

A set of steps had been placed against the side of the platform, and he was pushed up them until he was standing above the crowd with his attendants at his side. One of them stepped forward, thin-faced and stiff—the Senior Elder. The silence deepened. When he spoke, his voice in the cold air was like a fingernail scraping glass.

"Good people of this Community, you know why you are here today. To bear witness to the proper punishment of one who has denied his Maker and corrupted your young. One who fornicates and would have spread his foul ways among the innocent."

Here the prisoner made a movement as if he would have protested, but the man on his left jerked him by the arm and he subsided. The voice began again.

"Punishment is ordained as follows:

"*For fornication with a servant woman: ten strokes of the lash.*

"*For publicly declaring, in the presence of young people, that fornication is not against the will of the Maker: ten strokes of the lash.*

"*For denying the Maker, in public, and in defiance of admonition: twenty-five strokes of the lash.*"

As they registered the total, there was a shocked murmur from the crowd. Alis felt her head spin. How could she watch this? Surely the man would die. Why had she not stayed with Sarah instead of putting herself forward so foolishly?

Now the two captors who had been holding the prisoner were untying his hands and pulling him over to the whipping post, turning him round so that he had his back to the crowd. One of them ripped open the white smock and tore it away so that the skin of his back was exposed. Then they bound him to the post. When it was done, they all descended, leaving him there alone.

For a long moment nothing happened; then there was a movement in the crowd as it parted to give passage to someone else—a bull-necked, shaven-headed monster of a man in a sleeveless leather jerkin that showed the great muscles of his arms. He was carrying a whip. Although her parents had never beaten her, Alis had seen implements of punishment in the houses of her acquaintances: thick sticks, thin canes, or leather horse whips. But she had never seen anything like this. From the handle emerged a dozen long leather thongs. In the gray light she could see clearly that they were studded with glinting points of metal.

The whip carrier was on the platform now and had shed his jerkin. He looked down and received a nod from the Senior Elder. Grasping the handle in both hands, he swung round and raised the whip. The muscles of his torso and shoulders moved under his skin like living things; the thongs whistled in the thin air as they descended. They met the victim's back with a spattering sound like sudden hail on dry ground. The prisoner cried out, and at once spots of blood bloomed on his white skin. Again the whip was raised. Again the lashes fell. Again the prisoner cried out. Again. Again. Again.

Alis longed to shut her eyes, but she could not. She was hypno-
tized by the terrible rise and fall of the whip. The blows fell in a steady
rhythm, and now each one elicited a high-pitched scream from the
victim. His back was crisscrossed with bloody lines. There was not a
sound from the crowd.

By the time he paused to refresh himself from the tankard passed
up to him, the man wielding the whip was breathing heavily. Blood
flecked his shaven head and mingled with the sweat running down
his face and chest. The whipped man had sagged as far as the ropes
binding him would allow; his back was raw meat. At some point he
had turned his head so that his face was now toward where Alis stood.
His lips were bloody where he had bitten them in his agony, and his
eyes were shut. He must, however, have been aware of what was happening, for when his tormentor put down the tankard and took up
the whip again, he shrieked aloud. At this, Alis's resolve broke. She
had lost count of the number of lashes delivered, but however few
were left she could bear it no more. She turned, pushing her way
blindly through the crowd, and fled out of the square, thinking only
to escape the dreadful sounds that pursued her as the punishment
began again.

4

When, gasping for breath, she could run no longer, she was somewhere in the network of streets around the square. The houses were silent and there was not a person to be seen. She leaned against a wall, trying desperately to still the shaking of her limbs, sucking the air into her burning lungs. At last her breathing quieted and she began to wonder what she should do. Thomas would be ill pleased that she had run off. She shuddered at the thought. If only she could go home. Once more she was overwhelmed with longing. She wanted to be a little girl again, to see her mother reading in the lamplight on a winter evening, to feel the comfort of her father's arms when she was afraid of the dark. But she could never, never go back.

Suddenly there were voices. A woman whose face was familiar: Mistress Elizabeth, the Minister's wife, tall and dignified with a still-beautiful face and her silken gray hair coiled neatly at the nape of the neck. She and a boy of about seventeen had turned the corner and were coming toward her. They had been arguing, but on seeing her, they ceased. The woman smiled in recognition. "Why, it is Alis, is it not? What are you doing here alone, my dear? Are you lost?"

Alis nodded, not trusting herself to speak. The other looked more closely at her, frowning now.

"Have you been in the square? Is the dreadful business finished?"

Alis swallowed and said huskily, "I was there but it was too terrible. I ran away and now I don't know what to do." Her voice trembled.

"You had better come home with me, my dear." The voice was kindly, firm. "Sarah will be in no fit state to care for you, and as for Thomas—"

The boy broke in angrily, "Grandmother, have a care. She may tell him what you say."

The Minister's wife looked at him sardonically.

"I am too old to guard my tongue now, Luke. And I will not be frightened into silence. Now come, let us go home. There will be work for us to do later, and this child needs refuge."

And so saying, she tucked Alis's arm under her own and they made their way back toward the square. As they came near, Alis could hear the murmur of many voices and felt herself begin to shake. She could not go on—it was too horrible. But Mistress Elizabeth seemed to know her young companion's dread; though the Minister's house fronted the square, they did not go that way. They passed instead along a narrow lane between the backs of houses, through a wooden door, and into a large kitchen garden with neat rows of vegetables and tall bean plants. Beyond, through an archway, was a walled yard with potted plants and shrubs. Alis moved in a daze, content to be told what to do. They went into the kitchen, where pans of different sizes hung from hooks from the wall.

An elderly servant woman in a black dress and white cap was sitting by the stove. At their appearance, she jumped up in agitation. "Oh, Mistress Elizabeth, where have you been? I thought some ill had befallen you." And seeing Alis, her eyes widened. "And this is not wise surely. Is this not the girl who is at Master Thomas's?"

Her mistress nodded, smiling.

"Yes, Judith, this is Alis, and she has seen what no child should have seen and is in need of comfort. Let her sit awhile by the stove, and warm up some broth for her to drink. I must speak with my husband and see what is to be done for poor Samuel. And Luke, you must stay here, too. Your grandfather may have tasks for you, and how will you do them if you are running about here, there, and everywhere?"

The youth scowled at this and his grandmother shook her head at him.

"Ah, Luke, do not look so. There will be man's work for you soon enough in the dark times that are coming. Your grandfather and I will need you surely, even for our lives' sake, perhaps. Be patient a little."

She reached out and touched his cheek gently with her hand.

When she had gone, the servant, Judith, bustled about heating some soup, muttering fretfully to herself all the while. Luke remained, leaning against the doorpost, watching Alis suspiciously. For a while she did not notice him, still dazed from what she had seen, content that someone had taken charge of her and given her a resting place. At length she looked up and caught his eye. At once he looked away, flushing. He was a handsome boy, with smooth brown skin and dark hair.

Judith, having served the visitor, was hovering anxiously.

"Now, Luke, Mistress Elizabeth needs me I am sure, so I must leave you awhile with Alis, though I should not. I will set the door open so that you may be seen and heard."

He looked scornfully at her. "You need not fear, Judith. I am not likely to behave amiss with any friend of Master Thomas."

Shocked out of her dazed state, Alis exclaimed furiously, "I am no friend of Master Thomas! He is a wicked, cruel man and I wish I had never seen him."

Judith gave a cry. "The Maker protect us! For pity's sake guard your tongues."

Luke said proudly, "My grandmother says she will not be frightened into silence and neither will I."

"No." Judith was angry now as well as afraid. "And your grandmother is not likely to be taken into wardship and subject to particular discipline as you may be, if you persist in your foolery."

Luke hesitated. "They would not dare!"

Judith shook her head and looked at him pleadingly.

"They have dared much already. Who knows how far they will go?"

Luke's expression was stubborn. "I would defy them."

The old woman's face took on a sarcastic expression. "Like Tobias, you mean. Well, that will be mighty fine news for your poor grandparents. Think of them before you make yourself a mark, young Luke."

And she went out of the kitchen, shutting the door behind her with more than necessary firmness, quite forgetting she had meant to leave it open.

Luke glanced at Alis and then away again, saying awkwardly, "I beg your pardon if I have mistaken you. I supposed that, as you are dwelling with Master Thomas, you must be of his opinion."

Still nettled by his first assumption about her, Alis spoke sharply. "I am there at Mistress Sarah's request, not Master Thomas's, and it is possible to dwell in the same house without thinking alike. You are not always of one mind with your grandmother, it seems."

He surprised her by grinning suddenly.

"Well, well! Who would have thought you had so much spirit. You conceal your colors well. What are you doing then, in that house, if you are of our persuasion?"

Alis was still annoyed with him and not pleased to have been thought spiritless.

"I do not know what you mean by your 'persuasion.' Mistress Sarah came to visit her sister who lives in our Community and asked for me to accompany her home for a while."

"And you agreed?" He sounded incredulous. "Or perhaps your parents sent you and you had no voice in the matter?"

Alis thought bitterly that it was not in the matter of visiting Mistress Sarah that she had had no voice, but she could not tell anyone that, and especially not this arrogant boy whom she was beginning to dislike very much.

"It was my own choice. And I did not know then what I know now about Master Thomas, or perhaps I would not have come."

Even as she spoke, Alis knew this was not true. She would have done almost anything to escape. And now that she had seen what a husband might do, she was even more determined.

Luke was watching her curiously. It made her feel uncomfortable, as if he might read her secret in her face if she did not divert his attention, so she asked, "What did you mean by saying you thought I was of your 'persuasion'? Surely we are all People of the Book. Those who are not live without the protection of the Maker and at the mercy of the darkness, do they not?"

He nodded. "Yes, of course, except that my grandparents think— and I think, too—that Master Robert, our Senior Elder, and Thomas, and others like them, have come under the sway of darkness, though they think themselves purest followers of the Book."

It was clear to him that Alis did not understand, so he said, "In your Community would a man have been punished in the way that you have seen?"

Alis shook her head. "We have no whipping post."

Luke whistled in surprise at this.

"Well, we have always been stricter than that, but public whippings have been rare, and never so severe. It is a sign, my grandmother says, of what is to come. My grandfather is the Minister but his power is gone. And though the people love him, they are afraid. The Elders are determined to see that people keep to the rules of the Book more strictly. They come into the houses to inspect and investigate. They question the children. And those who are found to be at fault are punished with fines and the threat of worse if they do not mend their ways."

Alis was puzzled. "But the Elders have always had such powers, have they not? In our Community, my mother, who is Senior Elder, goes into the houses and asks questions if there is trouble or sin to be sought out, and the Minister or another Elder goes with her."

He nodded. "And what if the person questioned wishes for witnesses? What happens then?"

"Then they can ask to be questioned before all the Elders or even before the whole Community, so that all can see what is done and there can be no falsehoods."

For the Book said: *There is no justice behind a closed door. Let sinner and judge come to the meeting place and justice shall be done.* Different Communities had different ways of interpreting this injunction, but they all had some such arrangement as Alis had described.

Luke said heavily, "Here we do things differently now. The word of one Elder is enough to get a man or woman punished even to whipping. And he does not have to visit or question, though he must give reason."

"But"—Alis was shocked—"that is not what the Book says. How can they punish the people for breaking the rules when they are doing it themselves?"

"They say that judge and sinner meet at the prayer house when judgment is given, and punishment is public, so the rule is kept and justice is done."

She was silent. Then a name came into her head. "What did Judith mean about Tobias?"

He came to sit opposite her and did not answer at once. The wood shifted in the stove and settled with a soft sound. At length he broke his silence.

"You know that if parents cannot govern their children's conduct, or do not keep a fit household for them to grow up in, the Elders may take the children away and place them with those who will nurture them in virtue." Alis nodded and he went on. "Well, our Elders—in their wisdom—have decreed something called 'particular discipline.' Any boy or girl who is thought especially bad or troublesome is placed in the house of a wardmaster or wardmistress chosen for their strictness. Your Thomas would be one but it is thought, so my grandmother says, that his wife is not fit. It makes him very angry, too."

Alis shuddered. Was there nothing for which Thomas did not blame Sarah?

"And Tobias?"

For a long moment he sat staring down at his hands. At last he said, "Tobias was my friend." He stopped and swallowed, then went on. "We never liked restraint, though I do not think we did anything wicked. We climbed out at night sometimes, and took horses to go riding in the dark. Or we missed the prayer meeting and went exploring out in the woods to the south, beyond the edge of the settlement. We laughed too much and prayed too little, I suppose. And we did not fear a beating."

He stopped again. There was a brooding look on his face.

"Then Tobias was smitten with love for Miriam, the daughter of Master Robert, our Senior Elder. We talked often of whether he might consent to their marriage, but we feared that he was too proud to accept the son of a poor widow, so Tobias and Miriam met in secret for a while. And then—I do not know how—they were found out."

Alis waited for him to go on but he seemed lost in his thoughts. Softly she asked, "What happened?"

"Miriam was sent away north to her grandmother. But they took Tobias from his mother and made him a ward. The man who has charge of him is an expert in particular discipline, they say. Tobias came one night and threw stones at my window. He would not stand for any more bullying and beating, he said. He was running away and wanted me to go with him, but I would not leave my grandparents, though I longed to go. The Elders sent after him and he was brought back." There was a long silence. Then Luke said bitterly, "I do not know what they did to him. We see little of him these days. When he comes to the prayer meeting, he does not meet my eye, and he flinches if his ward master says his name. If he speaks at all, it is in a whisper; he looks at his master and cringes like a beaten dog."

Alis was appalled. "Are you not afraid that the same will happen to you, as Judith fears?"

"I do not think they dare, not yet anyway. But she is right. It may come. But I am not afraid. Whatever they did to me, I would never let them defeat me."

He spoke proudly and his fearlessness cheered her. She had found kindness and courage in the same household in spite of the cruelty that was all around. She thought of Tobias. Like her, he had run away.

"Luke, where did Tobias mean to go?"

He looked at her as if he were not sure whether to trust her, but something in her demeanor must have decided him for he said simply, "To the city. Until he thought to marry Miriam, he had always wanted to go there. We had talked of it often."

"Oh!" Alis could not suppress a cry.

Luke said anxiously, "You will not tell anyone that I said so. Judith is right. I must not draw the attention of the Elders and bring trouble on us all."

Alis shook her head vehemently. "I will tell no one, I swear by the Maker. Only, Luke, you must tell me how to get there, to the city."

He stared at her. "You? Why would you want to go to the city? It is no place for a girl like you."

There were sounds of movement and voices beyond the kitchen door. Desperately, for she feared missing her chance, she grabbed his hand.

"You *must* tell me, Luke. Promise me that you will. I have good reason, I assure you. I will explain. Now promise."

He looked at her in amazement. She was gripping his hand so hard that it hurt.

She said again, urgently, "Promise!"

Her eyes were blazing and her cheeks were flushed. He could not refuse. Wonderingly, his hand still in hers, he said, "I promise."

At that moment the kitchen door opened and Mistress Elizabeth appeared.

"Ah, Luke, good. You are still here. You must help me bring him in and then take your grandfather's mare and ride out to Woodland Farm. Ask Mistress Ellen to come here. Say that I need her. Tell her to bring leaves of self-heal, as many as she can, freshly picked. And Judith"—for the old woman had come clucking into the kitchen—

"put on pans to heat water, large ones. We must boil cloths to cleanse his back."

Luke said, "What is happening? Why . . . ?"

His grandmother was opening cupboards and taking out jars of ointment. "The Healers will not take the man. They say they have no authority from the Elders to treat him. I have had him brought here. He is likely to die if someone does not tend to him. And Luke, before you go, see that there is enough wood for the stove."

Her eye fell on Alis. "Alis dear, you must go back to Mistress Sarah's now. I have seen Master Thomas and explained; you have nothing to fear." And having dismissed Alis, she turned to the business in hand.

"Judith, we must put the man in the back bedchamber. Ellen and I can tend him, and you will have to take your turn, too. We must manage the days and nights between us, for he must not be left. If the Healers will not help, I doubt we shall find anyone else with the courage."

Alis took a deep breath.

"Mistress Elizabeth, may I not assist you? I have helped my mother with the sick, and I would repay your kindness if I can."

The Minister's wife hesitated. Then she shook her head.

"It is good of you, Alis, but the man is in a dreadful state. I doubt but you would turn giddy to see him and it is strong help that I must have."

Alis said quietly, "I will not turn giddy, Mistress Elizabeth. I am strengthened now, and surely the Maker has put me in your way to serve this need."

The older woman put down the jar she was holding and looked at Alis steadily.

"Now, Alis, if you can give your aid, we surely need you. But you must be certain. For if you faint and cry and I must tend to you, you will be a sore trouble and we have trouble enough. And remember this: the man may die when you alone are with him. Are you prepared for that?"

Alis nodded. Elizabeth's forehead creased in a troubled frown.

"Master Thomas will not like it. He has been a prime mover in this terrible matter, and you are a guest in his house, also. I wish I might consult with your parents but that is impossible."

Alis said hurriedly, "My parents would feel as you do, Mistress Elizabeth. They would think it only right that I should help to care for the poor victim."

There were more sounds—of wood scraping on stone, and a man's voice saying "Hold steady, now." Mistress Elizabeth made up her mind. "Very well. I will speak to Master Thomas myself, to ask his permission. I do not think he will refuse."

Alis let out the breath she had been holding. The Maker be thanked! She could stay near Luke, who had promised to tell her what she needed to know. But it was more than that: she longed to serve this woman who had reached out to her in kindness in her terror, and there was the man, too. She was ashamed that she had borne witness in silence, and ashamed, too, that she had not endured to the end. This time she would not run away.

5

A man appeared in the kitchen doorway, an old man in farm clothes, rough-shaven, with a weather-beaten face and bright blue eyes.

"He be set down in the upper passageway, Mistress Elizabeth. Hurdle won't go through chamber door I reckon. Shall us lift him?"

The Minister's wife shook her head. "Bide a moment, Matthew, and I will come. We must move him carefully, for he bleeds." And turning to Alis: "I shall need you in a moment, my dear, and it is a grim sight. Be prepared now and do not fail me."

Alis heard her go up the stairs and then her voice saying, "Now Matthew, you and James must lift him, one at each end. Keep him facedown. Luke and I will link hands underneath him so that his back does not bend. Gently now . . ." Her voice faded. They had passed into the bedchamber. Alis could hear their steps upon the floor of the room above her head. In a few moments there were feet upon the stairs and the man Matthew appeared again at the kitchen door.

"If you be Alis, you be wanted above." He jerked his head toward the ceiling.

Her heart beating at the thought of what she would see, she mounted the narrow stairs. Even before she went into the room she could smell the injured man—a chamber-pot foulness that caught in the throat and made her want to retch. He had loosed his bowels in his agony. She held herself stiffly and entered. She caught only a glimpse of the man, his back a mass of red and black, before the Minister's wife spoke.

"Alis, go down and bring back the large bucket—Judith will show you where it is. We must get these soiled breeches off him and you must give them to her to be taken tomorrow to the wash house, for they cannot be done at home. And then we will need clean cloths to bathe him and the green ointment—it is on the side table—though I do not think we will be able to use it. Ellen will judge. But wash your hands well before you touch the cloths. Hurry now."

Alis did as she was bid, glad of what her mother had made her do in tending the sick. Judith threw up her hands in horror when she knew what the bucket was for, but she fetched it from the scullery and took it without a word when Alis returned.

Luke had disappeared, and now Alis must make good her offer: there was the foulness to wash away, and then they must bathe the flayed back in preparation for laying on the leaves that Mistress Ellen was to bring. Alis went up and down, taking basins of water—hot first for the simple washing, and then cool for the poor, raw flesh. In the kitchen and scullery, Judith could scarcely keep pace with their need. No sooner was one basin of clean water ready than it came back stained, and fresh was needed.

At first the man did not stir, but when they began on his back he groaned piteously, turning his head this way and that, whimpering like an injured animal. There was no skin at all on his back and shoulders where the whip had fallen so cruelly. In some places, thick blood had dried purple or black, but at the least movement, the crusts broke and the fresh red oozed up again. The flesh was gouged, too, as if the embedded points had fallen repeatedly in the same places, and these places bled worse than the rest. Ribbons of skin, ripped loose but not torn away, marked the edges of the great wound. Alis kept her thoughts still, concentrating on what must be done. She did not ask yet what kind of Maker it was in whose world such things were done, and in his name, too.

At length Mistress Ellen arrived. Seeing the man from the doorway, she stopped abruptly and her hand flew to her mouth. "The Maker preserve us! What have they done? I did not dream . . ."

The Minister's wife went to her and embraced her.

"Ellen, I thank you for coming. I have none to help me but Judith and this brave child here. Can you stay? Who will tend the animals?"

The newcomer put down the covered basket she was carrying. "My neighbor Saul will see to it. He is not of my mind in this matter"— she gestured toward the figure on the bed—"but I have done as much for him in times of trouble, as we farmers must. Besides he loves the beasts. He will not have them suffer for the follies of humankind. Now we must be about our business here. You have bathed him?"

The other nodded. "Then we must lay on the leaves and pray to the Maker for healing."

She took up the basket and removed the cloth cover. Underneath lay a mass of the thin green leaves of the plant self-heal, which is used on cuts and wounds, especially those that will not mend. Ointment is made from it, too, which the Healers use in their work. Alis picked up the jar that she had fetched, but Ellen shook her head.

"The flesh must dry, if it is to heal. We will lay on the leaves and nothing more, I think."

Very gently she began placing the leaves, overlapping them so that gradually the man's back was covered. All the while she kept up a soothing murmur as he moaned and shuddered.

When at last it was done, she turned to the Minister's wife.

"Go if you wish, Elizabeth, and tend to the household or whatever else you must. I will sit with him. But send up some fresh water and a dry straw, for he must drink. I fear he will take a fever if he does not, so hurt as he is."

They looked at him. He was quiet now, lying facedown, his head turned sideways and one hand hanging slackly over the side of the bed.

Elizabeth gestured for Alis to accompany her, and together they descended the stairs. The kitchen was full of steam and there were cloths hung to dry on racks under the ceiling. Judith at once burst into fretful protest. "Oh, Mistress Elizabeth, I doubt but you have done unwisely to bring him here. The Elders will not like it and perhaps he will bring trouble on us all. It is a fearful thing to go against the Elders, so hard as they are upon us now and—"

Her mistress broke in sharply. "Well, Judith, if you are afraid, I give you leave to go to your brother. Ellen and I will make shift to manage without you; we have Alis to help us. Go, and take your fear with you!"

The old servant's eyes filled with tears.

"Oh, Mistress, you will not send me away after all these years. I do not mean to fail you, only"—here she could not suppress a sob—"you are so fearless. I think you would defy them even with the whip at your back, and who knows that they would not dare even that? Who is to say them nay?"

Elizabeth put her arms around the other woman. "Forgive me, Judith. I am unkind to you. It is only that I am tired with all that we have done and all that is still to do or I would not make so poor a return for your goodness. Do not weep"—for the old woman was crying in earnest now—"you shall not leave me unless you wish it. I should not know how to manage without you. Come now. You are weary, too. Go and sleep awhile, for I shall need you in the night, I daresay." Gently she shepherded Judith from the room, and they heard her slow footsteps on the stairs.

Elizabeth sat herself by the stove on the stool that the old servant had vacated. She rubbed her forehead wearily. "I must mend my temper. Poor Judith. These are cruel times for such as her. But her fearfulness will shake my courage if I let it, and that must not be."

Alis was dismayed. "Are you afraid, Mistress Elizabeth?"

For a moment the older woman sat silent, gazing at the fire. At length she said, "No, my dear, not as Judith is. Do not trouble yourself. Now let us eat and fortify ourselves, and then I will return to Ellen."

She busied herself about the cupboards and drawers, placing upon the table portions of cold meat pie and some crusty bread. Alis had not thought of food, but despite what she had seen that day, she realized she was hungry. She was glad to eat.

When night came, Elizabeth would not let Alis sit up but sent her to join the snoring Judith in the attic chamber. She thought she would lie awake, but instead she fell immediately into a deep sleep.

The days passed slowly for Alis. She ate, slept, and cared for the injured man. He must have his bodily needs attended to, as well as being fed and washed. It was often unpleasant, and more often dull. Elizabeth insisted that he must not be left alone: he suffered from fever intermittently, crying out and muttering by turns.

"He must be healed if it can be done," Elizabeth said, "and someone must be there if he seems likely to die. He must not go with none to comfort him in his last moments."

Ellen had returned to her farm, and Judith was so fearful that Elizabeth and Alis did the nursing between them. Alis did not mind. Elizabeth had saved her that terrible day, and she was glad to be able to show her gratitude. Nevertheless, although she saw Luke sometimes, they were never alone together, and as the days went by she grew fearful. Surely her parents would expect her to return; they might even send to fetch her if she stayed away too long. But what could she do? Even if she had been willing to leave Elizabeth without explanation, she had no more idea how to get to the city than when she had arrived.

One night, she woke suddenly to the sound of groans. Softly, so as not to wake Judith, she felt her way out of the attic and down the dark stairs to the landing below. The door of the back bedchamber was open. Huge shadows swelled and sank on the visible parts of the wall and ceiling, as those within moved about in the lamplight. Elizabeth came out carrying a chamber pot covered with a cloth. She was drawn and pale but she smiled when she saw Alis.

"Are you awake, my dear? Then go in and keep my grandson company. In ordinary times I would not permit it but I must tend to my husband, who is sick, and Luke may need your assistance."

When she entered the chamber, Alis found Luke kneeling beside the bed, holding a cup of water and guiding a straw to the man's mouth so that he might drink. He sucked in the water desperately, noisily, like a man in a desert place who finds the spring that will save his life. When he had done, he closed his eyes as if exhausted and his head dropped forward. He lay on his side, for his back was still raw and he could not lie upon it.

Alis and Luke sat in silence for a while. Their charge stirred and moaned intermittently, but whether in sleep or not was impossible to tell. At length, he fell silent and his breathing seemed to steady. Luke whispered, "My grandmother has given him some of the potion that Ellen left to ease his pain—something powerful, she said."

"Is he asleep?" Alis asked.

Luke nodded. "I think so. The potion acts swiftly, Ellen says, but in such cases it does not act for long. And the stuff is dangerous. He must not have it too often. He has a fever, too, and my grandmother thinks he may die, otherwise she would not have left us together unwatched. No doubt she expects that you will know what to do for him if the end comes. She thinks much of you: you are brave, she says, and good."

Alis felt herself flush. Mistress Elizabeth did not know that she planned to run away in defiance of her parents and her Minister. But she was alone with Luke and here was her chance. She was about to reopen the subject of the city, when Luke did it for her.

"And now that we will not be overheard, tell me why you want to go to the city. It is not a place for one such as you. Why must you go there?"

Alis wondered how much she should reveal. She did not know him. He might tell his grandparents, who would surely send her straight back to Freeborne. He was watching her curiously. Sensing her unease, he said, keeping his voice low for fear of disturbing the sleeper, "*I* trusted *you*."

She nodded. It was true. He had told her what he and Tobias had planned, taking the risk that she would report to it Thomas. At last she said, "My parents have agreed to a marriage . . . and the man . . . I cannot marry him."

Luke nodded. "A forced marriage is no marriage, my grandmother says. But did your parents give you no say at all?"

Alis shook her head.

Luke whispered angrily, "Why must they rule our lives? Even my grandparents sometimes, though they would never force me to marry against my will. But it is hard for a girl. A boy can run away and make a life for himself—"

"A girl can run away, too," Alis broke in fiercely. "I will not go back."

He looked at her. "Are you not afraid? The city is a dangerous place, they say. People disappear and are never heard of again. Without friends, how will you live and be safe?"

"My brother is there," Alis said firmly. "I will go to him."

"You have a brother? In the city? What is he doing there? Surely your parents do not permit him to live there?"

"He ran away."

Luke raised his eyebrows. "And you know where he is? You could find him?"

"I will find him," Alis said stubbornly.

"But, Alis . . ."

"I will find him," she repeated. "And if you will not help me, I will manage without you. But you promised! Will you refuse me and perhaps betray me? I will not go back, I tell you. I would rather die!"

Her voice had risen and they both looked instinctively toward the bed. The sick man had not moved, and his eyes were still shut.

Luke said softly, "I will not betray you. I will help you if I can but . . ." He stopped uneasily. "I would come with you if I could, but I cannot leave my grandparents, especially now."

They were silent for a while. Then Luke said, "Since the reformers—as they call themselves—grew in power here, we have had one or two such marriages. In the past it would not have been permitted. Is that how it was with you?"

Alis shook her head. Freeborne was not like Two Rivers.

He went on. "What did they say to you? Did they not explain why you must marry the man?"

Bitterness rose in Alis's throat. "They said it was the will of the Maker, an honor."

"And the man? Who is he? Is he well known to you?"

"He is our pastor, Minister Galin. I have known him all my life. As my minister. And he is forty years old!"

"Forty!" Luke was appalled. "But that is more than twice your age, nearly three times."

Alis nodded. "So you see why you must help me. I cannot marry him."

"So Pastor Galin is *your* minister. I have heard of him," Luke said slowly. "Our reformers speak slightingly of him. They say he is too easygoing with sinners, that he does not think the Communities need purifying. Why would he, of all people, insist on marrying a girl who does not wish it?"

"My wishes do not come into it," Alis said furiously.

Luke was frowning. "It does not make sense."

"Whether it makes sense or not"—she was angry with Luke now: what was the point of trying to understand—"I will have to marry him if I go back, and so I must go elsewhere. Unless . . ." A new thought occurred to her. "Do you think your grandmother would let me stay here with her?"

Luke shook his head. "Your parents know where you are and would send for you. Our Elders would never countenance your defiance, and my grandmother would have no power to prevent their sending you back. Even if we were leaving, I doubt she would let you come with us in opposition to your parents. But we shall be here until we are driven out. My grandfather thinks he may persuade the reformers to reconsider! He is ever the optimist and sees good in the worst of people. My grandmother knows better, but of course she will not go without him, and they are both determined to serve the people here while they can."

"Then there is no help for it," Alis said decisively. "I must go to the city to find Joel, and you must show me the way."

He looked troubled. "A girl on her own in the city is . . ." He stopped and swallowed. "How will you find your brother? You will not know who to ask, who is to be trusted. I have heard . . ."

"What have you heard?" She was angry again. What business of his was it to hinder her?

He began again hesitantly. "Alis, this marriage. Is it so dreadful?"

She gasped and would have interrupted him but he went on hurriedly, "Only they say that for a girl . . . there are dangers . . . worse even, than such a marriage." Again he hesitated. Even in the flickering lamplight of the sickroom she could see that he was flushed.

"Tell me what you mean." She was afraid now.

"There was a girl here once. She was older than me but I remember her. She was wild. They could not hold her: she feared nothing and no one. She disappeared one day and her father went looking for her. He was a man of means and he spent freely to find her."

He stopped again. Alis held her breath. He had turned his head away from her.

"She was in a house where the men of the city come when they want . . . a woman for . . . pleasure. There are those who keep a lookout for innocent runaways and trick them with promises of work and shelter. Her father would have brought her back but she would not come. She was too ashamed, he said."

Alis did not speak. She hated him. How could she go to the city now? He was still speaking.

"I am sorry, Alis. If only you were a boy, it would be different."

"If only I were a boy," she repeated angrily. "What use is that? If

I were a boy I would not be in this trouble. Minister Galin would certainly not want to marry me!" She paused. "Well, I do not care. I mean to go to the city, and I will."

"My grandmother is right about you. You have courage." Luke's eyes were shining. "Oh, Alis. If only I could come with you. There are great houses there I have heard, and street upon street, and shops, too. If you have money, you may buy anything in the world. The rich people parade up and down in fine clothes such as we are not allowed to wear. And the sailors come ashore from the merchant ships. They speak strange tongues and do not dress as we do. What would I not give to see it all! But my grandparents need me."

He would have said more but the door opened and Ellen came in. She raised her eyebrows at the sight of the two of them, but she said only, "Your grandmother sent for me to come. She thinks he is worse."

She went over to the man on the bed and stooped down beside him, examining his features, rolling back his eyelids to look at his eyes.

"He will sleep awhile yet," she said. "And you must do so also, if you are to be useful. I will watch now. Begone, the pair of you."

Outside Luke said in a whisper, "Good night, Alis. Do not fear, I will not fail you."

Back in the attic, awake to the rhythm of Judith's snores, Alis lay with her eyes wide open. Luke's face came before her with its smooth olive skin and eyes bright in the lamplight of the sickroom. He would help her, he had said. And she believed him.

6

The man Samuel's injuries were healing slowly, but he would not speak or help himself at all. Alis tended him carefully, helping to dress his back and bringing him food. He had not yet moved out of the room. It was clear, however, that he would not die, and she was gradually freed from watching.

She waited in dread for Elizabeth to say that she must return to Thomas's. She knew that the Minister's wife had sent word to him on the evening of the whipping. He had been ill pleased, but she had not been sent back, and the next morning Lilith had appeared at the door with an armful of Alis's clothing. That same afternoon, Mistress Elizabeth had accompanied Alis on a brief visit to Sarah and Thomas, so that Alis might thank them for their hospitality. It had been an ordeal to go, and a relief to come away again. But Alis felt guilty, too. Poor Sarah had so wanted her company, and now she was alone with her husband once more.

A few days later, on an errand, Alis had met Thomas in the square. She nearly turned round when she saw him, but it was too late. The familiar sneer greeted her.

"So you work as a servant now, Alis? You would not have to do so in my house. What is it, I wonder, that is so enticing about the Minister's household?"

Her stomach churned, remembering the last time she had been this close to him. But she would not be cowed. "The man must be tended to, surely, Master Thomas. That is the rule everywhere, is it not?"

His expression darkened and he came closer to her.

"Have a care, girl. You would do better to return. It is not wise to be numbered among those who make light of sin."

She wanted to tell him it was a sin to whip a man near to death but she did not dare. She only said, "I am sorry you do not approve, Master Thomas."

He turned away without another word.

She returned to the Minister's house, deeply grateful that she was permitted to remain there. The thought of living close to Thomas again terrified her. Besides, she had grown to love Elizabeth who had given her refuge when none had seemed possible. And then there was Luke.

When she got back, he was chopping wood for Judith. She told him what Thomas had said. He swung the ax so that the blade bit hard into the log, and then he straightened up, looking angry. "You are not a servant. You are my grandmother's helper, and a very good one. What does Master Thomas know? Lilith is his idea of a servant and I am sure he treats her ill. She would not be so sullen if he were gentler in his ways. She dropped her basket once in the square and I helped her pick up what had fallen. It was nothing, but she thanked me as if no one had ever done her a kindness before."

This was not the Lilith that Alis knew, but she did not say so, and their talk moved to other matters.

They had a plan of sorts now for getting Alis to the city, but they must wait for the reappearance in the area of an old acquaintance of Luke's.

"Will he help me, do you think?" Alis asked.

Luke hesitated. "Do you have any money?" he asked at last.

Alis shook her head. "My mother gave Mistress Sarah the money for my journey. And what is left, Master Thomas has for safekeeping. But this man that you know, must he be paid? He will not do it for friendship's sake?"

Luke looked troubled. "He might, perhaps. I met him first with Tobias, out tracking in the woods when we should have been safely abed. We thought we had been caught for sure when he seized me from behind, and Tobias would not run, though I shouted to him to be gone. But this man—Ethan is his name—seemed mighty amused when he knew that he had two truants to deal with instead of the thieves he had feared. He has no love for the rule of the Book. He said once to me"—Luke lowered his voice—"that he thought there was no Maker; it was just a story to frighten us all into doing as the Elders wished."

Alis was silent. She could not believe that there was no Maker. What other explanation could there be for the world and all that was in it? But she was no longer the child she had once been, believing in the kindly creator who punished only when he must and who loved his people. What she had seen in the square had changed all that. This Ethan, perhaps, had reasons like hers for his unbelief. Luke had paused but now he continued.

"He could never bear to live in a Community, so he found himself a traveling trade that he might be free to come and go. In the city, he buys ointments and medicines made from plants that do not grow in these parts. Then he goes from place to place and sells them. He comes here two or three times a year, but always in early spring when the Healers need new supplies after the winter. I see him then. He likes to hear the news, and he knows that I am no lover of the rules either, especially since Tobias . . ." He stopped. The subject of Tobias was always painful. "But there is no more than talk between us, and a little rabbit trapping. Whether he would help us in this matter, I do not know. When he comes, I will ask him, and we must offer him what money we have. Until then, we must wait."

So Alis waited, fearing the summons back to Thomas's—or worse still, home to Freeborne—but also wishing more and more that she might not be parted yet from Elizabeth. Or from Luke.

Although they were seldom alone together and never without the danger of interruption, the bond between them grew. Sometimes she caught him looking at her admiringly, which pleased her very much. Once, their hands brushed accidentally as he handed her a dish at the table, and she felt the blood burn in her veins. He spoke slightingly of the girls of Two Rivers: they had no spirit, he said, and she knew that he was comparing them unfavorably with her. For the first time in her life, she used the mirror not merely to check that she was tidy but to see whether her looks might please. Each day she brushed her long, fair hair until it was smooth and glossy. No, she did not want to be parted from Luke.

One morning, as Alis went down the stairs, Elizabeth called to her from the large front room that looked over the square. It was here that the Minister met sometimes with the Elders or gave counsel to the troubled in his congregation. Elizabeth was standing with her back to the window, and opposite her, so that the light fell upon his face, was Thomas. Alis felt her stomach clench at the sight of him. Had the moment come? The Minister's wife held out a hand to her and drew her near.

"Alis, my dear, Master Thomas has come with some news for you that I fear is not good." Alis had no time to speak before Elizabeth went on. "You must be longing, I know, to see your parents, but he tells me"—here she smiled at Thomas as if he were the pleasantest of visitors—"that word has come of fever in Freeborne. Your parents wish you to stay here until it is safe for you to go back."

"And I"—Thomas spoke loudly, as if he thought he had stood long enough while Elizabeth delivered this message—"wish to know whether you propose to return to my house, where you are a guest, or whether you will take up residence here to the inconvenience of the Minister."

Alis would have spoken, but once more Elizabeth was before her.

"It is no inconvenience to the Minister or to me to have Alis here, I assure you. She has been of great service. Perhaps we might keep her a little longer if you would be so good? My poor Judith grows old and needs her rest, and there is much to do in a Minister's household. You have Lilith, do you not? I am sure she is a goodly support to your wife."

For a moment Thomas did not answer. He looked baffled and furious as if he would refuse but did not know how. At length he said stiffly, "So be it. Let Alis come for the rest of her possessions."

As if she knew how little Alis would care for this, Elizabeth said, "Will you not send Lilith with them? It is only across the square and there cannot be much. Alis has her clothes already."

Thomas flushed, and Alis could see a pulse beating in his temple. His voice was tight with anger. "I will not have Lilith lose her time running after an idle child. If Alis desires her things, let her come for them. If not, I will dispose of them."

And he was gone from the room.

In the silence Alis listened to the blood beating in her ears. For a moment she could not take in what had happened. Was it really true that she was not to go back to Freeborne, that she could stay in the Minister's household and not be parted yet from Luke? Elizabeth's voice broke into her daze.

"I am sorry, my dear, that you cannot go home. But you must not worry too much about your parents. They are not sick themselves, Thomas said. We must pray to the Maker to keep them well. He has left the letter for you to read, and there is one enclosed for you, also."

Alis was aware of a moment's guilt. In the rush of feelings aroused by Thomas's visit, she had given no thought to the danger her parents might be in. Besides, she must not think of them; she must put them

out of her mind. But unbidden came a memory of childhood sickness, and of the little wooden horse her father had made for her. He
had tied a piece of rope around its neck, and when she had been well
enough to leave her bed, she had played for hours, pulling it along
behind her. She would not be separated from it even at night. She
slept with the end of the rope tied around her wrist, so that the sound
of the wheels rolling over the floorboards entered her dreams.

Her eyes filled with tears. She would never see her father again.
And who would love her as he had? He would not have wanted her
to be forced into marriage. It was her mother's doing, she was sure.
Elizabeth, seeing her grief, put an arm round her saying in her kind
way, "Do not weep, my dear. We will take care of you."

Alis swallowed hard and smiled through her tears at the older
woman. "You are very good to me, Mistress Elizabeth. I wish I may
be worthy of it."

For she had an uneasy sense that she meant to deceive the Minister's wife, and that it was an ill thing to do.

Later that day she crossed the square to Thomas's house. Fearful
though she was of facing him, she would not be terrorized out of
repossessing what was hers. Nevertheless, as she approached the front
door, she hoped that he might be out. It would not take her long to
collect her things, and then she need never speak to him again.

Lilith answered her knock, glowering as usual, and conducted her
up the stairs without speaking.

In the little attic room, Alis collected the few small items and
was ready to leave again. But when she turned to go, Lilith, who had

watched her in sullen silence from the low doorway, did not move. Alis felt her heart beat faster—she was anxious to be away. She took a step forward but the other girl remained where she was.

"What is it that you want?" Alis asked sharply.

Lilith stared at her, and then said hoarsely, "Tell me what you do there."

Alis stared back. The girl's face was thin and sallow in the dim light of the attic but there were patches of color on her cheeks and she was panting a little.

"What do you mean?"

"In the Minister's house. What do you do there?"

Alis felt her temper rise. Was this girl, who had never given her a friendly word in all the weeks she had lived in the house, to delay her with silly questions until Thomas returned?

"Let me pass, Lilith. I have business elsewhere and you are hindering me."

Lilith's lips twisted in a sneer.

"You weren't so haughty before you took up with the Minister's wife." Her face took on a slyly satisfied look. "And you wouldn't be so haughty now if Master Thomas had the ruling of you, I can tell you. He is much angered. You'd best be gone before he comes home." But she made no move to let Alis pass.

Alis did not know what to do. She did not want to push Lilith away from the door, nor did she know how to persuade her to move. She said again, "What is it that you want from me?"

Lilith's look darkened. "I want to know what you do there, in the Minister's house."

"I help in the household," Alis said, thinking it best to humor the girl's desire for knowledge, though not in the least understanding why Lilith should care what she did.

"And you talk with him?" Again the color was up in her cheeks, and her breath came and went quickly.

"With the Minister, do you mean? I scarcely see him. His health is not good and—"

Lilith interrupted her savagely. "Not the Minister. Why would I want to hear about that old man? Master Luke, I mean. Do you talk with Master Luke?"

At last Alis understood. She chose her words carefully. "Sometimes I do, but Mistress Elizabeth will not have us left alone together. She is strict in such matters."

Lilith continued to stare at her suspiciously. "You have never been alone with him?"

Alis hesitated, and the other girl shot out a hand and gripped her arm so tightly that she cried out.

"You have!" Lilith hissed at her. "What did he say to you? Did he tell you about me? What did he say?"

"He never mentioned you. Why should he?" Alis struggled to free herself from the fingers digging themselves painfully into her arm.

"Because he is my friend, even though he is the Minister's grandson and I am nothing but a servant here. And you've no right to be there with him when you should be taking care of Mistress Sarah, as you were brought here to do."

She gripped Alis's arm even tighter and leaned forward so that Alis felt the hot breath on her cheek. Lilith's voice dropped to a menacing whisper. "Have you done what you should not with him? You'd best beware if you have. The Elders have their eye on him. And on you, too. I have heard Master Thomas say so."

Saying furiously, "Let go of me," Alis wrenched her arm free and attempted to push her way past Lilith. For a moment they were locked together in the narrow doorway. Then somehow, Alis was through and going down the stairs as swiftly as she could.

She hurtled across the square, in through the Minister's front door, and up the stairs to the attic room she shared with Judith, slamming the door behind her. With her bundle still in her arms she stood, waiting for her heart to slow down. *Have you done what you should not with him?* Her cheeks burned.

Supper was done and Samuel settled for the night. Shaken by her encounter with Lilith, Alis was relieved when Luke went out alone—on an errand, he said. His grandmother forbore to question him. When he had gone, she said to Alis, "I fear he will fall into some trouble. He was ever impatient of check and discipline, but I cannot keep him at home as if he were a small child. What is this errand—do you know, my dear? I see that you are becoming fast friends."

Alis felt herself redden.

She was not able to speak privately to Luke until the evening of the next day. They sat in the kitchen and spoke in whispers, wary of Judith, who was dozing beside the stove, her white cap askew on her head.

"Ethan has come," Luke murmured. Alis felt her heart jump.

"Will he take me?" she asked, dreading what she would hear.

Luke looked worried. "Not for the little money that we have, he says. The danger is too great and the reward too little."

She could feel only immense relief. Keeping her voice very low—for it would not do to wake Judith—she said, "Do not be sorry. You would not wish me gone, surely?"

They were leaning toward each other, their heads close together so that Judith might not hear them. He whispered vehemently, "No, of course not. But I do not want you to go back to Freeborne and marry that man, either."

She felt the blood come up in her cheeks. Suddenly, with an extra loud snore, Judith opened her eyes, and Luke and Alis started away from each other. The old woman looked suspiciously at them and eased herself up out of her chair. It was time they were in their beds.

Judith was already asleep when Alis blew out the candle. She was not troubled by Ethan's refusal. There was time enough. Fever always lasted for weeks and weeks.

aster Robert was there, Thomas, and another of the
Elders, a fair-haired woman with the long-nosed features
of a shrew. They faced Elizabeth across the room that looked out
onto the square. This time the Minister was there, too, leaning on a
stick, his gentle old face troubled.

"My dear Robert, surely you can wait a little? His back is not fully
healed, my wife tells me; he hardly speaks. And we must not give up
hope that he will return to faith and be one of us again. How can that
be, if we send him away?"

Alis remembered the Senior Elder from the day of the punishment. It was his thin voice that had pronounced sentence, his stiff
face that had watched impassively as the flesh was flayed: it was fruit-
less to expect pity from him. His dry, rasping tone grated on the ear.

"Indeed, Minister, we must always hope for repentance, but the
man was not chastened by admonition. Neither, it seems, has punish-

ment effected any change in him. Mistress Elizabeth would doubtless have told us if words of penitence had fallen from his lips."

He paused but Elizabeth did not speak. He turned toward Alis, who had been standing by the door, expecting any moment to be dismissed from the room. He looked at her coldly. "Alis, is it not?" He did not wait for her answer. "You have been tending the man. Have you heard him express contrition for his ways? If so, speak."

For a moment her voice would not come. Then she cleared her throat and said a little huskily, "No, Master Robert. He has said nothing."

She was trembling. He turned away again. The Minister looked at him out of faded blue eyes.

"We must give him more time, Robert. I will strive with him. Let us not despair of his soul lightly. Besides, he has barely recovered. He is not to be harried."

The other man's thin face did not change. "We have been patient, have we not? None has troubled him while he has lain in your house these many weeks."

Elizabeth moved abruptly. "Does not the Book say, *Like years under the sun are the days of the Maker while he waits for the sinner to turn*? If the Maker can wait for years, surely you can manage a few more weeks."

Robert made no sign that he heard her but addressed the Minister again. "It is an ill thing for the man to remain in the Community, Minister. It will seem that we repent of our rigor." He paused. "Which we do not."

The Minister turned to the shrew-faced woman. "Mistress Rebecca, assist me to persuade our Senior Elder. Master Robert is rightly for discipline, but a little gentleness, too, will surely serve our ends as well or better. You have children. This man is some woman's son, too."

"And it is because I have children that I will not countenance his presence among us any longer." Her voice was loud and hard, at odds with the weak face. "Shall we let unbelief, like a fever, infect our young? Let him be cast out, as we have agreed."

The Minister looked startled. "Agreed? It has not been agreed. You have come to discuss it, have you not?"

Robert gave the woman a sharp look. "The Elders have spoken together, Minister, and we are of one mind. The man must go."

The old man had been leaning heavily on his stick, but now he straightened up, and the benevolence was gone from his voice.

"Since when did the Elders meet without the Minister to settle so grave a matter?"

"Forgive us, Minister." There was no courtesy in the formal words. "Your views are known. They were considered."

The old man was clearly angry now. "But I was not there. There is much I might have said."

For a moment Robert looked at the Minister out of his cold eyes. His dry voice scratched the stillness of the room. "It would have made no difference."

They had gone and there was time to digest defeat. Elizabeth looked grimly at her husband. "We must get Samuel away in the morning, and then we must make plans to be gone ourselves, Jacob. I doubt we shall be safe here much longer. And if our power is gone, we can do no good."

The old man said pleadingly, "Let us not despair yet, Elizabeth. Surely there are some of the Elders who may be swayed?"

She took her husband's hand in hers. "Dear Jacob, if there are others who think as we do, their voices have not prevailed. No doubt, means have been found to persuade or silence them. And think of this: we have one grandson—all that is left to us of our dear daughter. How long do you think it will be before they move against him if we resist? And that is supposing he does not himself provoke them. They will want little enough excuse, and they watch for the chance, I am sure."

Alis jumped. This was what Lilith had said.

The Minister was nodding. "You are right, Elizabeth. I am foolish. And it is not only Luke." He was smiling but his lips trembled. "You yourself are likely enough to provoke them, my dear wife, as fearless for good as you are. And it would be death to me to see you hurt."

He turned his head away to hide the tears that rolled down his old cheeks. Alis thought with loathing of Robert and Thomas.

The next morning at sunrise, Luke brought Samuel's oldest horse into the square. He and Elizabeth had gone the previous afternoon to fetch a few belongings from the farm that was already occupied by new tenants.

"They were ashamed," Elizabeth said with satisfaction. But it was all the satisfaction there was. Of the young woman Samuel called his wife, and to whom he had given the name Iri, there had been no sign since the day they had come to take him from the farm. She was said to be half-witted and almost without speech. She had appeared one year on the edge of the settlement and he had taken her in. She was with child now, though not yet near her time.

A small crowd had gathered. The Elders were there, of course, one or two looking uneasy. Alis had expected some kind of formal casting-out but there was none. In silence the people watched as Samuel mounted his horse, wincing as the movement pulled at the newly formed scars on his back. Then he was moving out of the square, the old horse plodding gently across the cobbles, disappearing between the houses and out toward the open farmland beyond.

"Where will he go?" Alis asked when they had gone indoors again.

Elizabeth shook her head. "I do not know. There are farms and villages that do not belong to the Communities of the Book where he might find refuge. But he bears the signs of his punishment and will meet with mistrust. Besides, they have broken him. How can he be a man among men again? If he had the woman to care for, it might be something, although she would be a burden, too, but no one knows where she has gone. And now, Alis, my dear"—she smiled sadly—"you must go home, I think, despite the fever. We shall have to leave here soon."

Alis could not speak for a few seconds. The moment she had dreaded for so long had come. "Must I go straightaway? I . . ." She could not stop her voice from breaking a little. "I shall be very sad to go."

"There is a wagon going north in five days' time. And you will be glad to see your parents, will you not? I hope you will find them well. I wish I might keep you here until we had word that the sickness was over, but that cannot be." She got up slowly, wincing at the stiffness of her back. Her face was lined and weary.

Alis looked at Luke, who had not spoken a word since Samuel's departure. He had listened to his grandmother with close attention. He did not meet Alis's eye but said quietly to Elizabeth, "Grandmother, if you do not mind, I will ride over to Mistress Ellen's. She has been preparing her old wagon for you and might be glad of help."

Elizabeth did not oppose his going, and he went swiftly from the room without so much as a glance at Alis. He had said he would not fail her, Alis thought miserably. Now he was ashamed to look at her.

The day passed in a dreamlike strangeness. She could not believe that her departure was really so close and she still had no way of getting to the city. After so long, she had come to think of finding her brother as a distant certainty: how it was to be accomplished she had not known, but somehow it would be done.

Now the future was upon her and it was not as she had planned. She tried to tell herself that Galin might have died of the fever. She thought again of confiding in Elizabeth about the marriage and begging to be taken with them when they left. But it was impossible. Elizabeth would surely send her home to obey her parents.

There was much to do in the household, for Judith had taken to her bed when the Elders had arrived the day before, and she would not leave it. She had been with Elizabeth for forty years. If the Minister and his wife went away, she would go with them. Alis envied her.

There were four days left. She thought of starting the journey to Freeborne and then leaving the wagon on some pretext as soon as she was clear of Two Rivers. But word might get back. Girls of her age and kind did not travel without protection—at the very least the wagon driver would be charged with watching over her. She wondered if she could steal a horse, but horses were valuable and she would surely be pursued—and fall into Thomas's hands or Robert's! She shuddered. Round and round it went in her head as she sorted bed linen and scoured pots—for she was doing Judith's work now—but no solution came to her.

In the late afternoon, Luke came back briefly. They were alone in the kitchen for a few minutes. He looked anxious. "Alis, I am going to speak again to Ethan, to see if he will change his mind."

She put down the pot she was drying. She knew she must get away before she was sent back to Freeborne, but her heart was heavy at the thought that she would see Luke no more.

"I wish I need not go," she said, feeling the ache of tears in her throat.

He reached out and touched her hand. "I wish it, too." His voice was so sad she was almost comforted. He minded as much as she did.

He did not return that evening. Had Ethan refused?

Sleep would not come and the attic was stuffy. Noisy, too! Judith had dosed herself into insensibility with some remedy of her own. She lay upon her back, shaking the bed with her snores. Softly Alis made her way down the stairs.

Nothing stirred in the kitchen. She opened the door, crossed the little yard with its shrubs and pots of herbs, and went to breathe the cool air in the vegetable garden.

Restless in her misery, she thought she would walk a little, so she let herself out through the wooden door in the wall and stepped into the back lane by which she had arrived at the Minister's house, six weeks before. How long ago it seemed. Now she must leave them, must say good-bye to Luke. And to think that she had disliked him at their first meeting! Troubled though she was, she could not help smiling when she thought of him leaning against the door frame, apologizing awkwardly for calling her a friend of Thomas's. Then her heart beat faster as she remembered the touch of his hand that afternoon.

She walked on. Above her head, the clear spring sky was dusted with stars. When she had been a little girl, her father had told her that the Maker lived up there.

She found herself by the side of the prayer house, which stood apart from the houses of the square in a plot of its own. She thought she would go in and sit for a while. The building was never locked. Perhaps she would ask the Maker for help.

Quietly she felt her way through the vestibule and into the main chamber. A little starlight glimmered in the windows, but the body of the hall was velvety dark. She sat down on one of the benches. She could not think how to pray. Surely the Maker knew what she wanted. What difference did it make if she put it into words? So she gave up that idea and sat quietly, wishing that the tranquil night would never end. After a little while, she stretched out on the bench and lay looking up into the blackness of the roof.

She was dreaming of dry leaves crunching underfoot as she walked with her mother through the woods that edged her uncle's farm. They were falling like snow from the great trees, slowly at first, then faster and faster, whirling through the air, more and more of them so that she could no longer see the path. She tried to cry out to her mother, but leaves filled her mouth, bitter and dry to the taste. She could not swallow or spit them out. She was choking. She could not breathe.

Abruptly she woke. She could see nothing. But the crackling of leaves was loud in her ears and her mouth was burning dry. For a moment she was bewildered, thinking herself still caught in the dream.

Then with horror, she knew: the prayer house was on fire. Covering her mouth and nose with her hand, she stumbled toward the door to the vestibule. In the thick smoke, she felt for the latch. She could not find it. The wood of the door was hot. She could hardly bear to touch it but she *must* find the latch. Again and again she passed her hands over the surface. It was not there! It was not there! She was whimpering in terror now. She would never get out; she would die. Even if she found the latch, there was fire behind the door. She would not be able to go that way. Desperately she prayed to the Maker.

Then she remembered that there was a door to the old graveyard behind the building. She could get out that way. But she could not remember where the door was. There were corridors and meeting rooms behind the main hall. The fire would catch up with her and she would be trapped.

The windows—that was it! She could get out of a window. She knew there was a passageway down the center of the hall. She inched forward with her hands out before her and found the back of a bench, then slid her hands along the top until, with a sob of relief, she found the space.

As fast as she dared in the thick darkness, she stumbled her way to the front, where the smoke was less dense. The left-hand window. She knew it opened easily. The Minister had asked her to open it before the last prayer meeting. There was a bench below it she could stand on. Her hands encountered empty space. For a terrible instant she thought she had lost her way, then she hit her elbow on something—yes, it was the lectern—and knew where she was. She found the bench and the window, running her hand up the side to the clasp. It yielded and she felt a rush of air. At the same moment, the door to the vestibule burst and fire roared inward, irradiating the smoke.

Desperately she pulled herself up and over the high sill. She meant to jump down, but her balance was gone and she fell, grazing her arm and landing awkwardly on the soft ground below. For a moment she was completely dazed, unable to move, but fear that the fire would find her gave her strength, and she knew that she must raise the alarm.

She staggered round the side of the building. Smoke was pouring out of the roof though—extraordinarily, it seemed to her—no flames were visible. She tried to shout, but her throat was so dry she could barely croak. She must warn them. They must come.

She made her way on trembling legs to the nearest house and hammered on the door. At first she could make no one hear. But then a window opened, then another and another. Soon there were voices and movement. The smell of smoke was in the air now, and the flames were visible. She stood by as people rushed to and fro, until a chain was formed to pass buckets of water from the pump. The smoky, flickering light danced upon their features, and their voices were lost in the roar of flames.

She staggered out of the square and at once the sounds became distant, the air cooler. Her throat was dry and raw, and her limbs ached. She must go home to Mistress Elizabeth.

8

She wandered confusedly through the back alleyways to the rear of the Minister's house. Surely, word of the fire would have wakened the household. Mistress Elizabeth would be waiting in the kitchen to tend to Alis's grazes and give her a soothing drink for her sore throat.

The narrow lane was very dark. Alis slowed her pace, fearful of falling in the blackness. Stretching out her hand to find the door into the kitchen garden, she felt the smooth leaves of the creeper that trailed over the back wall. Nearly there. Step by step. Feel for the latch.

Suddenly she was seized from behind and a hand went hard over her mouth. She froze in shock, and before she had time to resist, a voice whispered right in her ear, "Alis. It's me, Luke. Don't make a sound."

She stood still, her heart hammering. His voice was no more than breath.

"They're waiting for you. You mustn't go in."

Who was waiting? Elizabeth and Jacob? Her brain could make no sense of his words. He was speaking again.

"Make your way to the new burial ground. Don't let anyone see you. I'll meet you there."

He released her. Now she thought she understood. Someone had come for her: her father, or Galin perhaps. And Luke had, after all, managed to persuade Ethan to help her. For just a second, she hesitated. Once more the longing to see her father swept over her; then Luke gave her a little push and she knew she could not. Quietly she made her way to the far end of the lane where it gave onto a wide road. The moon had risen, and she must stay in the shadows of walls and duck as she passed windows, in case someone was peering from behind the shutters. It was torture to her to go slowly, but there were a few people about now. Sometimes she had to stand motionless in the dark, willing them not to notice her. Once, a woman came flying round a corner and straight into Alis, but she was gone again in an instant, calling an apology over her shoulder as she ran.

At last she was free of the houses and walking the tree-lined lane to the burial ground. At the gate, she paused. Beyond, surrounded by a low wall, the graves lay quiet under the moonlight. A little breeze stirred the leaves from time to time; other than that there was no sound or movement. She withdrew into the shadows to wait.

She had grown cold and stiff. Fearful, too. Ethan had said he would not help them. Why should he have changed his mind? Could Luke have thought of something else? It seemed a long time before she heard the faint clink of a harness and saw him come along the lane leading two horses, their coats burnished by moonlight. She stepped out so that he could see her, and he brought the animals to a halt.

"Alis. I'm sorry I've been so long. I had to get hold of some clothes for you and go out to Ellen's for this other horse. Quickly now. You must get away before they come looking for you." He was checking the saddle and tightening the girth.

"But Luke, where am I going? What is happening? Has my father come for me?" She felt panic rising. Everything was happening so fast, and all of it a mystery. Must she ride off into the darkness, without direction and alone?

He held the horse steady for her to mount. "Thomas and Rebecca came. You were suspected of starting the fire, they said. Someone had seen you. You were to be taken away and questioned."

For a moment she was made speechless by the absurdity of it. "But it was I who raised the alarm."

He nodded. "So they told my grandmother—a clever trick to cover what you had done!"

Her stomach lurched suddenly. What would happen to her if they caught her? They had broken Tobias. They had no mercy in them. She began to scramble into the saddle. In a moment Luke, too, was mounted, and they were away.

Alis could ride, but she was only used to the gentle pace of her father's mare. Galloping at speed along an unknown road, she clung fearfully to her horse's mane and prayed she would not fall. The beating hooves, the sound of her own panting breath in her ears, terror of the pursuers who were surely behind. And ahead? She did not know.

At length the farmland gave way to scrub; then they were among trees, and Luke slowed his horse to a walk. Alis was too breathless to speak, glad simply that they were no longer exposed on the moonlit road. They went on in silence until, through the trees, a faint light showed. They were on the edge of a small clearing. She could see the silhouette of a man seated on the ground by a fire that he was feeding from a pile of sticks at his side. Luke slid from his horse and held out a hand to Alis. Her limbs trembled so, she could hardly manage them, landing awkwardly despite his assistance. He tied up the horses, while she stood by in a daze. The figure in the clearing had not shown any sign of being aware of their presence.

"Ethan," Luke called softly.

Without turning, he raised an arm, black against the light of the fire, and waved them over. Alis hesitated and Luke drew her forward. She was shivering now, and the warmth of the flames was very welcome as they came close. Crouching opposite him, with the fire between them, Alis examined the man. Lit from below, his face was all shadows and highlights, the whites of the eyes gleaming out of the dark sockets, the cheeks hollowed out. He had a roughly trimmed, gray-streaked beard, and longer hair than she was used to, but he was not shaggy like the wandering tinkers and basket makers she had occasionally seen. He did not look at Alis, but jerking his head in her direction, said roughly to Luke, "Why have you come? I told you I would not take her."

Luke was opening his pack. "I have the money, and also something that you might sell."

From a small cloth bag he tipped into his hand a ring, a worn circle of yellowish metal made of two intertwining strands. Ethan took it and examined it, holding it close to the flames.

"Whose is it?" His voice, low and a little hoarse, gave nothing away.

Luke said firmly, "It is mine."

There was a pause. Ethan held up the ring, turning it in his fingers. Then he looked steadily at Luke. The boy met his gaze. After a moment the man gave a short, hoarse laugh. "Well now, friend Luke. You have delved into your box of treasures for me, it seems. And you have come here at a wild pace the pair of you, if appearances do not lie. So you had best tell me what has happened. Particularly"—he stopped, and for the first time his gaze rested on Alis—"if I am to risk my life to get your companion away from here."

Luke said eagerly, "Will you take it then?"

But the older man shook his head. "Not so fast, young hotblood. Two days ago you told me she was for finding her lost brother. And that there was a husband she couldn't stomach. But you didn't bring her with you. And this afternoon I told you again that I would not risk my life for a few coins, and you went away drooping, for you knew I meant what I said. Yet here you are, and the girl with you. So something has surely happened. And if I'm to take her from under the noses of the Elders, for which I shall surely hang if they catch me, I need to know the truth."

Luke's eyes widened with sudden hope and Alis's heart beat faster.

Ethan listened impassively as the boy described the night's events. He had returned to the Minister's house and found the door of the meeting room shut. He had recognized the voice of Elder Rebecca and stopped outside to listen. The Maker be praised for giving the woman a hard, loud voice! Of his grandmother's words he could make out nothing, but Rebecca's came through clear: Alis had set the fire; she had raised the alarm to hide her sin by a seemingly virtuous act; she was to be taken to Master Robert's house and there kept and questioned. "And," Luke ended desperately, "if you will not help her, I do not know how to save her from them. They mean her ill, I am sure. It is Thomas's doing, or Robert's, because he hates my grand-parents."

Ethan was silent for a while when Luke had finished. At length he said to Alis in his harsh, low voice, "Did you do it?"

She cried out in protest, "No, indeed I did not. What reason should I have?"

He was silent again, then turning to Luke he asked, "And the ring? How did you come by it?"

The boy's dark face was desolate in the firelight. "It was my mother's marriage ring. It is all I have of her. My grandmother gave it to me."

Alis felt tears prick at her eyelids, but Ethan appeared unmoved.

"Will she know it's gone, the old woman? Add theft to abduction, and I can expect a raw time before they hang me."

"My grandmother will not know unless I tell her," Luke said.

The fire had burned down and the air was cold. Ethan was again weighing the ring in his hand. At last he held it out to Luke. "Keep it. I will take the girl to the city."

Alis gasped in relief. "Oh, thank you, Master Ethan."

Luke said fervently, "You are a true friend, Ethan. There is no one else to help us."

Ethan nodded dismissively. "Yes, yes. But mind you do not tell your grandmother. I'd not have my name on her lips when they decide to question her. And no doubt they have ways of getting the truth out of old ladies in these days of rigor."

Alis shuddered at his words. Surely they would not dare to harm Elizabeth?

Luke was asking questions. Would Ethan help Alis find her brother? What if she could not? He would not abandon her in so dangerous a place, would he?

Ethan looked sardonically at him. "Do not trouble yourself, friend Luke. It pleases me to thwart them. I will do my best by the girl, never fear."

Ethan would say no more. He must leave them awhile to conceal his wagon. Provided Luke kept his mouth shut, it would be thought that Alis was hidden somewhere in the area, and the search would give them time to get away. He got to his feet, a stocky man, slightly bowlegged.

"What of the horse she came on?" he asked. "Is it stolen?"

No. It was one that Mistress Ellen had rescued from Samuel's place after he was taken from the farm. Luke had begged it of her in his grandmother's name. When she knew what had happened, she would not grudge the horse to save Alis from Robert and the others.

"How will you go?" Luke asked Ethan.

"Across country. I know the ways through the forest. We must avoid the main highway until we're much farther south, or they'll surely hear of us. And," Ethan added grimly, "that is all I will tell, for what you do not know, they cannot get out of you, do what they will."

He disappeared into the darkness. Luke and Alis were left alone.

Very soon they must part. Not knowing how to thank him, her voice catching in her throat, Alis said, "I am glad Ethan did not take the ring."

Luke nodded. "It was hard to think of giving it up. I had hoped there might be some other way. But when I heard Rebecca and realized that they were there, waiting for you . . ."

Suddenly fearful, Alis said in low voice, "Ethan will not fail me, will he? I can do no other than trust him."

"He did not like the rule of the Elders, even in the days before the reformers took hold here. I think he will be glad to save one they would persecute."

And now Ethan was back, leading his horse, and the time was come.

Luke said sadly, "You must go. The Maker keep you safe. I had no friend after Tobias until you came, and you are more to me than he ever was, though I loved him dearly. Oh, I wish I could come with you! But I will not leave my grandparents to face their enemies alone." He took her hand.

Alis felt her throat swell so that it was hard to speak. "We shall meet again. We must. When you go from Two Rivers, you can leave word for me with Mistress Ellen, to say where you are headed. Once I have found my brother, Ethan can bring me news when he comes again to the city, if he will. Tell your grandmother I am sorry for bringing trouble on her. And, oh, Luke, have a care: they will be so angry. I will pray to the Maker to protect you."

She put her arms about his neck and held him close, feeling the softness of his face against hers. Their lips touched.

Ethan stamped out the embers of the fire and the light died. She stepped back. Luke's face was the faintest blur in the darkness. He did not speak, but pressed her hand in farewell.

"Stay here awhile and let us get away," Ethan said to the boy when Alis was mounted and he stood at the horses' heads, ready to lead them off. "Then if you are seen riding back they will not so easily pick up our trail. In autumn I will be here again. I will bring what news there is to Mistress Ellen's. Do as the girl says and leave word for me there."

He pulled gently on the reins and murmured something to his horse. And they moved off into the blackness under the trees.

9

Their route lay mainly through the forest. It was slow but safer: pursuit would be confined to the main highways. Occasionally they came to small settlements where the people had cleared a little land and lived on what they could get from the forest. Ethan was known in some of these places, and so they had a bed for the night. Otherwise they slept in the open. Alis grew used to being tired, hungry, and cold, and she did not complain.

As they got near to their destination, Alis wanted to know about the city and told Ethan what Luke had said. He smiled at that. "He's right enough in some ways. The merchants who make their money from trade have great houses and do as they please. And they dress themselves in finery and think it makes them fine folk." He looked at Alis sardonically. "But you'll know how it is, surely. Have you not been warned what a terrible place the city is—*where the Maker is mocked and all manner of sin triumphs?*"

Alis nodded. Murder went unpunished there, and crimes too terrible to recount were committed.

"Yes," said Ethan. "That is what I was taught, too."

"Is it not so?"

"Only in part. On the north side, there are merchants who trade with foreign lands, and crafts folk, and tradesmen. Aye, and the Communities buy and sell with them for all their high talk. There are laws and taxes, courts to try offenders, and a prison to keep them in. Over the river it is different. Only the poorest people live across the bridge now—and those who have something to hide."

"My brother will not be there, I hope," Alis said rather anxiously.

Ethan did not answer.

Joining the wagons and horses on the northern approach to the city, Ethan was nervous. She was his niece from one of the forest settlements if anyone asked—her mother was sick and he had taken charge of her.

"How will you be called?" he said.

Distracted by the jostling crowd, she snatched the first name that came to mind: Sarah. Afterward, she wished she had chosen differently.

They reached the crumbling wall and passed under the remains of the gate-arch shored up by thick wooden poles, then into a roadway bordered by low shops. Most were open-fronted, with tables of goods or provisions for sale. The noise was tremendous: the vendors shouting their wares above the jingle of harnesses and the shrill cries of the ragged children who ran among the crowd, almost under the horses' hooves. Alis concentrated on keeping close behind Ethan as he edged his horse through the throng. Away from the gate, off the main thoroughfare, the crowds were less dense. Uneasily, she noted the number of passersby in the clothing of her own people.

After some time, they passed under an archway into an enclosed yard overlooked on all sides by windows. Here they dismounted, handing their animals to a bent-shouldered youth who received them with a grunt.

"Come," Ethan said to Alis, who was staring around her still stunned by the noises and sights. His expression was grim.

Inside, a passageway led to the inn's main room with trestle tables under a low ceiling. It was crowded with tradesmen and laborers sitting elbow to elbow at their midday meal. There was a good savory smell of meat and onions. A white-aproned woman carrying a steaming dish nodded her head at Ethan and indicated a side table. They sat there, and within a few moments she came over to them.

"You're back then. And who's this? Given up your lone ways, have you?"

"My niece," Ethan said tersely. "Her mother's sick."

The woman had a raw-looking red face, and wiry, dark hair threaded with gray strands piled loosely on the top of her head. She had been stacking up the dirty dishes on the table. At these words she stopped, a bowl in her hand. An avid look came over her face. "Niece? I never knew you had family. Thought you claimed no kin in the world."

He shrugged. "We're hungry, Moll. Is there food enough left for us?"

The eagerness in her face died and the last dish clattered loudly onto the pile.

"Well, I'm sure I can't see why you have to be so close with me. I've known you years enough. And let you have the little chamber at the top of the house so you needn't share bed-space with others. There's maybe some stew left, or bread and cheese if not."

And she turned away, calling loudly to a fat, red-faced man who had appeared at the door to the kitchen, "Two more, Jem, and draw some ale, too."

Ethan did not speak while they ate. Alis would have liked to question him, but he seemed preoccupied and she was anxious not to vex him. Her first view of the city had come as a shock. How was she to find her brother among all these people? She would need much help, and there was only Ethan to give it.

While he ate, Ethan looked watchfully about him. The tables under the blackened beams were emptying as the traders and workmen returned to their labor. A few lingered over pots of ale, taking their ease. At last, Ethan pushed away his plate. "Tell me about your brother."

"He is seven years older than me," Alis said. "He was named Joel, but I always called him Jojo. He is fair-haired as I am, with blue eyes. We are both like our father in that. And he is tall—Jojo, I mean."

Ethan looked skeptical. "Such a brother would seem tall to a little girl, but most likely he was of ordinary height."

"At fourteen," Alis said, "he was as tall as boys three and four years older—taller than some of them. My mother thought he took after my uncle who is above six foot."

"Tall, fair, blue-eyed." Ethan's expression was gloomy. "It is not much to go on. There is nothing else, no mark by which he might be known?"

Alis shook her head. She remembered very clearly the boy who had been her brother, but he would be a man now. Perhaps she would not even recognize him. The thought chilled her heart.

Ethan was frowning in concentration. "It's fortunate that the people of this region are mostly small and dark. Such as your brother are not common, except among outsiders who have settled here. And Joel is not a name given to children outside the Communities. We must hope he has kept it, so that he may be easier to find."

He was silent once more. Then he said, "Had he a skill? Was he destined for any particular trade, do you know?"

Alis said slowly, "My father is a master carpenter, and Jojo was good with his hands. But whether he would have taken to that work, I do not know."

Ethan nodded. "I'll try the guild of carpenters. It's a starting point, at least." He got up. "I'd best bestir myself."

"Shall I come with you?" Alis said eagerly, but Ethan shook his head.

"It's better I don't have to explain who you are. I'm not over-practiced at lying. You stay here. I'll have a word with Moll so that she doesn't pester you with questions. She's kind enough for a city tavern-keeper, but she likes to gossip. Remember the story now: your mother is sick, maybe dying. If Moll wants to know anything—you're too grieved to talk."

Alis nodded. Once more, she was engulfed with longing for the old days when she had trusted her parents. She turned her head away to conceal the tears that sprang into her eyes. There would be no falsehood in saying that it distressed her to speak of her mother: it was misery even to think of her.

For three days, Ethan came and went, and always he returned shaking his head. None of the guilds had anyone called Joel on their list of craftsmen. The city authorities kept records of residents, too, for the northern sector, which could be inspected at a price. These also yielded nothing. At last, however, he came back with news. He had come across a man who ran a gang of searchers—boys who lived rough, knew the poorer parts of the city, and earned a few coins by finding people. One of them knew of someone who might be Joel. Ethan was to meet a lad who would show him the way.

"Let me come this time," Alis pleaded, but Ethan shook his head.

"I must find out more first. Perhaps this is not your brother."

They were sitting at a table in the main room, conversing in low tones so as not to be overheard. Suddenly, the door opened to admit two men dressed in familiar dark clothing. Alis's heart jumped. They looked like Elders.

Moll was leaning casually on the bar, chatting to a thin man with a set square protruding from the pocket of his leather apron. He slid guiltily away as the newcomers approached. One of them was of middle height, with a slightly weather-reddened face under a bald pate. He looked like a farmer, but he carried an inkhorn and a large black ledger. The other was taller and thinner. He had a long, narrow face as if his head had been squeezed between boards: above thin lips, the blade of a nose jutted out sharply. Dark hair, cut short. He searched the room with his eyes, then greeted the landlady.

"Good day to you, Mistress. All is well here, I trust. Have you anything to report?"

Alis started, but Ethan gestured to her to be still. Moll straightened up.

"Nothing much, Master Bartholomew. We're full up. No newcomers these three days, since Ethan there"—she raised her voice as she nodded in his direction—"and his niece. He always stays here—a traveler in remedies for the sick—I've known him for years."

Ethan stood up and rested his hand on Alis's shoulder as the two men crossed the room. Stopping by the table, the man Moll had called Master Bartholomew inclined his head in greeting. In his narrow face, his eyes seemed too close together. His voice was high, slightly pinched, nasal. "Master Ethan. You are welcome. And this is your niece, I understand. What does she do here in the city?"

Ethan looked steadily at him. "Pardon me, Master. You'll tell me maybe, by what authority you ask questions of me? I am not a member of any Community."

The thin man nodded his head. "You are quite right to ask, Master Ethan, and I will tell you. The Community of the northern quarter—whose Elders we are—has purchased the lease of this inn. Naturally we wish to be sure that the establishment is well conducted. It is for that reason that we take an interest in who comes here. If you have nothing to hide, you have nothing to fear from questions, surely."

His glance slid across to Alis and away again. She held herself rigid. Ethan's hand was steady on her shoulder. Now he said guardedly, "Well, Master Bartholomew. As you know, my name is Ethan. My sister is sick, and I am taking my niece to stay awhile with her aunt who lives in the eastern quarter, close to the river."

The red-faced man had seated himself at the table and was making an entry in the ledger.

His companion looked directly at Alis for the first time. "And what is your name, child?"

She felt the warning pressure of Ethan's hand.

"My name is Sarah, sir, but I am c—c—c—called Sally at home." She knew she was blushing, but he did not seem suspicious.

"Well, Sally, I hope your mother will soon be recovered. Master Ethan, I am sorry that this young woman must be lodged in the eastern quarter. That part, especially near the river, is not as well ordered as it should be, though we have begun to remedy that."

He turned to his companion. "You have the record? Yes? Then let us be gone. We have much to do. Good day to you all."

He smiled, but the other man gave Alis a long stare before gathering up his materials and moving away. It occurred to her suddenly that the names Sally and Alis sounded very much alike, and she shivered.

The heavy wooden door swung shut behind them, and Ethan let out a long breath. Moll served two of the men at the table with more ale and came across the room. Ethan looked at her, frowning. "What's all this, Moll?"

She sat down at the table with them, brushing some loose strands of hair from her forehead with the back of her wrist. "You've seen nothing yet! I went to pay the rent last quarter day and found the lease had been sold. Instead of old Cora with her cap and leather bag—counting on her fingers and never forgetting a copper piece—there was this long-faced Master Bartholomew and a young'un with a quill writing it all down. Now we must abide by strict rules or the place'll be taken from us. You never know when they'll turn up either, asking questions and poking about. The good times are gone, I tell you, Ethan. Some drinking houses shut early now. Soon we'll all have to be abed when the Elders say and go to prayer meetings, I shouldn't wonder."

Ethan raised his eyebrows. "The city authorities, they are content with this?"

Moll shrugged. "And why not? It saves them the trouble of keeping order themselves." She got up. "Well, I must be about my work. You'll be biding a day or two, Ethan?"

"Maybe, Moll, but I must deliver this young'un to her aunt soon, and maybe I'll bed down there for a night or so. You'll keep the horses stabled for me?"

She nodded.

When she had disappeared into the kitchen, Alis seized Ethan's arm in terror. "We must leave at once. Perhaps they have news from Two Rivers. They will take me back there—to Thomas and Robert."

"Steady now." His craggy face had a brooding look. "Our Master Bartholomew has no reason to mistrust that you're my niece if I say so. Still, you cannot stay here much longer, I agree."

"I cannot stay at all! Oh, Ethan, I beg of you, let us go now, before it is too late. They may be back at any moment, and there is danger for you, also."

She could not bear his sitting there still, when they might be safely away. He looked at her without moving. "There is danger in staying here, it is true, but this lad I spoke of—I do not know if he is to be trusted. Maybe he can lead us to your brother, maybe not. I am to meet him by the bridge and cross the river into the southern quarter. It is an ill place. There is more danger for you in going there than staying here, maybe."

"I do not care! I will come with you. Whatever happens to me, it cannot be worse than going back." Seeing that he still looked doubtful, she added desperately, "Ethan, how can I stay here alone? Suppose they return while you are gone."

At that, he pushed back his chair. "Come then. I'll not leave you behind. Fetch the bundles, while I speak to Moll. She must think you are going to your aunt, so that she may tell our inquisitive Elders as much."

Alis went quickly up to the tiny room at the top of the house and collected their few possessions. When she came down again, Ethan was waiting for her. He took his bundle and pack, and knelt down to check the fastenings. Still shaky with fright, she said fervently, "You are good to me, Ethan. I am sorry we had so little to give you, Luke and I."

Ethan shrugged. "I've a soft spot for the lad. As for you, I wouldn't risk myself to save you from marriage, but I'd not leave a girl to the mercy of Masters Robert and Thomas—I have heard too much of their ways."

He finished securing his belongings and stood up. "Come then. Let us be gone."

They took up their bundles and went out into the sunlit streets.

10

They passed along a paved street of fine houses—merchants' houses, Ethan said—and then crossed the grand main square. Alis would have stopped to gape, but fear of Master Bartholomew drove her on. Leaving the square, they entered a district of tradesmen's shops—carpenters, boot and harness makers, chandlers, glove makers, taverns and pie shops, places selling lengths of cloth, hat makers, bakeries, apothecaries' shops. She was dizzy with it all. More houses, of a modest kind, and two rows of what Ethan called charity dwellings—built for the poor by merchants hoping for the Maker's favor, he said.

"Do the people here worship the Maker?" Alis asked in surprise.

"Your parents would not think so, but there are places of prayer of all kinds, though they do not follow the ways of the Communities. The world has more in it than you have been taught."

Alis was silent. She was beginning to feel that she knew nothing at all.

When at length they came to the bridge, it was still too early for the boy to be there. Alis leaned on the parapet to watch the choppy water slapping the bank.

"That way is the sea," Ethan said, pointing. "There was a port here once, but the river's been silting up for years. Now the seagoing ships unload onto barges downriver, on the coast."

She savored the smell, a muddy wetness with a tang of fish somewhere. Gulls scooped the air above the water and dived suddenly at invisible prey. Their harsh cries mingled with the voices of boatmen and with the more distant sounds of cargo being unloaded at the dock farther down.

For a little while, Alis was content to be away from the tavern, but as time went on and there was no sign of the boy, she became nervous. Master Bartholomew might, even now, be on their track. The open spaces and the sunlight, which had been such a pleasure at first, now seemed threatening.

It began to grow cooler. People came and went across the river. Still the boy did not come. Ethan said nothing, his face gloomy, but just as they were giving up hope, a ragged child sidled out from behind a couple of passing workmen. He was no more than ten years old, small, and very dirty. He stopped in front of Ethan, saying in a hoarse voice, "Man for Joe?"

Ethan said, "Joel. A tall, fair man called Joel, or Jojo maybe. You know him?"

The boy did not answer but jerked his head in the direction of the bridge and held out his hand. Ethan said, "Where's the other boy— the one I spoke to this morning? Did he send you?"

The child nodded. Ethan reached into a pocket and produced a single copper coin that he held out. The child looked at it but he did not move to take it.

Ethan said, "You'll get another one afterward. You understand? When we find Joel."

Almost before he had finished speaking, the child had snatched the coin and shoved it away inside a tattered shirt that had once been white. Then he set off at a trot across the bridge without looking back. Ethan and Alis followed him.

On the far side, the boy led them along the embankment, stopping from time to time so that they did not lose sight of him. Blocks of mean-looking houses and shops, separated by alleyways, faced them on the other side of the roadway. On one corner was an inn with a faded sign showing a crudely painted sail and a coil of rope. The boy darted across the road and gestured to them to follow. They turned down one of the alleyways.

Almost at once they lost sight of the river, and there was no more breeze to freshen the air. Ethan looked about him uneasily as they hurried along in the child's wake. The narrow streets twisted and crisscrossed. Fearfully, Alis wondered whether they would be able to find their way back if they needed to. The late-afternoon sun was already too low to penetrate the narrowest lanes, and in places the upper floors jutted out over the cobbles, making a kind of early twilight that seemed full of shadows. The few people they encountered either ignored them or stared suspiciously. Already they looked out of place—clearly better dressed than the locals, and their bundles showing them to be strangers, too. Ahead of them, the boy was visible only as a blur of limbs and a flutter of tattered shirt. Alis kept close to Ethan as they were drawn deeper into the maze of cobbled lanes. On the corner of a square, a woman with a heavily painted face put her hand on Ethan's arm and murmured an invitation. He shook her off and they hastened away down yet another narrow passageway in the thickening dusk.

The boy had halted for them at the next turn. Before he could dart off again, Ethan called urgently, "Wait!"

When they came level with him, Ethan held up another copper coin—out of the boy's reach. "It is getting too late. You must take us back to the bridge. We will come again tomorrow, in the morning, when it is light."

The child said in his strange, hoarse voice, "T'ain't far now," and made as if to go on but just then a man rounded the corner. He glanced at the little group and stopped abruptly, glaring at the boy. "Why you little—didn't I tell you not to come round here again?"

He made a grab for the boy's arm, but the child kicked out viciously, freed himself, and was off. With a roar of rage, the man charged after him. In seconds, he was out of sight. They heard the thud of his boots briefly, then there was silence.

They listened intently, but there was no sound of returning footsteps. Alis looked at Ethan nervously. "Do you think he'll come back—that man, I mean?"

"I doubt it," Ethan said quietly. "And maybe it's best that we aren't here if he does. Alis, we must turn back. I can go no farther without a guide, and besides, it will be dark soon. Come now. We will try again tomorrow."

She did not protest, for of course he was right, but her heart was heavy. Surely they had been close to finding her brother, and perhaps now they had lost their chance. "Do you know the way?"

"No, but we've been heading south. We must go north again, find the river, and cross the bridge. We'll not go to Moll's. There are other inns."

They turned back along a narrow street of crumbling houses. Walls bulged out or leaned at dangerous angles. Missing doors made mouths of blackness. There was no sound of human activity. Fearfully, Alis hurried along in the gloom.

Suddenly, a foot hooked itself round her ankle and she lost her balance. Someone caught her as she fell and a hand covered her mouth. At the same time a ragged figure came between her and Ethan. There was a thud and a groan as Ethan went down. A girl emerged abruptly from a doorway. She was no taller than Alis, but she was holding a knife whose blade glinted in the dull light. The newcomer joined the ragged figure who was kneeling over Ethan.

Panic-stricken, Alis struggled, trying to dig her elbow into her captor's belly, but he was too strong for her. Still off balance, she could not prevent him dragging her away from where Ethan lay on the ground. Then the hand over her mouth slackened its hold slightly, and she bit hard into the soft flesh at the base of the thumb. With a curse he let go. She seized her chance and fled.

She was between high walls, stumbling on slimy cobbles. At once she was lost. Footsteps behind her urged her on. Left. Right. Back on herself. Right again. And again. She ran in blind terror. Down an opening on the left—too late she saw the blank wall at the end.

Trapped! But no. There was a passageway running along the wall. She turned right out of it. This time she really was in a dead end.

Sobbing for breath, she turned back. The knife girl barred her exit. She turned again. Yet another passageway, and at the far end, the silhouette of a tall youth. She swiveled round: knife girl one way; tall youth the other. Alis stopped. They would kill her, but she must breathe, she *must* breathe.

Her pursuers looked older than she was. Not one of them was out of breath. They watched her as she recovered, cutting off the escape routes but not coming any closer. The girl was nearest: thin, raggedly dressed, with spiky fair hair. The tallest of them was almost a man, with a pocked, battered-looking face and long dark hair tied back with a scrap of cloth. When she met his eye he grinned, revealing broken teeth. She looked away, frightened. A skinny boy, clothed in a colorful array of mismatched items, was performing an elaborate dance on his own on the cobblestones. His feet beat a pattern that ended in a pirouette and began again immediately. He stopped suddenly and stared at her. Then he held out his hand. "Dance?"

She stared back with a sense of nightmare. After a moment he began again, feet pattering lightly on the cobbles. The others continued to watch her in silence.

Someone came into the passageway from the far end, carrying bundles—hers and Ethan's, Alis realized. The tall youth said at once, "Let's go. It's too light still, for 'angin round."

"What about her?" It was the spiky-haired girl with the knife. Her voice was light and sharp.

"Leave 'er." It was an instruction.

The dancer left off his routine and said protestingly, "Not safe, not kind."

"Don't be a fool, Dancer. She ain't nothin' to us." His pockmarked face was ugly in the half light.

Alis said suddenly in a loud voice, "I'm looking for my brother."

She did not know why she had spoken. She felt giddy with fright. The one called Dancer said sorrowfully, "Not this side of the river. Only derelicts. Shouldn't come this way. Not safe."

"He's called Joel." Her voice seemed to have a life of its own. It would insist on talking.

The knife girl said spitefully, "Joel! Nobody gives himself a name like that this side of the river."

"When I was little I called him Jojo." Why was she telling them this?

They had turned away, but now they swung back and were staring suspiciously at her.

"She's making it up," the fair girl said at last. "It can't be true."

"What's 'e do, this brother o' yours?" the tall youth wanted to know. He seemed to be the leader.

Alis's voice was shaking. "I don't know. He came here years ago and now I've run away. I've got to find him."

They were looking at each other uneasily. Finally the tall boy nodded. "Bring 'er along. We better be sure. We c'n always get rid of 'er."

Dancer took her arm. He had a beautiful, heart-shaped face, half-hidden by ragged locks of dark hair. His voice was coaxing. "Come with us. Much safer. Bad place. Worse at night."

In a sudden panic she pulled back. What was she doing? They had decided to leave her, and now she had made them change their minds.

"No! I must find Ethan. He's hurt. You've hurt him. Perhaps he's dead."

The one with the bundles shook his head. He was dark and heavy, almost a man, his neck so thick and short that his head seemed to grow out of his shoulders. "Nah. He'll be all right. He was coming round. We don't kill unless we have to. Ain't that right, Weasel?"

The tall youth grinned ferociously but said nothing.

Dancer held on to her and said soothingly, "Gone by now. Come with us. Much better. Danger in the dark."

She let herself be led away.

The light was gone by the time they stopped at the entrance to a small courtyard. A torch flared in a wall-holder, giving off a smell of pitch. The fair girl went first, taking the torch with her. The gate was old and grass grew at its base. It would not open all the way, and they squeezed through the opening one at a time, Dancer pushing Alis ahead of him. The courtyard itself was very dark, the ground uneven underfoot. Following the flare of the torch they came to an opening.

A voice spoke out of the shadows. "You've been a long time. And who is that with you?"

The girl raised the torch and it lit up a pale face framed by long hair: behind him a dusty staircase disappeared up into darkness. Alis saw him only for an instant as he turned away saying curtly, "Bring her inside."

Could this be her brother?

The room above was lit by a couple of reeking, smoky tallow lamps, and was furnished with nothing but a table and a few battered chairs. As they entered, voices called out greetings and questions.

Dancer pushed Alis forward. A hand lifted a lamp from the table so that it cast its light on her face, dazzling her. There was silence. Then the lamp was replaced on the table and she could see. He was older than the rest, lean and muscular, with the pale face she had glimpsed at the foot of the stairs. The others were quiet and still, deferring to him, except for the knife girl who said in her sharp voice, "This girl says she's looking for her brother. Claims she used to call him Jojo. We thought we'd better bring her back."

Alis was trembling with fright. Only Dancer's grip was keeping her upright. The pale face swam before her. Someone was speaking: "Who are you?"

She made an effort to focus her eyes. The young man who seemed to be the leader was standing with his arms crossed, looking at her. Was it Jojo? She strained to find the remembered face in his features. For a moment she thought she recognized him, and then he was a stranger again. She said as firmly as she could, "My name is Alis. I am looking for my brother, Joel. He is here in the city somewhere, I am sure, and I must find him."

She was afraid that they would kill her, or worse.

He said, "Perhaps I know him. Tell me about him."

She did not think he meant it; he was playing with her, before they did whatever they were going to do. And what could she tell him? Half her life had passed since Joel's disappearance and not a word from him in all that time. For all she knew he might be dead. And yet . . . surely there was something about the eyes, the shape of the brow. He spoke again. It was a stranger's voice, quenching her hope.

"This brother—this Joel—what is he like?"

"I have not seen him for seven years, since he ran away. He had fair hair and blue eyes. He used to carry me on his back."

He said dismissively, "He sounds like every older brother. Can you remember nothing more particular?"

Where memory should have been, there was only fear. Then a fragment of the past came back to her. "I bit him once when I was little. There was something I couldn't do, and he said it was because I was a girl. I said I wasn't going to be a girl anymore and he laughed at me. He was very good about it—it was bleeding, but he didn't tell. My mother would have been very angry with me. Now I have told you enough. You are surely not my brother, so let me go."

"Where did you bite him?"

Would he never leave off? What did it matter to him? "On the inside of his wrist." She could remember the surprising resistance of his skin between her teeth.

"Where are you from?"

"I am from Freeborne, one of the Communities of the Book." Too late it occurred to her that it might be a mistake to admit this.

"What is your mother's name?"

She gave in to his insistence. "She is called Hannah."

"And your father?"

"Reuben."

"Who is the Minister?"

"His name is Galin. Please, let me go." She heard the whimper in her voice. She had not meant to plead, but she could not help herself.

He held out his hand, palm up. On the inside of the wrist was a faint white scar. "You bit hard, little sister. I remember it well." He was smiling faintly, and his features were suddenly familiar.

"Oh!" She felt giddy with joy and relief. "You *are* Joel."

He said quietly, "My name was Joel once. And I came from Freeborne. My mother was called Hannah and my father, Reuben." His expression hardened. "Have you been sent to tell me that the Maker forgives and that I should return home? Surely you have not come with the Elders at your heels to fetch me back after all these years!"

She shook her head. "I need help."

"What help do you seek? I have nothing. I cannot go back there, whatever your trouble is."

"I cannot go back there, either. They have driven me out and I thought to find refuge with you."

He looked startled. "What could you have done that they should drive you out? And how have you managed to get here?"

The knife girl broke in impatiently, "Jojo, we're hungry. You can ask questions later."

He did not take his eyes off Alis, but he nodded. "Yes, we must eat. Dancer, fetch a chair, and one of you get her something to drink, and food, too."

He held out his hand. "Come, Alis. You look exhausted. Sit down. Do not be afraid. I am very glad to see you again, and if you need refuge, you shall have it."

Fear had killed her appetite, but she drank gratefully while the others talked and joked. Joel sat watching her, and she noted uneasily that he frowned from time to time. She glanced covertly at the others, remembering how they had attacked her and Ethan. Joel was their leader. No wonder he had not embraced her, or spoken the loving words she longed to hear. He was a different person now.

When they had finished eating, Joel demanded to hear her story and she complied. Her listeners were mostly quiet while she spoke, although Galin's age drew a hiss of fury from the fair-haired girl whose name was Edge.

There was silence when Alis stopped talking, then Joel said, "You are right. You cannot go back. You must stay here."

Before she could thank him, there was a voice from the shadows. "We don't need no one else." Weasel thrust forward into the lamplight, his face hostile. There were murmurs of agreement from some of the others.

Joel looked at him steadily. "She's my sister. I will not turn her away."

"She ain't any good to us. Chuck 'er out now."

Edge was playing with her knife, turning it this way and that, catching the light. Now she turned the blade so that it flashed in the speaker's eyes. "Lay off, Weasel." He turned his head away with a curse.

Joel looked at his Alis. Her face was white, and there were huge shadows under her eyes. "Put her to bed," he said to Edge, and the fair girl led Alis away to somewhere dark and quiet.

II

When she woke she was lying on a thin mattress under a woolen cover that smelled faintly damp. She could feel the floor beneath her, and her shoulder ached. Across the room a bundle of blankets and a dented pillow showed where someone else had slept. Groggy, and desperate to relieve herself, she staggered across the bare boards to the half-open door. The corridor outside was silent and empty, but a shutterless window halfway along looked down into a courtyard where a girl was drawing water from a well.

Outside, she realized that it was one of the girls she had seen the previous night—a tall redhead called Shadow. She gave Alis a sour look.

"I need . . ." said Alis.

"Over there." She jerked her head toward the far side of the court. "And make sure you use the ash to cover. It will stink otherwise."

When Alis returned, the girl said grumpily, "I suppose you want something to eat."

They went back up the splintered staircase. The room where they had eaten the night before was empty except for its battered bits of furniture and a scattering of clothes. Shadow brought her a hunk of bread with some strong-tasting cheese, and ignored her while she ate. When the meal was done the other girl said, "I have to go out. Jojo says I'm to take you with me."

Alis was glad to be away from the stale rooms. As they crossed the courtyard to the gate, she looked about her. The building ran all the way round. There were open stalls at ground level, like stables without doors, and a single story of rooms above. The place was in poor condition, with gaping holes in the roof at some points, and it seemed to be unoccupied. Alis wondered why aloud.

"Fever," Shadow said tersely. "Whole city had it four years ago. Worse on this side of the river, of course. Emptied the place out. Won't last, though."

They made their way through narrow streets to a kind of market, a few poor stalls selling cooking pots, bits of cloth, knives, and some food. Shadow bought here and there, spending only in small coins that she took from a belt round her waist. Later they searched musty shops full of old clothes and battered pots until Shadow found someone willing to give a good price for Ethan's jerkin. Poor Ethan. Alis wondered what had happened to him and longed to know that he was safe. It was her fault if he was not. But he was used to the city, and the boy they called Mute had said he would be all right. Surely he would find his way back to the inn where the horses were stabled, and the woman Molly would look after him.

❖ ❖ ❖

Over the evening meal, Alis learned that there were seven in the gang, including three girls. There had been eight but one of the boys had been killed the previous month. No one seemed to care much except Shadow, who pushed her food away when the death was mentioned.

Edge was making tiny punctures on the back of her forearm with the point of her knife. Weasel, sitting next to her, was arguing with Joel about something. After a while Edge stopped what she was doing and looked at him sideways. Then she reached across and rested the knife on the back of his hand.

He stopped speaking and looked down. She was pressing hard with the flat of the blade. Everyone went silent. Weasel sat quite still, his face tight with fury. Joel said warningly, "Edge," and after a moment she put the knife away. Dancer flapped his hands and said reproachfully, "Not nice, not safe," and some of the others laughed. But Weasel looked murderous. Later Alis watched them cross the courtyard in the evening sunlight. Edge was throwing the knife up into the air and catching it as it fell: the others left a wide circle around her.

Left alone, Alis wondered anxiously what she should do. Her first joy at finding Joel was turning to dismay. Her brother was a leader of thieves. Perhaps they were killers, too. She could not stay in such a wicked place, and the girl Edge terrified her. But she could not go out into the city alone. Even Ethan had not been safe. She had been taught to pray to the Maker, but over last few the months she had not dared to do so. Hesitantly she began: *O Maker of the world, hear my prayer and help me in my trouble* . . . She paused. Was anyone listening?

She did not try again.

❖ ❖ ❖

The next day was hot. Shadow sat in the sunny courtyard with another girl, Fleet—slender, dark-haired, with an elfin face and long dark lashes. They had taken a blanket and spread it on the tussocky ground, propping up a couple of moth-eaten parasols for shade. There they remained all day, sometimes sleeping, sometimes talking with their heads close together. Lonely and fearful, Alis did not dare join them.

When evening came, the two of them—plus Dancer, Weasel, and Edge—prepared to go out. Hours afterward, lying sleepless, Alis heard them come back. From the room down the corridor, there was laughter and the sound of money being counted.

For a week or two, Alis spent most of the days sitting in the court-yard or wandering through the endless neglected rooms. Sometimes she went with Shadow on her domestic errands. Then, one evening, as Weasel and the others prepared for their night's work, Joel gave instructions that Alis should go with them. To her he said, "You're going to have to learn to be useful so you'd better see how we work. But stay well back; don't get in the way."

As they were leaving, he said softly so that the others could not hear, "Take care, Alis."

Under their wraps, Fleet and Shadow had on only the skimpiest clothing. Dancer wore a pair of loose green trousers, with a grimy waistcoat of red silk over a ragged shirt. When they stepped from the courtyard into the street, he bowed extravagantly to Alis and offered her his arm. Fearful of offending him, she took it.

The heat of the day lingered in the air as they made their way through the warren of lanes and alleys. In places the cobbles were slimy with filth, and the central gutters ran with foulness; Alis was glad of Dancer's arm. Nearer the river there were crowds of people, and among them, some who were obviously visitors from the north side—groups of men conspicuous by their clothing and a certain bravado. There were stalls set up along the embankment, and the sound of laughter and shouts was in the air. Fiddle players and jugglers vied for attention under flaring torches. Now Dancer went ahead, leaving Alis with Weasel and Edge. Fleet and Shadow wandered along arm in arm, giggling and exchanging banter with the stallholders: the others stayed back a little, always keeping the two girls in sight.

Farther on, Dancer had stopped to watch two men trying their skill at hoop and stick: three hoops on a stick and you got a thimbleful of liquor. The girls stopped also, and Shadow let her wrap slide off her shoulder. Soon they were throwing hoops and laughing loudly at their own inaccuracy. A thickset middle-aged man, who might have been a tradesman or a master craftsman, was paying for everybody and was already flushed with drink. His arm was round Shadow's shoulder. Once more her three hoops missed the pole and she wailed in mock dismay.

"Have another go," he said, pulling out a purse attached to his belt by a cord. She shook her head.

"Put it away, fool. You'll be robbed. Don't you know thieves come specially when the fair is on?"

Fleet was holding hands with the other man, looking up at him lasciviously from under her long dark lashes. He had a dazed smile on his face, as if he couldn't believe his luck. They all moved on, followed at a careful distance by Dancer and the rest. The group ahead stopped to buy sweetmeats, and Shadow, sitting on her escort's lap, had her fortune told by a grubby old woman who turned over cards and promised her riches and long life. Now they had gone the whole length of the fair. Fleet detached herself and tugged Shadow's arm. They ought to go, she said, it was getting late. Shadow nodded and turned sadly to her companion. He protested at once. Surely she didn't want to go home. She must know the area well. Couldn't she suggest somewhere where they could eat and drink, enjoy themselves? The girls conferred. Then Shadow took her companion's arm again.

Away from the fair, the crowds thinned out. Down this street, under that archway, through this passage—a shortcut, just a little farther, nearly there. The streets were quiet now. Shadow drew her companion into the shadow of a doorway and put her arms round his neck. Fleet's partner stopped.

"Never mind them," she whispered. "She knows where we'll be." She took him by the hand and they disappeared round the corner.

A few moments later, Shadow gave a sudden cry and pushed the man away from her. At once Weasel, Dancer, and Edge surrounded him. Weasel grabbed him from behind with an arm round his neck, Edge kicked his legs from under him, and almost before he was on the ground, Dancer had found the fat purse and cut it free. Alis, watching in horror from the corner, could not believe the speed of it all. The others were up and running at once, Shadow catching her hand and pulling her along. Seconds later they were joined by Fleet minus her man. A few dark passageways and they slowed to a walk. Alis had no idea where they were.

"All right?" Shadow asked Fleet.

"No trouble." She laughed softly. "He'll think he dreamed me. And see!" She held up another purse—not stuffed like the first but clinking agreeably.

The summer weeks passed and Alis struggled to become used to a new life that appalled her. Joel, seeing her expression once when they were planning a raid, said sharply, "Do you want to starve on the streets? It's easy enough." So she kept quiet and learned to mask her feelings. She did not want to die, and she had nowhere else to go.

To her horror, she found that she was to be the gang's lookout, taking the place of the boy who had died. It was not easy. She did not know the streets and alleys as they did and was terrified of being left behind. Each time her brother said she was to go with them, her stomach churned and she could not eat. Joel ruled the group strictly, insisting that the knives were for purse cutting and intimidation only, unless they were used in self-defense. Nevertheless, Alis was haunted by the thought of blood, and learned to be grateful that Mute was so handy with his great fists. To see a man felled by a blow to the head was bad enough, but it was better than knowing he had a blade between his ribs.

The weather grew cooler, and Alis wondered how long she would have to stay with her brother. Ethan had spoken of finding honest work for her, but he had not thought it safe for her to remain in that part of the city where she might have found it. Even if she had been brave enough to risk venturing out on her own, she knew no decent person would employ her. Already she looked ragged, and though she drew water for washing every day, she could not keep her clothes clean as she had done at home. She told herself she would wait until she was more familiar with the city, but she felt her hope fade with the days.

Joel did not ask about their parents, and he was reluctant to talk about the past. Only once, when she wanted to know whether their mother had driven him away by harshness, he paused.

"Harshness? No, not really. Just, there were too many rules. And the dreariness. All that studying of an old book, and then the future stuck in one place. Our father would have had me work with him, but I wanted to see more of the world, learn something different. I meant to go back to see them, and you, when I had made my fortune." He grimaced.

"So you are not . . . glad? It isn't a better life?" She spoke hesitantly, fearing he would resent her questions, but he only shrugged.

"I do as I please, at least. And I needn't stay here if I don't want to." He looked at his sister. "And what about you, Alis? Is it a better life for you?"

She did not answer at first. Then she said slowly, "I could not bear to marry Galin. I have been saved from that."

He nodded. "Well, I am glad to have you here, and while I am leader, there is a place for you. But don't expect too much. I can't protect you from what we have to do, and it's not always pleasant, as you've found out. Besides, the others already think I favor you. If I lose their loyalty, there'll be nothing for either of us."

She nodded. "When you first came to the city, did you look for . . . work of a different kind?"

He laughed briefly at her expression. "Well, I was set upon as soon as I arrived, and what little I had was stolen from me. I lived rough for a while. Then I met Dancer and he taught me how to pick pockets. It's as good a living as any."

"You didn't miss home?"

He made no answer and she could not help adding, "I missed you."

She had put it away long ago—the misery of those first weeks. Now it came back to catch in her throat so that her voice trembled when she spoke.

He looked uncomfortable. "I thought of you often. And I kept the name Jojo. No one but you had ever called me that."

She wanted him to say more, but the others came in and the moment passed.

Often a feeling of desolation came over her. There was nothing to look forward to, and only a hard, dangerous way of life to learn. Dancer was kind enough in his strange fashion, but Fleet and Shadow were unfriendly, and Weasel openly resented her presence. Edge never took any notice of Alis, but she was unpredictable and the ever-present knife was alarming.

In the small dark hours, afraid and sleepless, Alis could not escape the thought that Ethan might never go back to Two Rivers. And even if he did, he could not bring her any news, not knowing where she was in the city. Most likely he was glad to be rid of her after what had happened. Luke was lost to her: it was punishment for her wickedness. The Maker had turned his face from her, and there was nothing before her but to die eventually and go alone into the dark.

Slowly, however, she became used to her new life. Her brother was kind to her when he was sure no one would notice, and if the others disliked her, they did nothing about it.

One night, having successfully relieved a lost stranger of his money, they stopped to catch their breath in a shadowy doorway. Suddenly Alis noticed that Edge was no longer with them. Nervously she pointed this out to the others. Weasel merely shrugged, and Shadow said tartly, "Edge can take care of herself, as she's always telling us. Come on, let's go. I'm cold."

"But she always comes back with us," Alis said.

"Well, this time she 'asn't." Weasel sounded irritable. "We can't do nothin' anyway."

"Something might have happened to her." Edge knew the city better than anyone, but Alis could not bear the thought that they might be abandoning the fair-haired girl when she needed their help. Her own dread of being left behind in the dark squares and alleyways had not diminished. "We could just go back and look."

Dancer, who was performing a neat sidestepping routine to and fro on the cobbles, broke off to say, "Quick look. No harm."

Alis added quickly, "Then if she doesn't come back, we can tell Joel we tried."

That decided them. They retraced their steps cautiously, catching sight from time to time of other stealthy figures like themselves or a lone person slinking by.

Then they saw her. Light spilled for a moment from a tavern door, and there was Edge, limping slightly and clutching her jacket close about her in the chill night air. Weasel whistled softly and she looked up, startled.

They joined her, Shadow saying, "Why are you walking like that? Are you hurt?"

Edge shook her head. "Turned my ankle, that's all. I couldn't run. Didn't expect you lot to come back, though. You needn't have. I can manage on my own."

"See!" Shadow gave Alis a hard shove. "We could've been back home instead of out here in the cold."

Dancer made a little sound of protest. "Can't run is dangerous. Bad people like us about." The others laughed and Alis felt foolish, wishing she had kept quiet.

But the next day, Alis was drawing water from the well when Edge came through the grass-choked gateway. The other girl stopped and then made toward Alis. She was carrying something wrapped in a piece of cloth. "Do you like plums?"

Alis nodded, surprised. Edge sat down with her back against the stone well, motioning Alis to join her. She opened the cloth. "Three each," she said.

12

E dge's support did not make Alis any more popular with the others, but it was a comfort. It pleased Joel, too, and Alis felt closer to her brother. It was not that Edge was friendly: she said little and was prone to black moods when not even Joel dared to disturb her. But Alis knew that the ever-present knife would not be turned on her, and in the dangerous byways of the city, the fair-haired girl could be relied on.

One morning Joel and Dancer were out somewhere. Shadow and Fleet sat murmuring to each other in a corner, while Weasel and Mute bickered over a card game. With nothing to do, Edge paced the room until Shadow looked up and said irritably, "Go out, can't you? It's like being shut up with a mad beast." She glanced at Alis. "And take her with you."

Alis felt herself flush, but before she could respond, Edge swung toward her, saying flatly, "Come on. It's time you learned your way around."

They went through a part of the city Alis had never seen before, along narrow streets to a crowded market. At one end, farm women from outside the southern wall sat on the ground, keeping watch over small piles of parched-looking vegetables and fruit. Some of them had tiny pens containing three or four scrawny chickens with their feet tied together. The birds pecked listlessly at the dust as if they knew their time was nearly up. Farther on, there were dozens of rickety stalls selling cooking pots, lengths of cloth, needles and thread, knives—all of poor quality. There were food stands, too. And everywhere, a press of people—pushing, arguing, haggling.

Alis kept close to Edge as they made their way between two lines of food stalls. Some of these had fire buckets with bubbling pots perched on top, adding to the pungent mix of smells. Alis watched a stallholder wipe a used platter with a cabbage leaf and begin ladling out a fresh portion of the greasy mixture from his pot. A couple of skinny lads handed over some coins and crouched down between the stalls to share the food.

Suddenly, a hunched, ragged-looking man barged his way to the front. His face was flushed and his eyes bloodshot. He demanded loudly to know the price of the grayish stew, and when the stallholder named it, he turned away with a curse. As he did so, he jogged the elbow of one of the squatting boys. The platter tilted, and the remains of the stew slopped onto the ground. With a screech of rage, the lad leaped to his feet, fists up. The man swung his arm and the boy went down, howling. At the same time, the stallholder kicked out at a mangy dog licking up the spilled food. He missed, and his foot caught the ankle of a thin-faced housewife instead. The woman yelped in pain, and the man at her side—her husband perhaps—gave the stallholder a violent shove. Within seconds, blows were being exchanged amid a clamor of angry voices.

In the rapidly growing crowd, Alis lost sight of Edge. She was struggling against the throng to find her again, when a man in sailor's clothes grabbed her arm. "No good, this. You come along wi' me," he said roughly, hauling her away. Panic-stricken, Alis jerked her arm in an attempt to free herself, but he held on firmly. A woman stallholder said doubtfully, "Here now," but the sailor winked at her. "She's mad wi' me for not buying her a ring, see. Womenfolk!"

He clamped his arm around Alis's waist and half lifted her off the ground. "You come along, my girl. I'll gi' ye more than a ring, don't ye fret."

He was holding her so tightly and she was so frightened that she had no breath to scream. Within a minute, they were away from the heaving market crowd and he was dragging her down an alleyway with washing strung between the upper stories.

Her voice hoarse with terror, she twisted in his grasp crying, "Let me go! Let me go!"

A couple of roughly dressed young men came toward them. They looked at her as they went past and laughed coarsely. One of them said, "You've got an armful there, sailor. Want some help?"

The sailor grunted. "I can manage this 'un, I reckon."

He swung her round, pushing her into a short passageway that ended in a blind wall. He let her go then and stood still, blocking the exit. She backed away from him, giddy with terror, the blood thundering in her ears. "Leave me alone!"

She could hardly get the words out, her throat was so dry. He grinned and came toward her, a big man with sun-weathered skin and blackened teeth. Her back to the wall, she put up her hands to fend him off, but he seized her wrists in one great paw and stretched her arms above her head so that he could press his body into hers. He smelled of sweat, tobacco, and clothes long unwashed. Desperately, she attempted to heave him off, but he only laughed and put his face down to hers. She jerked her head sideways, but he got his mouth against her lips, pressing, trying to force his tongue between her clenched teeth. His breath was foul. Only the fear of opening her mouth prevented her from vomiting. After a few seconds, he leaned away from her and said coaxingly, "Come on, now. Be a good girl. I'll gi' ye a present for it."

She tried to kick him, but there wasn't room and it only made him laugh again. With his free hand, he took hold of the front of her shirt, pulling at it so that the fastenings began to tear away. As the thin material ripped, horror gave her strength, and she spat in his face. His head jerked back in surprise, and at the same moment a voice shouted urgently, "Alis! Alis! Where are you?"

"Here!" she screamed. "Help me! Help me!"

The sailor put his hand over her mouth but it was too late. From the end of the passageway, Edge said sharply, "You'd best let her go, sailor. She's got a brother who won't like what you're up to. He and his mates are on their way. This is their patch."

The sailor released Alis and turned round. Hesitantly, he stepped toward the exit. He was blocking her view but Alis heard Edge say, "That's right, sailor. You keep coming. You're in a trap now, and if I were you, I'd be out of it when the boys arrive. Nasty things knives, especially when it's three to one in a little space like this."

He took a couple strides and was out of the passageway. Edge shouted, "This way, you lot! Quick!" Alis caught a glimpse of the knife in her hand.

A pair of boots clattered on the cobbles. Then there was silence.

Trembling and sick, Alis clutched her tattered shirt to her. She leaned against the wall, her legs shaking so much she did not think she could walk. Edge was still silhouetted in the opening, keeping watch. "Come on! We must get away."

When Alis did not stir, Edge said urgently, "He might come back if he guesses he's been fooled, and this is a bad place. Move, Alis."

Shakily, Alis took a step, and then another, forcing herself forward.

Edge grabbed her by the hand. "Straighten up," she said tersely, "and try not to look as though something's happened."

Alis did her best to comply. Dazed, she looked round for Joel and the others, saying hoarsely, "Is my brother . . . ?"

"No, of course not! I was bluffing. Now let's get away from here."

Alis hardly noticed the route they took. She clung to Edge, terrified that the sailor would reappear. No one troubled them, however, and after a while, they emerged from the twisting alleyways into a district of squares and ruined buildings. There were children playing in the dirt and women going to and fro with baskets. After a while she said, "I can't go any farther." She sat down on the pedestal of a broken fountain.

Edge looked round warily. "All right," she said. "But we shouldn't stay too long."

Alis felt as if the ground were moving beneath her. The smell of the man was on her skin. She could taste him on her lips and feel the coarseness of his fingers on her breast. She leaned forward and vomited into the dirt. Over and over her stomach heaved and her throat convulsed. It seemed as though it would never stop.

When it did, her mouth remained full of foulness, though she spat into the dust until she could spit no more. At last Edge said, "Let's move on."

The tavern was down a flight of steps, in the cellar beneath a chandler's shop. It was crowded, but Edge was obviously a regular. She made straight for the yard at the back, where there was a well. Alis splashed her face with cool water and drank a little to freshen her mouth. She was still trembling, and she felt exhausted.

When they went back inside, two old prostitutes sitting at the bar made room for them. A tankard of something cold was put before Alis.

"Try it," Edge said. "You'll feel better."

One of the women, thick face paint clogging the creases in her skin, jerked her head at Alis and raised her plucked eyebrows. "What's up with her?"

"A sailor tried it on," Edge said. "We got away, though."

The woman nodded. "Men," she said without feeling. "All bastards." She stared moodily into her drink.

Alis took a sip from the tankard before her. The bitterness of the dark brown liquid took her by surprise, and she thought she would be sick again. She drew a deep breath, and after a moment the feeling passed, to be replaced by an agreeable warmth in her belly.

She lifted her head and saw that Edge was looking at her without expression. She felt her eyes fill with tears. "You saved me," she said tremulously. "If it hadn't been for you . . ." She could not go on.

Edge shrugged in her usual way. "No point escaping from the minister man to be banged up by a sailor."

The prostitute lifted her head from her drink to say to Edge, "Came to her rescue, did you? You're a tough 'un all right. Friend, is she?"

The fair-haired girl hesitated briefly, then nodded. She caught Alis's eye and looked away, flushing faintly. She lifted her tankard. "Drink up," she said. "Time we were on our way."

Back with the others, Edge merely said that they had been attacked but had gotten away. The girls and Weasel showed little sympathy, while Dancer fluttered round them uselessly until Edge turned on him. Joel looked grim and said they must take better care. His eyes rested on his sister anxiously, but he said nothing. Alis retreated to the room where she slept, feeling soiled and ashamed.

For a few days, she would not go out. She shivered with fever on her thin mattress, and in her dreams the sailor came toward her, his features monstrously enlarged, hands everywhere. Eventually, Edge, who had tended her for nearly a week, lost patience.

"Nothing happened, and you can't stay here forever. I've brought you water to wash in and here's a shirt you can have. You can burn the other one if it makes you feel better. Now get up!"

So the matter was ended. Alis felt herself harden toward the world. She looked about her distrustfully and thought that perhaps all men were vile. But Edge was her friend—there was no doubt of that—and she owed her a debt that could never be paid.

13

As the year went on, the Elders tightened their grip on the northern side of the river. Some of the empty rooms around the courtyards acquired occupants, and other groups began to move into the territory that Joel had claimed for his own.

Late-summer rain chilled the air, making the streets and alleys slimy and dank. Tempers in the group frayed. They had spent the money so easily acquired earlier, and when rats got into the food store, they were even worse off. Alis still slept where she had the first night. Sometimes Edge slept there also. When she did not, Alis understood that she lay with Joel, just as Fleet and Weasel shared a bed.

Joel called them all together. They needed money and they must make plans. Weasel indicated Alis and said, "She oughta do more."

Mute, sitting with his arm round Shadow, nodded, and the red-haired girl gave Alis a scornful look.

Joel said evenly, "She keeps lookout."

"Lookout!" It was Shadow, sneering. "Anyone can be a lookout."

Fleet, sitting at Weasel's side, leaned forward to join in. Her pretty face with its dark eyes and lashes was hard. "Why's she special? The rest of us do the real work. Shadow and me put up with dirty men pawing us to bring the money in. She eats, same as everyone else."

There was a murmur of agreement. Alis looked at Edge, who usually stood up for her these days, but Edge, with her elbows on the table, was pulling at her fringe and chopping bits off it with her knife. There was a little pile of blonde tufts in front of her.

Weasel looked hostile as usual. "It ain't fair that she's treated different."

Joel's face was cold. "Fair or not, I'm leader here. And if you don't like it"—he looked at Weasel—"you don't have to stay."

There was a sullen silence in the room.

Alis went fearfully to her bed: what if they attacked her in the dark, while she slept? She could not stay awake forever.

In the room, however, she found Edge preparing for the night and was pleased. When she was ready, she blew out her candle and lay down. She allowed herself to think of Luke for a moment and was overwhelmed with longing, but eventually she fell asleep.

When she awoke, the other girl was sitting cross-legged on the floor watching her. There were two knives between them on the bare boards. She pushed one toward Alis. "Yours," she said. "I'll teach you to use it."

In the room where they slept and out in the courtyard, they practiced. For this they used an unsharpened knife, but that did not mean it was blunt. If she turned the edge toward her when it should be away, if she were clumsy in handling the blade, she could and did cut herself. She did not care. The fair girl said it was the best way to learn.

"If you know it'll cut you, you'll watch more carefully. That way you'll learn more quickly."

When they went out on a job, Edge would not let her carry the weapon. "Not yet," she said. "If you don't know how to handle it, it'll be turned against you maybe. Wait."

And so she waited, glad enough for the delay. In truth, she knew very well that she would never be able to use the knife. She was not dexterous enough to cut a purse, and as for defending herself or anyone else with it, the idea of the blade cutting through flesh sickened her.

Summer turned to autumn. In the dark alleys and passageways of the city, Edge stayed close to Alis. When food was short, she saw that Alis got a share of what there was. The others did not like it, but with them, Edge remained her old unpredictable self.

The days shortened; it was colder at night. Then it was winter: icy drafts through the broken shutters, bitter wind, fewer people abroad at night, and less to steal. They went farther afield and took more risks. There was boredom as well as hunger to fuel resentments. One evening, coming back from the privy, she encountered Weasel in the narrow upper corridor. Instead of passing her, he stood blocking the way, baring his broken teeth at her in a mocking grin. Suppressing her fear, she said firmly, "Let me by please, Weasel."

He did not move at once. "Not very friendly, are you? Ain't I good-looking enough for you?"

Then he stood aside for her, and she felt his eyes on her as she went along to the room where she slept.

"How can Fleet bear to lie with him?" she asked Edge later.

"It's what most girls do," Edge said. "For protection."

Alis asked, "What about you? You and my brother?"

Edge said sharply, "I don't need protecting; I can look after myself. I go with your brother for my own pleasure."

They were silent for a few minutes. Then Edge said, "And he doesn't expect me to go on the streets. Weasel would have Fleet sell herself to any man with a purse, if he could."

Alis had seen the women in their flimsy clothes waiting in doorways and on street corners. Disturbed, she said, "Weasel would do that even though he and Fleet . . . ?"

"Most men would. Jojo's unusual."

Alis thought of the people she had known before. She could not imagine her father or Luke behaving like this. She shook her head. "It's a different world."

"You think so?" Edge sounded scornful. "What were your parents doing when they said you had to marry the minister man?"

Alis was shocked. "They weren't selling me. He wasn't paying."

"Oh no? He was getting you for his bed, and your parents were getting power, importance. Doesn't seem so different to me."

She felt sick. She did not want to think about it. To turn Edge's attention from her she asked, "What were your parents like?"

"Never knew my father; he went off when he knew I was on the way. My mother kept me fed as best she could, and taught me to speak nicely." She grimaced. "I ran off myself when I was ten."

"What happened?"

There was a long silence. Eventually Edge said reluctantly, "Where we lived, the landlord had rooms in the same house. He was always leering at my mother and making remarks. I think she sometimes, you know . . . when she didn't have enough for the rent. And then he began on me—how pretty I was growing, what lovely hair I had; it was long then. I was scared of him. I tried to tell my mother but she didn't want to know. Didn't dare offend him in case he threw us out. One day I was there alone. I can't remember why. Maybe I was sick. He came into our room, pretending to be nice and all the time trying to touch me."

Her face was twisted with loathing.

"I picked up a knife off the table and said I'd kill him. He laughed at me and tried to take it from me. I suppose he thought it wasn't sharp, but my mother was funny about knives; she wouldn't have them blunt even if we only had bread to cut. So he grabbed for the blade and I pulled and it cut his hand. He was angry then, cursing, calling me foul names, and saying he would put us out on the street. But he went away."

She stopped speaking and swallowed. Alis waited.

"I didn't know what to do. I thought he'd throw us out and my mother would blame me. I was so frightened. I wanted to get out of the house, but I thought he might be waiting for me on the stairs."

Again she stopped. Her face was that of the ten-year-old child she had once been, full of pain and fear.

"I waited a bit, but in the end, I crept onto the landing. There was no sign of him so I got out and ran. When I stopped running, I walked until I couldn't walk any more."

Beyond the broken shutters the winter afternoon had already darkened. Outside snow began to fall—large, soft flakes descending steadily in the windless air. Edge said in a tense voice, "Let's go out for a bit. It'll feel warmer now that the snow's started again. I need to walk."

They both owned boots, purchased at summer's end with the last of the easy money, so they wrapped themselves up in whatever they had and went out. Beyond the gateway, they turned in the direction of the river, walking arm in arm. For a long time they said nothing. At last Edge said bitterly, "I wasn't any better off really. There was a place I knew—a building had collapsed and there were kids living in the ruins. When I made her angry, my mother used to tell me I'd end up there." She gave a short laugh. "Anyway six or seven, mainly girls, were sitting on the steps to a kind of basement. I went right up to them. I don't know what I was going to say. They just stared at me; someone spat. And then one of them said, 'Is that blood?' They'd seen the knife. I was still carrying it. The blood from his hand had dried on the blade. I told them I'd stabbed him in the stomach."

They had reached the river now and were leaning on the parapet looking down into the dark water. Edge went on wearily, "I thought my mother would come looking for me, but she never did. Perhaps the landlord told her some lie, or maybe something happened to her. I don't know. I stayed there for a while. It was better than nothing, but I wouldn't wish it on anyone. The ones who were brothers and sisters did best—most of them looked out for each other. You needed someone. The older boys—they were like the landlord really, only they were younger so it didn't seem as bad. One of them taught me to use a knife. After a bit I moved on. There was a man who took a fancy to me. He kept me for a while—he ran a tavern on the southern edge of the city. I fetched and carried for him until he threw me out for drawing my knife on a customer who'd turned nasty."

The snow fell softly. It was very quiet.

"After that I lived as I could. A girl on her own in the city doesn't stand a chance. I was nearly killed once, by a man I'd gone with. I kept telling myself I wouldn't do it anymore, but it's hard when you're hungry. After him, I wouldn't, though. I chopped my hair short and lived on what I could get with my knife."

Alis asked how Edge had come to know her brother.

"I was looking for somewhere to sleep. I saw the gate. There was a fever sign up but I didn't care. The place was almost empty—everyone had died or gone. Jojo and his lot were already living there, although I didn't realize it that night. When they found out I could use a knife, they said I could join them."

They began to walk back. After a while Edge said, "I wonder sometimes if I should have stayed with my mother. The landlord was disgusting, but he was no worse than other men I've been with."

"No!" Alis was distressed. Surely it was better to have tried to save yourself?

Edge looked at her sideways with something of her old scorn.

"What about you? You ran away so that you wouldn't have to marry that man. Will you be any better off in the end? What will happen to you—to all of us—when we're too old for this anymore?"

Alis had no answer. She lived from day to day, keeping alive the hope that she might one day find Luke and his grandparents again.

Edge wanted to know about life in the Community, so Alis told her: about her parents, about learning to read, about prayer meetings, about the daily and weekly duties expected of a good daughter of the Book. A dull, safe life it sounded. Edge had pushed back her hood; snow settled on the spiky tufts of her hair. She was sticking out her tongue to catch the drifting white flakes. After a while she said, "I couldn't live like that. But you should have stayed. Plenty to eat, a good bed to sleep in, and you'd have been important like your mother. People would have had to treat you with respect."

Alis thought of Galin. "But I'd have had to lie with him. Like you and the landlord. And he was forty."

Her companion said sharply, "You'll lie with someone in the end anyway. We all do. And have a kid you have to get rid of maybe, like Fleet. You've just been lucky so far."

Alis said stubbornly, "I don't care. I'm glad I ran away. At least I didn't give in." She was angry with Edge.

The fair girl shrugged. "Yes, all right. But all the same"—her tone darkened—"I wish I'd been a boy. It's better for them."

They came to the gate and went through. These days, the door at the foot of the dark stairs was kept shut and the heavy old key hidden behind a loose brick in the wall. They let themselves in. The others were gathered in the main room. Joel was lying on a makeshift couch near the fire, looking white and sick, his head wrapped in a blood-stained cloth and his eyes shut. The atmosphere was somber.

"What happened?" Edge's voice was flat, as if this was only what she had always expected.

Joel, Dancer, and Shadow had gone picking pockets on the north side of the river where the better-quality inns were. They'd nearly been caught, and someone had hit Joel over the head with a great stick. There was a deep cut and a dent in his skull where the blow had landed. But there was nothing they could do.

Edge said she would watch by Joel. Some of the others settled themselves to sleep in the room as they did when there was a fire—for the sake of the warmth. Weasel, however, went away with a calculating look on his ugly face.

14

"Here." Edge threw a clutch of small coins onto the table for Weasel to count.

He looked up at her. "About time."

Alis looked up anxiously. Joel had been sick all through the winter, and Weasel had not hesitated to point out that they could not go on supporting someone who ate but did not work. Edge picked up one of the coins from the table and was spinning it between her fingers. Weasel finished counting and nodded. "Not bad." He scooped the coins into an old pot and then reached for the one still turning under Edge's gaze. He whipped it away and her knife was out before he could move.

"Don't try it, Weasel. You'll be sorry."

He hesitated, then shrugged as if he'd meant to confront her but thought better of it. "All right. But keep it coming. Food costs."

Alis grabbed Edge by the hand. "How did you get the money?"

Edge looked at her. "How do you think? I was nice to someone and he paid up like a good boy! I'm going to see how Joel is. Coming?"

They went along the corridor together, but at the door of Joel's room, Alis changed her mind and made instead for the staircase down to the courtyard. It was not wise to go out alone, but she knew her way about now and no longer looked like a country girl, an easy target.

Once in the street, she walked rapidly toward the river, driven on by anger, misery, and fear. Joel might never get better—he might even die. Weasel was already making most of the decisions. And he hated her. Might she and Edge be able to survive together and support Joel, too? But she could not stand on a street corner and sell herself for the price of a meal. And yet if Edge did, then surely she must, too, if they were to make a living for themselves and Joel. She carried her knife now, sheathed at her waist, but she had never used it. She could not support herself that way.

When she got back the others were eating. Edge pushed a plate toward her, and she took it and ate without appetite. There was no point in going hungry; she might come to that soon enough. When they had finished, Weasel leaned his elbows on the table and spoke. It was time for Alis to prove herself. Jojo could not work; his sister must help to provide for him.

She knew it was pointless to protest that she did her share as lookout. "What do you want me to do?" Alis asked.

Weasel grinned at her as he had done on that very first day, showing his broken teeth. How could Fleet lie with him? "Take part, 'stead of just watchin'. You got a knife, ain't you? We all know Edge's taught you to use it."

Edge said sharply, "She's not ready. It's dangerous."

Weasel shrugged. "So what? If Alis c'n do what's needed, she's one of us. Otherwise . . . And Edge, you stay 'ere. She's gotta do this without you."

Alis would have protested but Edge shook her head at her. The time had come when she would have to prove herself.

The Elders had closed the brothels on the north side of the river. Men came across the bridge regularly now, looking for pleasure. The southern bawdy houses flourished. Weasel said they should find a fool of a shopowner or a merchant's son out for the night. That sort always carried money—and more than they needed, liking to show off their prosperity to the girls. Alis felt sick. She wished she could have consulted Edge before they set off, but the other girl had disappeared and Weasel hurried them out—herself, Mute, Shadow, and Fleet. As they went, she tried to imagine what she might do. A knife was frightening only if your victim believed you would use it. In her head, a voice light and sharp was saying, *Mean it. You've got to mean it.*

Watching from a distance as the girls eyed up the men, Alis shivered. Her pulse was hammering. She tried to breathe deeply to calm herself. Then she saw that Fleet and Shadow had a fattish elderly man in tow. He had an arm round each of them and he was laughing uproariously. Fleet whispered in his ear and he guffawed again. Shadow said something and pointed. He nodded eagerly.

The three began to move and the others retreated, drawing the man gradually away from the relative safety of the more populated streets to the slimy alleys and deserted squares. The girls led him on, and then in a small moonlit square Shadow drew him into a doorway and put her arms round his neck—her usual trick. Weasel whispered to Alis, "When Shadow cries out and pushes him off, we go in. Make sure he sees the knife. Slash at him if you have to, but make sure you don't get one of us by mistake."

Alis drew her knife. Her mouth tasted of dry metal; she could hardly breathe. Then Shadow cried out and they were running toward her. There was a confusion of movement, thuds, and grunts, and then the victim was propped against a wall, gasping. Weasel and Mute were on either side of him, holding him upright.

"Now," Weasel said. "'E's all yours. Stick 'im in the belly. Finish 'im off."

For a moment she could not make sense of his words.

"Go on," Weasel said. "What d'ya think a knife's for? Kill 'im."

Alis looked at the man. Eyes rolling in terror, he was fighting for breath; someone must have punched him in the stomach. She was still clutching the knife. She could not move.

They let the man go and he slid to the ground. Thrusting his face into Alis's, Weasel spat out, "Useless bitch!"

Then they walked away. Alis remained where she was.

Time passed. A voice said softly, "Alis." A hand touched her shoulders. She whirled round, the knife raised. A figure leaped back.

"Alis. Don't. It's me, Edge."

A stranger with spiky blonde hair. The voice said urgently, "Drop the knife, Alis. They're gone. It's all right. Let it drop."

Behind her, a man groaning, sounds of him getting to his feet. She must turn round. But in front of her, this stranger. There was something she must do with her knife. It was in her hand, she was ready. But she could not. It was no use; it had never been any use. Her fingers uncurled suddenly and the knife clattered to the cobbles. Dragging footsteps behind her. Going away. Hands on her shoulders. A face close to hers. The strange girl but . . . no . . . not a stranger . . . someone she knew . . . someone she trusted—and yes, now there was a name: Edge. Her friend. Memory returned. What was Edge doing here?

"Come on, Alis. You're frozen. There's somewhere we can go. Come on now."

She let Edge lead her away.

At the back door of the inn, the fat woman was smoking a pipe in short puffs, her eyes narrowed against the sudden jets of smoke.

Edge greeted her. "Missus Pike, we need a bed for the night, my friend and me. We can pay."

The fat woman contemplated them sardonically. The glare of an oil lamp on a hook by the door highlighted the bulge of cheek and the double chin. "Ya can, can ya? Let's see ya money."

Edge held up a coin. The woman removed the pipe from her mouth, spat into the darkness, and took it.

It was hardly more than a walk-in cupboard, but the fat woman threw down some cleanish-looking bedding, left them a candle, and even brought them a basin of hot water.

"Don't say Ma Pike never does nothin' for ya," she said tartly. "And mind you keep that blade o' yours outta sight. I know you and I don't want no trouble."

Edge thanked her and they were left alone.

Wearily Alis allowed Edge to arrange the bedding. When it was done Edge said, "I picked up your knife."

She held it out, but Alis would not take it. After a moment, Edge put it away without a word.

The fat woman returned with a steaming tankard. "Get 'er to take some o' this. It'll revive 'er. There's enough for ya both."

The spiced ale was comforting. Propped up and wrapped in bedding, Alis breathed the scented steam and felt warmth return to her limbs. With a sigh she passed the tankard to Edge. "He tried to make me kill a man."

"I know." Edge's face was grim. "I knew he was up to something as soon as he mentioned the knife."

"Suppose I had done it?" Alis shuddered, seeing again the gasping mouth and terrified eyes.

"He knew you wouldn't," Edge said. "And if you had, he wouldn't have cared. Besides, it's not that easy. You have to know how."

The ale was making Alis drowsy. "How did you come to be there?"

"I told you," Edge said. "I knew he was planning something. I followed. I was frightened for you."

Alis tried to reach out a hand but her arm was too heavy. She could not lift it. Sliding into unconsciousness she heard the murmur of Edge's voice, but the words were lost.

When she woke, Edge's head was on her shoulder. Alis lay for a long time without moving, feeling heavy and dull. She knew she ought to be afraid. She had failed the test: she had no place now. But where fear should have been there was only weariness. She had tried very hard, but it was no good. Edge stirred, stretched, and sat up, turning to look at Alis. "Hungry?"

Alis shook her head. She did not care if she never ate again. She just wanted to go on lying there. But Edge made her get up, saying that Ma Pike would want them out, and anyway, food would get rid of the aftereffects of the spiced ale.

The streets were cool in the early-morning light. Spring. A year since she had left Freeborne, Alis thought dully. She had been full of hope then. Edge bought bread, freshly baked and still warm, insisting that she should eat.

They sat on a wall in a patch of sunlight. For a long time they were silent. Then Alis said wearily, "Weasel's always hated me. Fleet and Shadow, too."

Edge nodded. "Weasel wants to be leader, and he doesn't like Jojo's ways. He'd rather be free to kill or have a bit of unnecessary fun with some poor fool. Me, I'm for taking the money and getting out fast. I'd rather not kill. I haven't yet." She was picking moodily at the flaking surface of the wall. "The others were angry because Jojo favored you, taking you in just because you were his sister even though you weren't much use."

Alis did not protest. She understood well enough.

Edge said, "I've heard of people going away, to a new life in another country, across the sea. I want to take Joel and go as soon as we can save money for the passage—a year perhaps. I'm sick of it here. Why should I die of fever alone in a filthy room or be kicked to death in a rat-infested alley? That's how it is: you have to be young and fast to survive and no one stays like that for long."

Edge was looking at her. "Come with us, Alis. Joel has a mind to try farming. There'll be work for us all."

For a moment Alis had a vision of freedom, far away from the city, beyond the reach of Galin and the rule of the Elders. She had never seen the sea.

Edge was still looking at her, waiting for an answer. Alis shook her head slowly. She would not cross the sea. Once, she had decided to search for her brother, and she had found him. Now it was time to find Luke.

15

With roads newly passable after the winter, there were crowds wanting to travel. Once more she had Edge to thank: she would never have gotten aboard a wagon on her own. But Edge had elbowed her way through the throng, ignoring the protests of those she shoved aside. Only once did she stop, to exchange insults with a thin, sour-faced woman in the sober dress of the Communities. For a terrible moment Alis thought the woman might know her for a daughter of the Book, but the cold glance passed over her contemptuously. Just one more ragged city girl; they ought not be allowed to travel with decent folk. Edge bargained with the driver for a place, handing over some money. That done, she thrust a bundle of possessions and a fistful of small coins at Alis, saying roughly, "Don't look like that. You can't starve. And you don't know how far you'll need to travel to find this Luke you've told me about."

So Alis had accepted the gift, stammering her thanks. Then the driver said, "Get in if you mean to have your place, or give it up. I can't be waiting all day for you to finish your gabbing."

The wheels were already beginning to turn as Alis took her seat, leaning forward to keep her friend in sight for as long as possible, but Edge had already turned away and was soon lost among the milling crowd at the wagon stop. Alis thought of her parting from Luke: at least they had said good-bye.

Wedged between a bony raw-faced youth who smelled powerfully of onions and an old woman with a basket on her lap, Alis slid in and out of consciousness, waking with a jolt from time to time when the wagon lurched and the side of the basket dug into her leg. Images from the night before haunted her sleep with sickening intensity. Dream voices blended with those of her fellow travelers in a constant, sinister muttering whose meaning was always just out of reach, though she strained and strained to grasp it.

At first the inns were expensive. Dismayed, Alis watched her small store of money diminish, went hungry for fear of spending all she had, and wondered what she would do if Luke and his grandparents were gone from Two Rivers when she got there.

Two weeks later she shook her head miserably when the plump, cheerful innkeeper asked her what she would take for supper. The woman looked at her appraisingly. "Aren't you thin enough already? Girl your age needs to eat. I should know. I've a daughter of my own and she could certainly put it away when she was a lass. Got kids herself now—all boys." She smiled proudly.

Taking a chance, for the woman had a kindly face under her

dark curls, Alis said, "The journey's cost more than I thought. I need to earn a bit to keep me going. If you need a hand here, I can work hard."

Again the woman—Jessie, she was called—examined her closely. "Well," she said at last, "you don't look like a thief, and as it happens I could use a bit of help, Mary having gone off with that good-for-nothing fellow she thinks will marry her, though he won't. I can't pay you much, but you can have Mary's bed for nothing till she comes to her senses."

She took Alis into the kitchen where a big, friendly-looking man was taking his ease with a tankard of ale. The suppers were mostly done, for Alis had stayed out of the way feeling it was too much to bear, smelling the food and watching the others eat when she was so hungry.

"Will," Jessie said, "here's someone to give us a hand for a few days. She needs a good feed before we set her to work. Let her have some of that cold pie and whatever else, and then she can clear the tables."

So Alis washed pots, changed bedding, cleaned floors, served food and drink. It was hard work but she ate well and she slept better, too. Once, tidying the best room that was kept for the few wealthier travelers, she stopped to examine herself in a mirror. She was taller than she had been, and thinner, too—that did not surprise her. But her face she hardly recognized. Mirrors had not been plentiful in the houses of Freeborne—they encouraged vanity—nevertheless, it was sometimes useful to be able to see that you were neat and clean, and Alis's mother had taught her to check her appearance in this way. She was familiar with her own face, with its creamy pale skin and gray eyes. Now the face that looked back at her was almost a stranger's. The hair that framed it was still long and fair but it was rougher, no longer glossy; the skin was duller, and the childhood roundness had gone. Pointed chin, sharp cheekbones: if she hacked off her hair she would look like Edge. Uneasily she examined the girl in the glass and thought she did not know her.

She was glad to eat well again but the delay tormented her. She must get to Ellen's and find out where Luke was.

One morning when she went into the kitchen, she found Will and Jessie trying to comfort a chubby, dark-haired girl who was crying hysterically. Will's usually cheerful face was creased with anxiety; he hovered helplessly as his wife attempted to extract a coherent story from the girl.

"Calm down now, Mary," she was saying, "and tell us plainly what's to do. Where's that fool of a man you went away with?"

Mary's response was a fresh outburst. Sobbing and hiccupping, she choked out a story of promise and betrayal: she'd trusted him, he was a brute, left her all alone, no money, hated him, wished she was dead. Another great howl, head on the table, shoulders heaving. Jessie rolled her eyes and said to Will, "You try. I must talk with Alis."

They went into the little parlor and Jessie closed the door, shutting out the sound of Mary's crying. Then she said, "Alis dear, you'll have to move on, I'm afraid. I'm sorry to take your place from you, for you're a much better worker than Mary, but she can't help being what she is, I reckon, with a mother like she's got. This is the only real home she knows. We'll pay you for what you've done, of course, and make sure you get a place with a trustworthy driver, though I can't deny I'll be sorry to lose you."

So the next day, Alis put up her bundle of belongings and Jessie gave her a loaf of bread, cheese wrapped in muslin, and the little money she had earned. Then she climbed into the wagon, and within a few minutes it had passed through the yard gates out onto the road going north, the wheels turning briskly in the crisp morning air.

In the predawn stillness Alis made her way along the lane to the farm. Ellen would be milking at this time, the cows gathered flank to flank awaiting their turn, their breath curling up into the cool morning air, tails swishing. Alis found she was trembling. In a few moments she would know where Luke was.

But as she crossed the yard, there was no sign of the animals: the packed earth was swept clean and the usually pungent smell was a mere memory. There was no one in the milking shed. She went up to the small farmhouse and knocked at the door. No reply. She tried the handle. It was locked. In desperation she went round the back and stepped up onto the back porch to peer in through the window of the kitchen. The big table was bare and the hearth empty. Ellen had gone.

For a few moments, Alis was stunned. How was she to find out where Luke and his grandparents were? Perhaps they were still at the Minister's house, though it was not likely after so long, especially if Ellen had been driven out. But she dared not go into Two Rivers itself. She might still stand accused of setting fire to the prayer house. At the thought of meeting Thomas—and worse still, Robert—her stomach clenched.

Suddenly she heard footsteps and drew back into the shadows as someone came round the side of the house. A figure in a voluminous wrap, with long hair and a sallow, bitter face. Her eyes were red as if she had been crying. Lilith! Alis froze in horror. There was no escape. The other girl stopped abruptly and squinted into the shadows.

"Who are you? What are you doing here?"

"I . . ." Alis could not summon a thought.

Lilith narrowed her eyes suspiciously.

"You're a stranger, aren't you? What do you want?"

Alis let out her breath. Lilith had not recognized her.

"I—" She must think of something quickly. But there was no need. The servant girl interrupted her.

"Well, whatever it is, you're wasting your time. There's no one here."

Before she could stop herself, Alis asked, "Where have they gone?"

Lilith looked away for a moment. There were fat buds on the shrub growing beside the porch steps and she picked one and examined it. After a pause she said, "You don't know what's happened?"

Alis shook her head. Keeping her voice low, she said, "I'm not from these parts. My grandmother—when she was a girl, she knew Mistress Ellen. She's sick, Gran is, and she wants to see her again before she dies. My mother sent me with a message."

Lilith was tearing away the layers of the bud, letting the white pieces of petal fall to the ground.

"Mistress Ellen's not here anymore. Nor the old Minister and his wife that was here with her. No one knows where they've gone. Their grandson, Luke, died of a fever last spring and then . . ."

For an instant Alis thought she would faint. Dead? Struggling desperately not to give herself away, she said, "How . . . dreadful. Did many people die?"

Lilith shook her head. "Oh, no. It wasn't like that. Only there was a fire—the prayer house nearly burned down and he was missing all night. When he came back the next day, he took sick. His grandmother nursed him but it was no use. A week after, he was dead. A whole year he's been gone."

She stopped, rubbing the back of her hand against her eyes. Alis stood up with an effort. "I . . . I must go. Thank you for giving me the news. My"—she struggled to remember what she had said—"grandmother will be sorry."

She drew her shawl about her face and went down the steps, not looking at Lilith.

Blindly, Alis went along. There were few people on the country lanes and she ignored those she passed, too dazed and sick to care whether anyone recognized her. Luke was dead. And it was her fault. He must have stayed out all night for fear that someone would see him and pick up her trail.

He was dead. It could not be true and yet it was. She had imagined him so often—tall and supple, with his soft dark hair and olive skin, his eyes shining with excitement to hear of her great adventure—and all the time, he had been dead. Now he lay quiet under the green turf of the burial ground. She would never see him again. She had not thought such pain was possible. She wished she might die, now, on the road as she walked so that she need not feel her great loss anymore.

But she was young and strong. The death that had come so swiftly and cruelly to him was not hers for the asking. She found herself at length on the highway again.

Sick with despair, she knew she could not go to Elizabeth and Jacob, even if she could find out where they were. How could she expect a welcome from them when Luke was dead because of her? The road south would carry her back to the inn where she had worked: Jessie and Will might help her. Or she could return to the city to rejoin Edge and Joel if she could find them again. But she would not go south. She had brought evil upon those who had helped her: Luke, Elizabeth, and Jacob; Ethan; even Joel perhaps, for her presence had set him at odds with the others, and it was only after her arrival that hurt had come to him. And trouble for Joel meant trouble for Edge also. No. She had defied the Maker and now He had punished her. She would not resist anymore. She would return to Freeborne.

It was once more early morning when Alis was set down by the cart on the road that led to her childhood home. A beautiful summer morning of soft wind, delicate blue sky, and the sweet gold of the corn ripening in the fields. Alis looked at it from out of a dark tunnel. It sickened her with its mockery. Her feet were sore, for she had walked a good many miles in the preceding weeks. Now her boots had rubbed the raw places bloody, but she welcomed the burning pain—anything to distract her from the agony within.

She followed the path beside the stream until she stood among the willows at the end of her mother's garden. As a child, she had loved to watch the tiny fish as they darted to and fro or dispersed in alarm when she disturbed the surface of the water. Her mother had been afraid that she would fall in and drown. Would that she had! Now she waited on the bank among the softly shifting leaves for the place to reclaim her. If it would not, she would stand there forever, in sun and rain, until she was no more than a tree herself.

After a long while the back door opened and her mother came out to feed the chickens. The silly creatures set to squabbling loudly over the handfuls of grain, but eventually the pail was empty and the birds were pecking peacefully. Hannah paused to look down the garden, shielding her eyes against the morning sun. Standing among the overhanging branches at the edge of the stream, Alis did not even know whether she was visible. But then her mother frowned and advanced a few steps before stopping once more to peer into the shadows. Evidently something had caught her attention, for she came on again, until she was standing only a few yards from the bank of trees. Alis did not move.

"Good morning, stranger." The voice was as brisk as ever. "Are you in need? Can I aid you?"

Still Alis did not move. Her mother came in under the shade of the leafy branches.

"By the state of your clothes, you have traveled far and perhaps you are weary. Will you come in and break your fast with us?" She smiled at the ragged figure whose face was half concealed by the shawl wrapped about her head. "Come. My hens are laying well. I will give you good fresh eggs, and new bread with honey from my own bees. And you shall rest awhile and tell us what we may do for you."

She held out her hand, and when there was no response, took Alis gently by the arm and drew her down the garden and into the house.

Seated at the table in the kitchen, where the meal was already spread, was a gray-haired man, somewhat rounded in the shoulders. He looked up in surprise as they came in. Alis gave a start. It was her father. But he had aged, and his face was etched with lines of melancholy. Her mother seated her beside the table and sat down herself, saying firmly, "Now my dear, won't you put up your shawl and we will say the morning prayer before we break our fast."

With a weary hand, Alis pushed back the wrap. She heard a sharp intake of breath from her father and saw her mother go still. Then her father's voice tentative, trembling, as if he dared not believe. "Alis?"

She did not look at him. She looked at her mother: a few more lines perhaps, a few more gray hairs, but she still had her strength. For a long moment they stared at each other. Then Alis said bleakly, "I have come back. I will do what you want. I will marry him."

16

In the weeks that followed she refused to answer any questions. Otherwise she was obedient. She submitted to examination by the Healers who declared that her body showed she had not yet lain with a man, and could therefore marry in purity.

And now the day had come.

Her mother poured the laboriously heated water into the wooden tub, and when Alis sat motionless in it, she soaped her body for her, moving her hands gently, anxiously, over the girl's skin, most unlike her usual brisk self. She washed the dark hair and rinsed it in herb-sweetened water. Then she dressed her daughter in the simple white-and-green bridal robe. Alis made no protest: she let her limbs be moved into convenient positions; she obeyed instructions to bend this way or that. But she said nothing.

When it was all done she went into the front room. Her father was there in his prayer-house clothes, gazing out of the window. He looked round when she entered and came forward to kiss her gently on the forehead. Taking her hand, he said, "I would not have chosen this for you, Alis, but sometimes our paths are chosen for us. He is not a bad man, and he has no choice, either."

If she heard the pleading note in his voice, she gave no sign.

Her mother came in with a plate of wheat cakes and a cup of milk.

"You must eat something, Alis. This is no day to go without sustenance."

Obediently she reached out and took a wheat cake. On her tongue it had no taste: she felt the dry flakes separate and the material turn to pulp. Her jaws moved it and her throat swallowed it. The milk in her mouth was wet and chill: she felt its passage down into her belly.

Alis stepped out into the gray, still day. No sun or sound of wind, nothing moving but she and her parents treading the path to the prayer house. She went a little ahead of them, alone, moving like a sleepwalker.

In the gray stone interior of the prayer house, the whole Community was gathered for the ceremony. Some of the women—especially the younger ones—had brightened their sober clothing with a touch of green in honor of the wedding—perhaps a fine kerchief kept for such occasions, or a spray of leaves. The chatter was less subdued than usual, for the people had not gotten over their surprise that the Minister was to marry the daughter of their own senior Elder.

Galin had been with them for twelve years: in all that time, not one woman had been able to attract his gaze, though many had tried. There was also the mystery of Alis's disappearance after the fire in

Two Rivers, and a rumor that the marriage had been ordained by the Great Council, which had decreed that every Minister must take a wife. Some thought it hard on the girl to be given to a man old enough to be her father—such unions were usually frowned on, sometimes forbidden. There was plenty to talk about.

Reaching the doorway, Alis stopped. The building dilated before her eyes so that the neat lines of wall and window swelled slowly into curves and arcs. Her father took her arm, murmuring something, and she went forward. At the table facing the crowded wooden benches, Galin was already seated on the left. He was pale. He did not look at her. Beside him, in the center, was the Minister appointed for the occasion, a thin-featured, raw-skinned man, completely bald. He looked up at her as she approached. His face seemed to be doing odd things, the mouth curving upward and the eyes wrinkling at the corners. She thought that he must have some sickness. She stared at him until he looked away. Her father said softly in her ear, "You must sit, Alis, beside the Minister."

She made to go round the table toward Galin but her father steered her to the other side. Of course! Galin was not the Minister today: he was the bridegroom. A spasm of nausea gripped her, sending bitter liquid up into her throat. She swallowed.

Now the Minister who was not Galin was standing up. The people ceased their chatter. The ceremony was beginning.

She went through it in a daze: yes she would be his wife; no she had not known another man; yes she knew the duties of a wife and would perform them faithfully; yes the will of the Maker was in all things her will, and so on. In a dream she heard Galin making his responses. His voice came to her from a great distance, oddly muffled as if she heard him underwater.

Of the feast she remembered nothing. And then it was time for them to leave together.

She had not yet spoken a single word to him. He went in front of her to make up the fire, which had burned down. When he turned, she was still standing in the doorway.

"Shut the door, Alis. Come in. This is your home now."

She did not move. She heard his voice but his words made no sense. He came over to shut the door himself. He could not have done it without brushing against her, but she took a step forward to prevent it. And so she came in and the door was closed.

He maneuvered past her and went back to the fire, kneeling down to fiddle with the wood, keeping his face away from her. At last he could do no more. "I told Martha not to come back today. I thought it would be . . . easier."

She remained standing. She knew she should speak to him but her lips would not open.

He said, "I'll fetch us some ale. You've touched nothing all day and I, too. Come with me and I'll show you where everything is kept."

She felt almost as if she were dead—still and cold. After a moment he turned away again and went out of the room.

In the interval she did not move. And then he was there again, carrying two tankards that he put down carefully on the polished wooden table.

"Come, Alis. Sit, and have your drink. You must be tired and you cannot stand there forever."

At last she moved, obedient to the simple command. She seated herself at the table opposite him passively. He pushed one of the tankards toward her.

"When you have refreshed yourself, I will show you everything. There's a garden—you didn't know that, maybe—at the back. It's neglected, I'm afraid, but you could grow herbs and vegetables— flowers, too, if you wanted."

He sounded doubtful, as if he were unsure what a girl of sixteen might want, and then added not unkindly, "Drink your ale. It will sustain you."

She looked at him at last. "I cannot." And she bent down her head, weeping in great gasping sobs. Through the sound of her grief she heard him speak her name.

"Alis, don't. I beg of you. How are we to go on together if this is how we begin?" She raised her head. He looked horrified, helpless, and she was glad. Let him suffer, too. He got up, as if to come round the table to her, and she stilled her weeping and stiffened. He stopped. The thought that he might touch her, even to comfort her, filled her with terror. She longed to hurt him.

"How else should we begin? I wish I had died before this day. You have taken my life from me."

Bitterly he replied, "I had no more choice than you. Why should you blame me? Do you not think I would have done otherwise, if it had been in my power?"

"I do not believe you. You are the Minister. You could have said no."

He sighed wearily. "Oh, Alis. Do you think the Minister of a little Community has so much power? Besides, it would not have mattered how important I was. This marriage is the Maker's will."

She turned her head away.

He spoke again. "I know you do not understand. We must talk of these things in the days to come."

At this reference to their future, she shuddered. He saw it and said angrily, "Do you think you alone suffer? Do you think I wanted to marry you?"

She stood up, summoning her pride, sorry that she had given way to tears. Coldly she said, "Show me the rest of the house. Since I am its mistress now, I had better know its ways."

All her childhood, his austere figure had been part of her landscape, and with her mother he had ruled her world. She did not believe that he had had no choice.

He took her through the simple house. Apart from the main room there was not much to see downstairs, just the kitchen with its store cupboards and the privy out the back. The top of the steep wooden stairs brought them to a narrow passageway with two closed doors, one immediately on the left, the other at the far end. The first room was a fair-sized chamber with a bed of the kind they called a marriage bed because it was wide enough for two. It was made up with the wedding sheets of good linen that her mother had prepared for her. She stared at it, sickened. She thought of the knife she had left behind with Edge. From behind her, his dry voice interrupted her trance.

"The other chamber is yours. I have made up a bed for you there."

She turned to him. She could make no sense of what he said; she could see only the marriage bed that was wide enough for two.

He gestured to the doorway and she went along the passageway to the other door. "Open it, Alis."

She did so. The tiny room contained a narrow wooden bed-stead, made up with coarse cotton sheeting and a rough blanket. On a small table beside the bed was the copy of the Book, a marriage gift from her parents. Nothing else. He stood beside her. In the narrow space they were almost touching. She held herself rigid. Then without looking at him she said, "What is this room for? What will I do here?"

"You will sleep here, if you wish."

Still she did not understand. "But I thought . . . the other room . . ."

There was a long silence. At length he said simply but firmly, "I will not force you, Alis. Know that."

And then he went away, his boots hard on the wooden staircase, and she was left alone in the little chamber with the bed and the Book.

17

For a long time she stood without moving. It was too much to take in, this sudden release from horror. Though she had promised herself that she would not weep again, the shock brought on tears. When she had finished weeping and dried her eyes, she did not know what to do: she was no ordinary bride with a joyful path laid out for her. Could it be true that she need not lie with him? Surely that could not be. But she would not think of that now. For tonight at least, she was safe. There was some good where she had expected none, relief instead of dread. She drew strength from it, and not knowing what else to do, went down the stairs.

He was sitting again at the wooden table with two tankards before him. He looked up when she came in. "Come and drink now."

She did as she was bidden, aware suddenly that she was hungry, too, though she had not thought she would ever want to eat again. Tentatively, not sure of her position, she asked, "Is there any food in the house?"

"Yes, yes. Martha will have prepared food for us, and there will be cheese in the store cupboard."

He spoke wearily, as if he did not care. In her newfound relief, she could feel something like concern for him. And a kind of pride, too. After all, she was a wife now. Her mother had not despised the traditional work of the household although she was an Elder and a scholar of the Book. "Are you not hungry? Shall I prepare something?"

He looked up. "Yes, if you please. Do so."

If she had hoped for gratitude she was disappointed. He spoke formally, distantly, much as if she were a servant who had requested instructions. Nevertheless it was a relief to have something to do.

In the kitchen larder she found a whole roast fowl under a muslin cover, and as he had said there was bread and cheese: simple, wholesome food, and the fowl a little luxury to celebrate this marriage that neither of them wanted. She suspected her mother's hand in that. Placing portions of the bird on the red earthenware platters, she swallowed down the tears that *would* rise despite all her efforts: the thought of her mother was like scalding water on tender skin.

He pronounced the blessing and they ate in silence. When they had done and all was tidy again, she returned to the table to sit opposite him. Now she would raise the subject that had preoccupied her during their sad meal. Hesitating, for she feared his answer, she said, "Will Martha not think it strange that I lie in the little chamber and not . . . ?" She could not bring herself to say "with you."

He shook his head. "In such cases it is common enough. She will assume that I summon you to me, or come to you myself when . . ." He broke off.

"Such cases? What does that mean?"

He was not looking at her. With his forefinger he was tracing a precise, small circle on the table over and over; he followed it with his eyes.

At last he said, "There have always been marriages made, not by mutual consent or for the high companionship that should exist between husband and wife, but for . . . other reasons." He stopped a moment, as if the subject pained him, and then went on.

"You know this yourself. Sometimes parents choose and insist, even though the Book rules otherwise, saying that marriage is no marriage where there is no consent."

She stared at him, unable to believe what he had just said. Then she burst out, "But if the Book forbids, how could I . . . how can we . . . ? Did I consent?"

"Wait, Alis. Do not interrupt. Let me finish."

He spoke sharply—he was again the Minister to whom she must defer. In the dry, reasonable tones she had heard so often when he and her mother had argued about some Community matter, he went on. "You say you did not consent to our marriage, but you came back from wherever you went, did you not? You took your part in the ceremony. You are sitting here now—the door is not locked; the windows are not barred."

Bitterly she said, "It was not true consent. What else could I do?"

"You could have stayed away." His hesitation made her wonder whether he knew that she had been to the city. Its ragged towers and stinking alleyways rose in her imagination. She thought of Joel and Edge. Perhaps they would succeed in crossing the sea to the new life she might have shared with them, or maybe the deep would swallow them up. She could have gone with them. She could not explain this to him.

He said softly, "You chose this."

She was silent for a while. She saw that he was right but her spirit rebelled.

"Then it is the same with you. You said that you had no more choice than I. But you also chose. You *could* have said no after all."

His finger was again tracing circles on the wood of the table. "You are right, Alis. I, too, had a choice."

"Then why?"

He was silent so long she thought he had forgotten her, but at last he said, "The reformers dominate the Great Council these days, and the Great Council decided that all Ministers should be married. When I would not choose a wife, they sent the Bookseers. You know how this is done?"

She nodded her head. She knew that decisions could be made by opening the Book at random and finding guidance in the text on the page. He went on, "It is a way of finding out what the Maker wishes, though the texts are not always easy to interpret. But in this case there was no doubt: three times the Bookseers let the pages fall open, and three times the signs were unmistakable. I could not but think that the Maker had spoken."

He got up and crossed to the cabinet with its shelves of leather-bound books. Carefully, he removed the largest volume and brought it across to the table.

"See." He had opened the book and was running his finger down the page. When he stopped, she leaned forward to read the text: *Who is the girl at the gate?*

He said quietly, "I was coming up the cart track from Master Amos's when the Bookseers rode into Freeborne. You were swinging on the gate at the entrance to the long field. We all saw you."

He turned the pages of the Book slowly and then stopped. At the top of the page she read the words: *The Elder has one daughter; she is the chosen one.*

She shuddered. It seemed as though her path had been laid out long ago. Had she ever had a choice?

He found the last text: *All life is sacred.*

She frowned. "What has that got to do with me? It is just a saying."

He gave a bitter laugh. "I thought so, too. I rejoiced for a moment, thinking that I was saved. For the three readings must agree or it is not binding. But look at the initials."

She saw at once: *A l i s.* Horror clutched at her throat. It was like being trapped in some dark place. Galin had closed the book.

"You see how it was. Your parents could have refused; I could have refused. But had we done so, there would have been no place for us anywhere in the Communities of the Book. We three, and you, too, would have been outcasts."

He paused, with a brooding look on his dark face, as if his thoughts troubled him. "Besides, we would not defy the Maker, and in any case the Maker is not to be defied. No doubt whatever He willed would have come about."

She considered this. If it was indeed the Maker's will that she should marry this man, she had certainly meant to defy it. But here she was, married to Galin after all.

"What is the point of our being able to defy Him, if He always prevails?"

He smiled grimly. "Perhaps our defiance is part of His will."

"But then, in truth, there are no choices. If we obey, it is His will, and also if we disobey? Whatever we do, He has willed it?" She gave him no time to speak but rushed on. "But what is the point of being alive at all? We are just—"

His face darkened. He said sharply, "Cease, Alis. There is blasphemy in what you say. And it is dangerous to think such things."

She had never truly considered any of this before. The Maker had been a remote authority, interpreted for her by others. Now her mind was full of questions.

"But I don't understand. How can it make sense? Is everything we do, every tiny thing, His will? Whether I drink ale or not? Whether I walk down to the stream or not? Whether I dabble my hands in the water or sit on the stones in the sun? And when I speak—if I choose this word or that—is He choosing for me? I am His puppet then and—"

He was on his feet, breathing heavily, his fists clenched. "Cease, Alis, I command you. Such words must not be spoken."

She was silent, afraid. What had she done? She had blasphemed. Would he whip her? Would he make her stand before the Community in the prayer house and confess? Gazing up at him in dread, she thought she would rather die than endure such shame.

He seated himself again, still breathing like one who has run a race, but his face, which before had been flushed with rage, was now livid, the great sweatdrops standing on his forehead.

"Alis, you are the Minister's wife. You, of all people, must not say such things."

She saw that she had frightened him. She longed to ask if he, too, had such ideas, but she did not dare. Husbands and wives were supposed to be equal but he was her senior by many years, and he was the Minister, too. He might think it his duty to punish her. She was afraid of him.

He did not seem disposed to punish, however. He looked exhausted. "Go to bed, Alis."

She stood up and then hesitated. Should she not bid him good night? But he looked up and said vehemently, "Go!" and she went.

Only later, as she lay in her narrow bed, did it come to her that he had not commanded her to her knees to beg forgiveness of the Maker for her wicked words. Nor had they knelt together to say the evening prayer.

She heard him come up the stairs slowly, as if his feet dragged with weariness. She tensed. Was he to be trusted? But the footsteps did not come along the passage. She heard the door of the other room open and close. There were noises from beyond the wall, and then silence. He was lying between the wedding sheets. Perhaps he was staring up into the darkness as she was. She could not imagine his thoughts. Now she must try to sleep. She must not think of Luke. That was done with. He was dead and the worms fed upon his flesh.

She put her hands over her mouth so that the man she had married could not hear the sound of her agony.

18

Nights and days were equally bad. Galin kept his word and neither came to her room nor demanded her presence in his bed. But that was the only relief. Always, she lay open-eyed in the dark until the small hours. If she slept, it was only to dream of Luke, and then she must wake to remember that he was dead. To get up, to face the day with its duties and encounters, was harder than anything she had ever done.

Her mother came to help her set up in her new home, bringing extra linens, a small spinning wheel that had been her grandmother's, pots of preserves, and other needful items. While she put away the things and inspected the household, Hannah dispensed advice. "I have made a copy for you of your grandmother's recipe book: you must cook dishes that are wholesome and good to taste but not over-indulgent to fleshly appetite. And I will inquire about a cast-iron pot for you, so that you can make your own soap when autumn comes.

Sift the ashes before you make the lye and remember that too much of it, and the soap will burn the skin."

Alis thought wearily of the long process of soap making.

When they went to put away the sheets and bedcovers, Hannah brought out some small muslin bags of sweet-smelling herbs, one of which she placed in the linen chest. "These bags must be renewed in the spring, for they will lose their power, and then the moths will get into your garments and bedding. And do not allow Martha to make up the bags but do it with herbs you have dried yourself. Or if not, I will give you what you need from my own store. This chest is of good cedar, which keeps out the moths, too, but the lid does not fit closely. Your father shall come and amend that."

Alis listened in silence. The moths might eat every stitch of fabric in the house for all she cared. On and on Hannah talked, casting anxious glances at her daughter from time to time, but Alis would not yield her a look or a smile. Why should she?

Galin had tactfully removed himself while all this was going on. He returned as her mother was making ready to go and Alis saw them exchange uneasy looks. When Hannah had gone and they sat at their meal, she said coldly to him, "You are not to talk of me to my mother behind my back. I will not have it."

He flushed a little. "It is only that we are concerned. You look as if you never sleep, you are so pale. And you scarcely eat." He indicated her plate. "You will surely make yourself ill."

She said nothing. If she became ill, if she died, they would be punished as they deserved.

He was watching her. When she remained silent, he said in a

neutral tone, "Your father is much troubled about you, too."

Again she did not reply. An image came to her of her father's face, the tears of joy in his eyes on the day she had returned to Freeborne. After a moment she took up her knife and began to eat.

Alis shrank from public scrutiny, but pride would not let her remain indoors. When the time came for the first prayer meeting, she dressed with particular neatness and gathered her courage to accompany Galin. He stood at the door of the prayer house to greet people as they arrived, but Alis went to the front bench where she had always sat with her parents. They were already there, seated together. She did not look at Hannah but slid in swiftly next to her father, squeezing his hand in reassurance. Then she bowed her head as if in prayer so that her mother would not try to speak to her.

When all the people had arrived, Galin took his place at the front. She had seen him there, week in and week out, all through her childhood; she could not believe that now she was a married woman and that this man was her husband. It seemed like a dream, except that she knew she was trapped in it forever.

He spoke the opening prayers and then said, "And now in silence, let us look within, and listen also, that we may know the truth of our hearts and hear the voice of the Maker."

Alis shut her eyes. The Maker would not speak to her, but at least she need not look at Galin anymore, or try to keep a proper expression on her face. She had been sitting stiffly upright, afraid that the congregation would notice if she wavered from her rigid posture. Now she could relax a little. Behind her, people bowed their heads, folded their hands in their laps, disposed themselves for silent contemplation.

Alis listened. She could hear her father breathing softly beside her. A child whispered and was hastily hushed. Farther back, a bench creaked from time to time. Occasionally a shoe scraped on the stone floor, or cloth rustled as someone changed position. Gradually the hall grew quite still and she sat quietly, grateful for the respite.

But of course, it was too much to hope that after the obligatory period of silence there would be no testifying. One after another, members of the congregation stood up to speak about the virtues and joys of marriage. The old baker, rambling enthusiastically in praise of the example Galin had set for them all, was silenced eventually by his embarrassed daughter. Alis sat looking straight before her, desperate for it to end. She felt that everyone was watching her, judging her behavior—her body ached with tension.

Afterward, though she longed to leave, Galin stopped to speak to several people, including a tiny old woman, recently widowed, her lined face full of sorrow.

"How are you today, Mistress Hester? You are keeping your spirits up, I trust."

Her lip trembled. "Ah, Minister Galin, that's what I shall not be able to do again in this life, I fear. I must bide now until I can see my Joshua again, if the Maker permits. I must pray He will—for whatever our sins, we loved each other well, and what's the use of love if it comes to nothing at the end?"

"Have faith, Mistress Hester, have faith. The Maker is good and knows what is in our hearts. And you have your friends to comfort you. I shall come to see you by and by. We will sample some of your seed cake, and sit and talk of Joshua."

A smile lit up her sad face for a moment. "You're a good man, Minister Galin, and a blessing to this Community. The Maker grant you as much joy in your marriage as I had in mine." She looked up at Alis. "Make much of him while he is yours, my dear. He's a deal older than you, and you'll be left like me, I daresay. My Joshua and me were the same age and yet he's gone before me."

The blood burned in Alis's cheeks. Fortunately, old Hester did not wait for a response but turned away to answer a neighbor inviting her to take the midday meal with him and his family. "Master Daniel, most kind . . ."

But then came fat, red-faced Mistress Dinah demanding attention. She had a gift for Galin—a crock of honey from the bees she kept in the apple orchard. She handed it to Alis, saying, "You will see that he eats some, will you not, Mistress Alis? I am sure 'tis no harm for a man so self-denying to taste sweetness once in a while."

When Alis thanked her stiffly, Galin frowned at her and broke in, covering her awkwardness.

The people admired him but they were in awe of him, too, and some were clearly very ill at ease. A thin-faced man with a shifty look left in a hurry as soon as the closing prayer was done. He had recently been brought before the people to confess that he had lain with his neighbor's wife. The burly miller, who had been admonished, first privately and then publicly, for his mistreatment of his two sons gave Galin a black look.

The young kept their distance. The girls Alis had known gathered in little groups, smirking and shooting glances at her when they thought their parents would not notice. Her mother's position as Senior Elder had always set Alis somewhat apart. Now that she was married to Galin, it was worse than ever. And Elzbet, who had been her dearest friend, had not come to the meeting. She was with child and very sick. Alis had been to see her, thinking to find some comfort there. But Elzbet, between bouts of terrible nausea, seemed overawed by Alis's new status, and the meeting had not been a success.

When, at last, she and Galin left the prayer house, he took her arm. She stiffened, but with a sense of eyes upon her, she knew she must endure it.

Back in the house she had not learned to call home, he said to her, "It must have been an ordeal for you, Alis. You did well."

She felt so lonely, she was grateful for his praise. He was a good man—she had seen his kindness to poor old Hester. And after all, he might have been like Thomas.

Martha, the servant girl, who had cooked and cleaned for Galin before his marriage, helped in the household still. Heavily built and plainer of face than she liked to think, Martha did not see why she should defer to someone younger. In awe of the Minister, she had not dared to neglect her duties before, but now that Alis was in charge, she dawdled, skimped, and looked affronted when she was given instructions. Galin noticed the difference, was displeased, and said so. It was clear that he expected Alis to deal with the matter.

She ran a fingertip along a ledge: it was dusty. In the kitchen

Martha was idly scraping the pots in water that needed changing. She stopped altogether when Alis entered.

"The cleaning has not been done. Leave that and do it at once. The Minister will be home soon and he will not wish to lay his books among the dust."

Martha dropped the pot back into the scummy water, sighed loudly, and reached for the towel. Alis stood still in the kitchen doorway and the girl found her way blocked.

"If you want me to do the work you'll have to let me pass, I reckon," she said scornfully.

Alis looked at her. "You may go home."

The girl stared back. "I can't go yet. I don't finish till the prayer-house clock strikes four." There was a note of triumph in her voice: no jumped-up minister's wife could get the better of her.

"You finish now and you don't come back," Alis said evenly. She was not afraid. She needed no knife for this.

Martha smirked. "You can't dismiss me. *He* took me on. *He* must tell me to go."

Somebody would slap her big, bold face one of these days, Alis thought. Calmly she said, "I think you will find that the Minister regards this as a matter for a wife. You may tell your mother you were dismissed for idleness and insolence."

Martha went white; she had not expected this. "There's no need for that. I meant to do the cleaning. I daresay I should have done it sooner, only the pots needed scouring. There's more to do than there used to be, now you're here."

Alis raised her eyebrows. "You can explain at home. I am sure your mother will understand."

Angrily, though her lip was beginning to tremble, the other girl said, "'Tis not fair. You ought to forgive me as we're taught, instead of getting me into trouble. I'm sure the Minister does not think ill of me. He never complains."

Alis said coldly, "The Minister has noticed your neglectful ways. He is much displeased. No doubt your mother will wish to know that, too."

This was too much for Martha. Her mother had never been slow to punish, and she held Galin in high esteem. "Oh, no. Please! I'm sorry, truly I am, and I'll not give you any more trouble if only you'll not dismiss me."

"Complete your work, then I will decide." Alis turned away and went out of the house.

She sat in the wilderness of the garden at the back, hearing the sounds of frenzied activity from indoors. The prayer-house clock struck four. Still she sat there. It had struck five, and six also, before Martha came out, disheveled and apprehensive, to say that she had done. Alis went indoors. Methodically she went through the house: examining surfaces, lifting chairs, checking corners. At length she looked at the waiting girl. Martha's hair had come loose and her big face was sweaty.

"It will do well enough," Alis said—the house was spotless—"but let me not have to speak to you again."

Later, waiting for Galin to come home, she felt sickened. What had her life come to?

When he arrived, it was only to say that he had to go out again immediately. He had promised Eli, the stone mason, that he would visit. But he noted the newly polished wood and dust-free books approvingly. "You have spoken to Martha already, I see."

Alis said sharply, "Of course. It is my job, is it not?"

He flinched at her tone and turned away without another word.

Afterward she was sorry. He had meant well, after all. And he was gone, for the third evening in a row, to sit with Master Eli, who was dying slowly and in great pain. She must try to be kinder to him.

It was very late when he came back. Alis had been sitting in the gloom wondering what had become of Edge and Joel, dreaming of Luke. It was a relief to hear Galin returning. Hurriedly wiping away her tears, she turned up the lamp. He stopped abruptly in the doorway when he saw her.

"Alis! Why are you not in bed? Are you ill?"

"No, I am quite well. Would you like a bit of supper? You have had such a long day, you must be weary."

For an instant, he remained quite still in surprise. Then he said, "That is kind. I am weary indeed." He came in and sat down heavily at the table. "But I do not think I can eat. To watch such suffering—"

"You will feel better if you take a little food," Alis said firmly. "I have made some broth. I will heat it up."

He made no further protest but sat staring blankly before him. When she placed the bowl on the table, he lifted the spoon slowly, as if his mind was still in the sickroom with the dying man. Nevertheless, he ate what she put before him, and when he was done, he said, "Thank you, Alis. That was good. Now you must go to bed. Midnight is long gone."

"Will you go to bed also?"

He sighed and shook his head. "I will sit up awhile. My spirit is heavy tonight."

He sounded so heartsick, she was prompted to say hesitantly, "If it would please you, I will sit up with you. I am not tired."

He looked up at that. For a moment she thought he would dismiss her, then he said, "Will you, Alis? That would be a comfort."

They sat in silence until at last he said, "I have prayed that he might die and be spared more pain. None who sees him could wish him to linger. And yet he lives. In his agony he cries out to me, to know what he has done to deserve this dying when others pass peacefully in their sleep. I have no answer for him."

She wanted to help, but she had no answer, either. Why had Luke died?

Angrily she said, "It is cruel and we must endure it. It is of no use to ask for reasons."

"But I am the Minister. Who should answer such questions if not I?"

"Well, you must tell them that all will be made well. The dying go to the Maker and their tears are wiped away."

It was what she had been taught as a child, but she was not a child anymore, to believe such a tale. There was sorrow, and at the end, darkness: that was all.

He was tracing circles on the table with his finger as he did when he was troubled, and almost arguing with himself. "The Maker is merciful. We must believe this. How else can we bear to live? But why must we suffer—the good and the sinner alike? It cannot be that the Maker is not good himself. Perhaps he is not all-powerful then. But . . ." He was silent once more.

She said, "You are worn out. You should go to bed."

He sighed and got up, rubbing his forehead wearily. Then he

looked at her and smiled faintly. "You have been kind, Alis."

She shrugged. "I have done nothing."

He shook his head. "I came home desolate but your company has cheered me. I thank you."

He went out slowly and she listened to his feet on the stairs. Then she put out the lamp and sat in the darkness thinking about him.

19

The next day was hot and when Alis had completed her household tasks, she remembered a book that Galin had wanted the previous day. It was on the shelf at the back of the prayer house where the volumes for borrowing were kept.

The heavy front door was open wide in the sunshine. Martha would be there with one or two of the other girls, taking her turn at cleaning as Alis had done with Elzbet long ago. The inner door was ajar and she was about to push it open when her attention was arrested by the sound of her own name.

"Well, you can say what you like, but it sticks in my throat to call her *Mistress* Alis."

That was dark-eyed Hetty, whose glossy curls always escaped from her cap. She was something of a ringleader among the unmarried girls, and she lived to gossip and make eyes at the young men.

A kinder voice replied—Betsy, the weaver's youngest daughter, mousy, fair, and thin. "'Tis hard on her, I say. I'd not like to be married to an old man."

"He's not such an old man," Hetty said, adding sharply, "and you've no call to speak for her, Betsy; she's as puffed up with pride as anything. Can't hardly bring herself to speak to us no more."

Alis felt her cheeks redden. Then Martha's grumbling tones took up the theme. "Hetty's right. You've not to work for her as I do. Why should I be servant to such as her? She's no better 'n me."

"Yes," said Hetty, "and my mother says she don't behave like a wife toward him at all. She's only took him so's she can set herself above the rest of us and give herself airs, I reckon."

"You're mighty hard on her, Hetty," Betsy protested. "She didn't choose him. 'Twas all arranged, they say. And even if she don't like it, she can't say so, can she? Besides Elzbet thinks—"

"Elzbet!" Hetty's voice was spiteful. "You do as I say, Betsy, and don't be talking to Elzbet. She'll only go telling tales to the Minister's wife. Always standing up for her, she is. She's not one of us no more."

Alis retreated silently, her cheeks burning. She knew well enough how she must appear to them, but if she seemed proud, it was only that she must get through her days without showing the world how bitter her life was to her. And poor Elzbet. They had been the closest of friends once, and now it seemed the other girls had turned against her on Alis's account. She would go to visit her and make an effort not be stiff and formal.

Full of good intentions, she turned away from the green, and went down the beaten-earth path along a row of cottages until she reached the one that Elzbet shared with her young husband Martin, the blacksmith's apprentice. The door was shut but the shutters were open. Alis knocked and waited. There was no reply. Resisting disappointment, for Elzbet might be upstairs or out back, she knocked again, more loudly. This time there were footsteps, and then the door opened.

Elzbet's pregnancy was well advanced and her belly bulged hugely under her apron. She looked flustered when she saw who her visitor was. "Oh, Mistress Alis, I beg your pardon for keeping you waiting. I was upstairs, and I move so slowly these days. Do come in."

They went into the cool interior of the cottage. Determined to reach out to her friend, Alis accepted refreshment and pressed Elzbet to say how she was finding married life. Things were well with them, Elzbet said—Martin was most loving to her at home, and the blacksmith thought highly of his work. Although she smiled when she spoke of her husband, she seemed reluctant to say much, and after a little while the conversation faltered. Then Elzbet said timidly, "And what about you, Alis? Mistress Alis, I mean."

Alis looked away from her. Once, as children, they had promised to be friends forever and tell each other everything, even when they were married. And now Elzbet called her "Mistress Alis" and thought of her only as the Minister's wife. It was no good.

She turned back to Elzbet, meaning to make a polite excuse and depart but the sorrowful look on her friend's face and the memory of Hetty's spiteful words made her say instead, "Dear Elzbet, we were such friends once. Will you not call me Alis and talk to me as you used to?"

She heard her voice waver at the end but Elzbet said eagerly, "Oh, yes, I should like that. I have been so troubled about you."

"Well, you shall hear all about me, but first, tell me truly how you are."

"Truly, I am well. And Martin and I are very happy together. He is so proud and joyful that he is to be a father soon."

Alis hesitated. "And you are not lonely? I have heard . . ." She stopped.

Elzbet looked down at her lap and sighed. "Well, you know, Hetty thinks me a dull old thing now that I am a married woman. And where Hetty leads, Betsy and half a dozen of the others follow, so I see little of them."

"What about Susannah? Surely she will not do Hetty's bidding."

Susannah was the cobbler's daughter, a big, kindly girl whom they had both liked very much.

"Poor girl," Elzbet said. "She lost her baby last year, and she cannot bear to come here. I understand very well how she must feel. To lose a child, it is what everyone dreads."

They spoke sadly of Susannah, and Alis promised to visit her, then with some hesitation, she approached the subject of what she had overheard that morning. It was typical of Elzbet to say nothing of the real reason for Hetty's spite and Alis wanted to show her gratitude for her friend's support.

"I think . . . I have heard that you have spoken up for me sometimes. It is good of you, Elzbet. I have not been much of a friend to you since—"

Elzbet broke in, "Oh, Alis, you must not blame yourself for that.

You have suffered, I know you have. You are so pale and thin. Will you not tell me all that has happened?"

"I will tell you everything," Alis said.

It was strange to relive it all. Elzbet was shocked by life in the city and troubled to hear of Edge's savage ways, though glad that she had helped Alis. When they came to Luke's death, Alis wept and Elzbet comforted her. It was such a relief to unburden herself that she was even able to speak of Galin calmly. Only when it came to her mother did anger overwhelm her again so that her voice lost its steadiness.

"She should not have agreed to the marriage. I am sure she could have done something."

"But Alis," Elzbet said reasonably, "what could your mother have done if, as you say, the Bookseers named you? She must have thought it the Maker's will, even if you do not."

Alis was silent for a moment. Hannah was powerful. People listened to her and did as she advised. How was it that she could do nothing for her daughter? She said bitterly, "She did not pity me, even. She just said it was my duty. I thought she loved me but she does not."

Elzbet gave a little cry of protest. "Oh, Alis, you are wrong. I am sure you are wrong."

Alis shook her head but Elzbet took both her hands and said urgently, "Listen to me. I will tell you how I *know* that you are wrong. When the news reached here that you were gone from Two Rivers, your mother came to see me. She guessed that you had run off, though she did not tell me why, and she hoped you might have confided in me where you meant to go. She begged me to tell her, but of course, I could not."

"She wanted to fetch me back so that she could make me marry, that is all," Alis said angrily.

But Elzbet went on. "No, that was not it. For she said to me, 'If only I knew she was safe, I would be content.' When I said again that I knew nothing, she looked so ill I wanted to fetch my own mother for I was afraid, but she would not let me. She sat awhile with her hand pressed to her side as if she were in great pain. Then she said, her voice very low, 'I do not think I can bear it.' After that she got up and went away. For a long time, she did not come to prayer meetings or do any of her work as an Elder."

"She recovered, though. When I came home, it was my father who had aged. She looked just the same."

"My mother says she put her sorrow away for your father's sake, seeing his grief for you and his fear that he would lose her also. But if you had seen her that night," Elzbet said, "you would believe me. Be angry with her if you will, Alis, but do not say she does not love you. I have seen and I know."

They sat for a long time in silence. The heat had gone and they were both weary. At last, with a quiet embrace and a promise to meet the next day, they parted.

Walking home through the evening sunshine, Alis found herself dwelling on the image Elzbet had painted of Hannah's visit. She wanted to go on being angry with her mother. She wanted to believe that her mother, who had once seemed all-powerful, could have acted differently. There must be someone to blame! But the image would not go away.

When she got home, the house was empty. Galin, she knew, was gone to take supper with her parents. They had both been invited of course, but she avoided her mother when she could: she had said she would not go. She went to the kitchen and opened a cupboard although she was not hungry. There was some bread, and a pot of preserved meat. She stood there, seeing nothing.

After a long time, she closed the cupboard and went upstairs. She poured water from the ewer into the basin and washed herself before putting on a clean gown and apron and descending again. Into her basket went a blackberry pie she had made—her mother liked blackberry.

Then she set off for her parents' house.

20

Her heart was eased by Elzbet's friendship and she was glad to have made some kind of peace with her mother, but still she felt as if her life were over. And though her days were better, her nights remained a torment.

Late one morning, coming back from seeing the dairy wife about the cheese and cream, Alis found little Deborah from Boundary Farm in the kitchen with a message: her father was bad again—raving about his sins, howling that he was cast into the darkness. The Minister must come: no one else could soothe him. Martha reported that Galin had a visitor and she was about to take in some refreshment.

"I will see to it," Alis said. "Stay here with the child." She put the tankards and the plate of cake onto a wooden board and carried it to the front room. The man sitting at the table with Galin turned his head as she came in. She felt the room spin and blur and knew she was about to faint.

When she came to, she was lying on the polished boards feeling weak and sick. Galin leaned over her, his pale face anxious. "Alis, you are not well. I will send for someone."

She shook her head, feeling the tears trickle out of the sides of her eyes and into her hair as she lay there. The dreams were bad enough. And now this. How was she to bear it?

She could hear Galin instructing Martha to stop cleaning up the broken pots and fetch one of the Healers. She struggled to sit up. "No. It was a moment's giddiness, no more. Martha, stay here and finish what you are doing. I do not need a Healer."

Galin protested but she would not hear of it. She would be better in a moment; she required no one. He helped her up. The visitor had disappeared. Remembering her errand, she told Galin that he was wanted. He looked troubled. He did not like to leave her. She made an effort to smile at him. Martha would take care of her; he must not neglect his duties. He agreed reluctantly.

"Are you fit to entertain the young man who has come? I am anxious to know his news but I must attend to Deborah's father first. He is not safe when these fits come upon him; I fear for the child and her mother."

He would have said more but Martha came through from the kitchen saying that the child was crying: her father would kill himself. Why did the Minister not come?

"Tell her I am coming," Galin said. "Alis, it troubles me to leave you. Shall I not send Martha to have someone come to sit with you?"

She shook her head. "No indeed. I am quite recovered. Get you gone before the man does violence upon himself. I will tend to our guest."

Her husband looked at her doubtfully. She was very pale, with dark circles under her eyes, but when did she not look so?

He went away and Alis sat for a few moments gathering her strength. Now she must deal with the visitor and if there was a resemblance, she must endure it. He was in the garden, Martha said. He begged the privilege of a few words with her if she were well enough. He was sorry to intrude. She rose, and as she did so the prayer-house clock struck four.

"Go now, Martha. I am quite well again. I do not need you."

The girl did not need bidding twice.

Alis went out of the door and stopped. The blood pounded in her head. It could not be true. "Luke?"

He was dressed in farm clothes—a man now, taller, broader in the shoulders, but with the same soft brown hair and olive skin. He said stiffly, "I heard you had married him. I came to find out why."

She stared at him, unable to speak. He looked away, saying in a lower voice, "When Ethan did not come again, I feared for you. I thought perhaps he was dead and you were lost somewhere with none to aid you, or even that you yourself were dead. I thought to tell my grandmother the truth so that I might come to seek you. And then we heard the news."

He looked straight at her, his face full of grief. "Oh, Alis! How is it that you are married to that man? You said you would rather die." His voice shook, and he stopped speaking.

She said in a whisper, "I went to Ellen's and there was no one there. Even the cows were gone."

He gave a strangled exclamation and slammed his fist into his open palm. "Fool that I am! I never thought of you coming back there by yourself. Ellen left word for Ethan with one of the Healers whom she trusts. She knew that having medicines to sell, he would go to see the woman and would learn where we were. We'd moved in with Ellen when my grandfather fell sick and the Elders said he could not be Minister anymore. But then my grandmother thought we would be safer with some friends of Ellen's who live outside the Two Rivers boundary, where it would be harder for the Elders to trouble us. Her neighbor, Saul, put Ellen's cows in with his so that she could travel with us to help care for my grandfather. It is too cruel that you should have come just then!"

Her throat closed up. "I thought you were dead." She could not go on. He was alive! He had haunted her dreams until she thought she would go mad with grief. And now he was here.

Luke looked baffled. "You knew we expected to go away. Why should you think me dead just because there was no one at the farm?"

"It was not because of that, but . . ." She saw again the shrub and Lilith tearing the petals, the litter of white fragments at her feet.

Lilith *had* known her, and had lied to get her out of the way!

Shyly she took Luke's hand—there was no one to see them. She had been cruelly misled, but he was alive, his hand warm in hers. "Come and sit here, and I will tell you how it was."

On an old bench, among the weeds and wildness of the neglected garden, they sat down together and she told him her story.

He clenched his fists at Lilith's lie. "But why did you believe her when she said I had died?"

She had to think. Not for a moment, then, or in all the months since, had it occurred to her to doubt what Lilith had said: the shuttered farmhouse, the girl's tear-reddened eyes, the sense of secret dread fulfilled, perhaps. And then the story fitted with events and seemed likely enough.

"Likely enough?" Luke scoffed. "As if a night in the open would kill me."

"I see that now, but at the time . . . Besides, I did not think Lilith had recognized me, and why should she lie to a stranger?"

"But even then," Luke said angrily, "when you thought I was dead"—she shuddered remembering it and clasped his hand more tightly—"why did you come back here? You could have found work at an inn as you say you had done before. Or you could have gone back to the city to your brother."

How easy he made it sound! She said slowly, "I thought it was meant to be a lesson, your death, because I had defied my parents and because I had not heeded the signs of the Maker's anger."

He looked at her uncomprehendingly.

She tried again. "Your grandmother, Ethan, Joel. Things went ill with them because they tried to help me. And I would not see it. Then when Lilith said you had died, it was as though the Maker was saying, 'Now do you see?' And although nothing could be worse than your dying"—she closed her eyes, remembering the horror of that day—"I would not bring evil on anyone else. We are to obey our parents, the Book says. So I came home at last, to obey."

Luke said furiously, "You should not have married him. You should have kept faith. You said you would rather die."

"Oh, Luke!" She was despairing. How was it that he did not understand? "If I had known you were alive, do you think I would have done it? I thought you were dead. I was like a dead thing myself, except for the pain. It did not matter to me whether I married him or not, only—I would not bring more grief to those who had been good to me."

He was not looking at her. He disengaged his hand and stood up. His mouth twisted bitterly. "Well, you are married now and no help for it. And I must care for my grandparents. Lilith cannot have dreamed her little trick would work so well."

It hurt her to hear him speak so. "Do not be angry. Think how it is for me. All this time I have mourned for you—it has been so dreadful." Her voice broke and his expression softened. "And now you are alive after all; it is like coming into the light and air after being trapped in a dark place."

She made a little sound, half laugh, half sob. He moved toward her as if he would have taken her hand once more, and then as if some unwelcome memory had arrested his gesture, he stopped. She looked at him. His face had gone hard.

"Are you with child?"

She was so startled she could not speak for a moment. "With child? No, indeed. Why should you think it?"

"You fainted. My grandmother says it is sometimes thus with women when they conceive—she did so twice when she was carrying my mother though she is strong and never sick."

Alis said firmly, "I am not with child, I assure you. It was seeing you that made me faint."

His expression did not lighten, however. He said viciously, "Well, if you are not, you will be soon enough, I daresay."

She shook her head.

He frowned. "How can you be sure?" And then in sudden distress, "Alis, you will not be foolish and do that which will harm you to stop a child from coming. Women die that way, I have heard."

She put her hand on his arm to stem the flow of words. "Dear Luke. You need have no fear. There is no question of that."

She could see he was not persuaded.

"How can you be certain there will be no child? When husband and wife lie together"—she interrupted him.

"We do not lie together, he and I. We have never done so."

He sat down again upon the bench and stared at her disbelievingly. She said gently, "He will not force me. He has given me his word."

Luke took a deep breath and let it out again. The hardness was gone from his face. Hesitantly he said, "You do not share a bed?"

She smiled. "I have my own chamber."

Luke shook his head wonderingly. "He must be a strange man. But Alis, suppose he changes his mind. What will you do?"

"He will not change his mind."

"You cannot be sure."

"I am sure."

His expression was mulish. "All the same, what would you do?"

"Oh, Luke! I don't know. I wouldn't let him touch me, you may be sure of that." She remembered her first sight of the marriage bed, and the nausea rose in her throat as it had done that day. "I think I would kill him. I know how to use a knife, I suppose."

He looked at her, appalled, and she hastened to reassure him.

"But truly, there is no danger of it. He has no desire for me. And though he says the marriage is the Maker's will, in truth I am not sure he believes it."

For a long time they sat without speaking. The sun left the garden and a little wind got up. She took him indoors and prepared food for him, assuring him that Galin would not be home for hours, for he said he could not endure to sit at table with the man who was her husband. While he ate, she asked for the news from Two Rivers. Luke looked gloomy.

"There is little good to tell except that you are no longer spoken of as starting the fire. They have blamed the mute woman who Samuel lived with before he was whipped and driven out. But Thomas is more powerful than ever. He and Robert have their way in everything. Sarah is with child again. My grandmother is unchanged, only grieved for my grandfather who is full of sorrow, and sick, too. They have made him so: he could not bear to see the people suffer, and yet he would not leave them until he was forced to. And the Elders are extending their power, buying up farmland closer to where we are living. We may yet be driven right away."

She sat opposite him at the table as he talked, reluctant to take her eyes from him for an instant, wishing that the meal might never end. But at length he said, "I must go. I do not like to leave my grandparents any longer than need be. Tell your . . . tell Minister Galin my grandmother bid me say to him that Freeborne is not far from Two Rivers and you should not think yourselves safe from the contagion of reform."

They went to the door and stood there. It was too cruel that they must part. They could not say, this time, that they would—*must*—meet again. She was married. She put her arms around his neck as she had done once before.

"Oh, Alis." His voice trembled.

She thought she would weep. "Don't say anything, Luke. It is hard enough to bear."

For a moment they clung to each other, then she was watching his tall figure stride away into the June dusk and biting her lip to hold back the tears.

Galin returned weary and vexed, and she had to hide her feelings. The farmer he had been to visit was tormented by ideas of sin since his widowed mother-in-law had come to live with them.

"I would that we could send her away again," Galin said, sitting down to the food she put before him. "The reformers rule where she has come from, and I would not have her spread their poison here. I suppose they have tightened their hold on Two Rivers also. What did the young man have to say?"

She told him the news and gave him Luke's message from Mistress Elizabeth. He looked gloomy. "These are ill tidings. I hope we shall not take the infection." He looked at her, and then went on a little hesitantly, "You are recovered from what ailed you earlier, it seems. There is color in your cheeks. You need young company. I hope you will see much of Elzbet, now that you have begun. You and she were inseparable once."

"Galin." She was looking at him intently, a plan forming in her head. "Why might not Luke's grandparents"—she would not say

Luke—"come here to Freeborne if they are driven even farther from Two Rivers?"

His face was somber. "They might, but it is usual for such moves to be agreed between the Elders of both communities, and I daresay those of Two Rivers will declare Minister Jacob and his wife vexatious. Then we would have to ask permission of the Great Council for them to settle here. And I do not think it would be granted. I have heard that Master Robert has friends on the Council."

She felt cold suddenly. "Will it be the same everywhere?"

He nodded. "Among the Communities, yes. There would be no place for them."

"Could we not take them despite the Great Council?"

She wanted him to say it was so—she was afraid for them—but he shook his head. "If we defy the Council, Freeborne would cease to be one of the Communities of the Book. I do not think our people would vote for that."

In her mind, she saw the three of them: Minister Jacob leaning on his stick, Mistress Elizabeth wincing at the stiffness in her shoulders, and Luke staring ahead. They had their backs to her and the empty road stretched away before them. There was a tremor in her voice. "Where would they go? How would they live?"

The oil lamp was beginning to smoke a little. Galin said, "As to where they would go—who knows? There are farms and villages outside the Communities, and forest settlements. The city, too. But"—seeing her distress, he sought to sound a more cheerful note—"perhaps it will not come to that. And they have their grandson. He will take care of them, surely."

He was trimming the wick of the lamp as he spoke, and the light burned clear and steady again. She was comforted. They were not without help. And as for herself? Luke had come, and he had gone once more, but he was not dead. They would meet again: she knew it.

21

Alis stared up at Galin in horror. "Thomas? Here in Free-borne?"

She was trying to clear the ground at the end of the garden where the brambles snaked over the other weeds and flourished their thorns in what had once been the vegetable patch. Lacking the appropriate tools but unwilling to venture out to borrow from anyone, Alis hacked away with a rather blunt old kitchen knife and made slow progress. Nevertheless there was already a considerable pile of barbed strands, some several feet long, when her husband came out to give her the news.

"He arrived yesterday, it seems, with his wife who has miscarried a child. They are with her sister Leah and he asks permission to remain."

Alis was crouching down to cut off a thick stem of bramble. As she stood up, it caught at her sleeve and it was only with difficulty that she detached it, scratching herself in the process.

"He will make trouble," she said, brushing earth and leaves from her skirt. "He is cruel and dangerous. When I was . . ."

She stopped. She had told Galin little of what had occurred during her year away from Freeborne and he had refrained from questioning her. She had gone from Thomas's house in Two Rivers to stay with the Minister's wife, and from there had disappeared on the night of the fire: this he knew but nothing more. Now he waited. She went on.

"When I was there, he dealt harshly with his wife, blaming her because their babies did not live. I think perhaps he beat her, though I did not see it. But whether he did or not, she was terrified of him. I should have become so, too, I think, if I had remained with them. Why has he come to Freeborne? It cannot be for his wife's sake. He hates her."

Galin nodded uneasily. "I have heard much about Master Thomas, and there is what the Minister's grandson said to you, also. The man likes power, and he has power in his own community. Why does he leave it for one where he will be a mere guest, unless he sees some gain for himself?"

"Can we not refuse his request?" Alis wanted to know.

Galin shook his head.

"His wife is sick after miscarrying a child and wishes to visit her sister. He is concerned for her in her melancholy condition and would attend upon her. What could be more natural or more praise-worthy? How could we refuse?"

Alis felt her temper rise. It did so often these days. "So Mistress Elizabeth may not come here, though she is all goodness, but if Master Thomas wishes to bring trouble among us, he must be permitted to do so. It is a topsy-turvy world, is it not? And if I ask you why, you will say the Great Council rules thus and therefore it is the will of the Maker."

Angrily she turned her back on her husband and heard him retreat toward the house. Seizing a long strand of bramble, she began to saw at it with her knife. Her first wild joy at Luke's reappearance had given way to bouts of misery and rage. She need not have come back to marry Galin after all. It was Lilith's fault, and her mother's, and Galin's—his above all. It was his failure to marry that had brought the Bookseers to Freeborne. And she would never forgive her mother, who should have defied them for her daughter's sake. All her bitterness toward the two of them had returned.

Over and over in her mind she replayed her encounter with Lilith. Why had she not realized? They had cheated her, the three of them: she hated them all. And now, as if things were not bad enough, Thomas had come to Freeborne!

The knife blade snapped off suddenly, and the bramble she had been trying to cut sprang up and scratched her face. Furiously, she flung the useless knife handle across the garden and stormed into the house. Where was Galin? It was all his fault. She would tell him so, let him do what he would. She was not afraid of him anymore.

But the house was empty. She stood in the kitchen, panting with fury. It was unbearable: she must do something or she would go mad. On the table was one of the red platters from which they always ate. She seized it, raised it high above her head, and hurled it down. With an immense crash it exploded against the flagstones, sending pieces sliding across the floor in all directions.

In the ringing silence she stared at what she had done. Fragments of red earthenware littered the kitchen. There were even some on the stove. The thought of having to clean it up appalled her. Impulsively she went toward the door, shards crunching under her feet. She must get away.

Tormented by the thought that she might still have been free, she walked until she was weary, finding herself at last at Boundary Farm, where her husband had been called away the day Luke had come. She was tired and hungry. With a little tremor of fear, she realized that her husband might by now have returned to the house and found the scene of destruction she had left in the kitchen. What would he think? Would he guess that it was an act of temper and not an accident? She did not fear punishment—that was not his way—but he could be very cutting when he was angry, withering her with icy words to which she had no answer. She shrank from that.

When she arrived back, he was eating cold pie and bread, sitting at the table in the main room. She paused in the doorway and he looked up, his face expressionless. Quietly he said, "You must be hungry. Come and eat."

He had laid a place for her.

"The kitchen, I ought to . . ."

He smiled a little at that. "I have done it. Come and eat."

After all her rage, she was touched. If only she were not married to him, she might like him very well.

When they had eaten and the table was clear, she said awkwardly, "I am sorry about the platter."

He raised his eyebrows in that way that he did, and his mouth twitched humorously. "I am glad I was gone from the house or perhaps Freeborne would need a new Minister now."

She laughed, a little startled. He was jesting, of course, and he could not know what she had said to Luke. All the same . . .

It was an unusually hot summer. The old people kept within or sat on their doorsteps, fanning themselves with their hands. The more easygoing mothers brought their little ones down to paddle in what was left of the stream. Shrieking and laughing, the children splashed each other. Elzbet and Alis walked slowly in the shade of the trees close to the water; Elzbet was near her time now and the heat troubled her.

They had been speaking of Thomas. He had created no such stir as Alis had feared but conducted himself courteously enough as a guest in the Community, though not concealing the strictness of his views. Some of the unmarried girls would have made eyes at him had they dared, Elzbet reported. He was a good-looking man, and his sternness excited them.

They seated themselves on the bank, watching Leah's children, Peter and Rachel, who were playing at the edge of the stream. Peter was already soaked. Little Rachel, more mindful of her clothes, was keeping well back on the bank. Her brother was capering for her amusement, pretending to extract fish from his pockets, shaking his head like a dog so that the drops sprayed everywhere. Rachel laughed and clapped her hands crying, "More! More! Do it *again*, Peter."

The boy broke off a long stem of willow and began flicking the surface of the water with it so that Rachel was showered in droplets, much to her delight.

Suddenly Thomas appeared from among the trees, looking stiff and hot in his dark clothes. "Come, Rachel, and you too, Peter. Your mother wants you home. The meal is nearly prepared."

Rachel came forward obediently, but the boy, who had crouched down at the water's edge to examine something in the mud, looked up briefly and went back to his play. Alis held her breath as Thomas stiffened, wondering whether she could intervene. Before she had time to speak, however, Thomas was beside the child. He grasped Peter roughly and hauled him to his feet. The boy let out a yell of protest and began to struggle. Thomas's face convulsed with rage. In an instant he had seized the willow rod that Peter was still holding and began to beat him furiously with it, gripping him by the arm. At once Alis was on her feet calling loudly, "Stop, Master Thomas! Stop this instant! Leave the child be! You have no right."

Thomas's head jerked up in surprise and taking advantage of the diversion, Peter wrenched himself free and ran to Alis, flinging his arms about her waist and sobbing with his face in her apron.

"Give the boy to me!" Thomas's voice was low and furious.

Peter tightened his hold on Alis and she stared at Thomas, her heart beating fast. Putting her hand gently on the child's head, she said in her most conciliatory tone, "Master Thomas, won't you forgive Peter? He has been sufficiently punished for his naughtiness, and he will go home quietly now like a good child, I am sure."

Red-faced with heat and rage, he stared back at her. "I will decide when he has been sufficiently punished. Give him to me."

She did not know what to do. She could not yield up the boy who was clinging to her desperately, but she could see that Thomas was not going to back down. To make matters worse they had attracted a small audience, mainly children and a few mothers, who were watching avidly.

When she did not move, Thomas said coldly, "The boy is under my authority. I will punish him as I see fit. The matter does not concern you, and when you are no longer a child yourself you will, perhaps, know better how to conduct yourself."

Alis felt her cheeks burn and heard Elzbet's intake of breath: no one spoke to the Minister's wife like that. She put her arm protectively over Peter's shoulder. "The welfare of the children of this Community is most decidedly my concern, Master Thomas, and I must tell you that however you do things where you have come from, we do not beat small children publicly for trivial offenses here."

He curled his lips in contempt. "Whether the offense is trivial is a matter of judgment. But since you object to his being punished where he has offended, I will take him home and attend to the matter there."

This was too much for Peter, who had ceased his sobbing and turned his head to listen. He slipped free from Alis's sheltering arm, shot off along the bank, jumped the stream, and disappeared at a run into the trees beyond. Rachel, who had been standing wide-eyed with fright, gave a whimper of terror. Thomas turned toward her but only said sharply, "Get you home, Rachel. Tell your mother that I will be there shortly."

She gazed at him white-faced, unable to move. Then from among the watchers, a young mother carrying a small girl on one arm stepped forward and took Rachel by the hand. She did not look at Thomas. Saying comfortingly, "Come along, little one. Let us go and find your mother," she led the child off. Another woman shooed the rest of the children away, leaving Alis and Thomas with only Elzbet as witness. He was still holding the willow rod. Now he tossed it aside.

"Well, Mistress Alis, if the boy should come to harm, no doubt you will feel able to explain to his mother how it came about."

"He will not come to any harm," she said with more confidence than she felt. "And if he does, I will most certainly be able to explain to his mother"—she paused—"and to the Elders, also."

Despite the heat, his face went white. For a moment he seemed to have difficulty breathing. "Do you dare to threaten me?"

Uneasily she remembered the prayer-house fire. Thomas had meant her to be blamed for that: he was dangerous. She said as calmly as she could, "I do not threaten, Master Thomas, but you know well that when a child goes missing, it is a matter for the Elders."

Now for the first time Elzbet spoke up. "I think, Master Thomas, that some of the older boys will know where Peter goes to hide. If he knows that he will not be any further punished, he will be persuaded to come home, I am sure."

Thomas hesitated. Then he said stiffly, "I thank you, Mistress Elzbet. Let the matter be closed. Obviously it is not my wish that any harm should come to the child."

They watched him walk away, and Elzbet let out a long breath. "What ails him?"

"He likes to rule," Alis said.

"But Peter is not even his own child. Surely Leah does not allow it?" Elzbet's face was indignant.

"What can Leah do if he says the boy is disobedient? She is already afraid that the Elders will think she lets Peter run wild, having no father at home."

Alis put out a hand to help her friend up. Elzbet hauled herself to her feet, panting a little and saying, "Well, I must speak to Martin. He has a brother just thirteen who will know the hiding places hereabouts. Let us hope the child has not gone farther afield."

Peter had not gone far. An hour's search found him, still tearful, curled up by the wall of the ruined hut in the woods.

Because he had been found so soon, the Elders did not concern themselves in the matter, but it caused a good deal of talk. Some thought that Alis had done well and that Thomas had been too hard on the child. Others said that Leah should be grateful to him; the boy was fatherless and needed discipline. Thomas regarded Alis coldly whenever they met.

It grew hotter and hotter. The fish lay gasping in the shrunken shallows of the stream, while above swarms of tiny insects danced in the stillness.

22

At last the heat broke. One night there was a storm. Great sheets of lightning lit up the sky. Thunder roared and cracked as if the world would split open. The water bounced off the dry earth and swept down the stream bed until it was more like a river. Then there were days of gentle warmth and blessedly cool nights when it was possible to sleep again.

Late one evening, Alis stood at her doorway breathing the scented night air. Galin was out at the bedside of a dying woman. Moonlight silvered the roofs and pathways, deepening the shadows between the houses. Here and there, a little lamplight glinted behind shutters, but mostly the houses were dark. She wondered what would happen if she made up a bundle, put on her shawl, and walked away into the night. It was tempting. But it would do no good. She had rebelled before, and it had brought only sorrow. She turned wearily and went indoors.

Some hours later she woke suddenly, not knowing what had

disturbed her. Perhaps Galin had come home, and the sound of his return had penetrated her sleep. She propped herself up on one elbow and listened. She could hear nothing, but maybe he had come in and was sitting motionless with exhaustion as she had found him on other occasions. Well, she would be a good wife for once and go down to him. Very likely he had not eaten, for he did not look after himself. He was a good pastor. If only he were not her husband!

She opened her chamber door and stopped. Someone was calling her name softly but urgently from outside the house; she could hear it now. Sick or in trouble, and wanting the Minister no doubt, but why did they not use the knocker? She felt her way down the stairs to the front door and unlatched it. She felt a weight against it as she pulled it open and then something fell in at her feet. A girl's voice said, "Hurry! Get him inside. I have hurt him."

Alis felt the world tilt madly. The voice was Edge's, and the figure at her feet in the flood of moonlight was her husband. She thought she had only dreamed her waking and that in a moment she would wake indeed in her narrow bed, but then the figure at her feet groaned. The light fell upon a tufted fair head as the girl half lifted him over the threshold and kicked the door shut. This was no dream. In the renewed darkness the voice that was Edge's said, "Light a lamp. He needs tending."

Dazed but obedient, Alis fumbled her way across to the table where the oil lamp stood ready with a tinderbox beside it. Her hands trembled so much she could hardly manage.

Edge, for it was indeed her, was kneeling beside Galin. "Help me get his shirt off. We must bind up the wound."

Alis stared in horror. His shirt was soaked with blood. Stupidly she said, "What are you doing here? What has happened?"

Edge looked up at her. "It was an accident. He took me by surprise and I went for him with my knife. Don't stand there like a fool. I need some help."

When Alis did not move she added savagely, "Do you want him to bleed to death? Fetch some strips of cloth, and hurry!"

The knife had laid his arm open from elbow to shoulder—as deep as the bone in places—and the wound yawned like a great mouth. They bound it tightly but still it bled.

"I must fetch the Healers," Alis said.

Galin groaned suddenly and opened his eyes. His face was gray in the lamplight and clammy with sweat. In a hoarse whisper he said, "Help me up."

"He's better off lying down," Edge said abruptly, but Galin began to struggle up, groaning in pain. They propped him against the wall. His breathing was ragged and the blood was already soaking through the outer bandage.

"Drink." His voice was a whispered gasp.

Alis brought him water. He looked deadly sick. "I'll go for help," she said. "You stay with him."

"No, I can't stop here," Edge said, terror showing on her face. "They'll take me."

In her confusion Alis had forgotten that it was Edge who was the attacker. "But I must get help. He'll die." She did not know what to do. How could this be real?

"Alis." It was Galin—hoarse still but stronger-voiced now. She knelt down beside him. He put his good hand on her arm. His eyes were shut.

"Who is she?" His breathing was easier and he spoke more clearly.

"She's called Edge. She's . . . she was my friend in the city. I don't know how she comes to be here."

"Friend?"

She hesitated for an instant in her horror at his injury, but her memory of all that Edge had done for her was too strong. "Yes. A good friend. She looked after me. I might have died without her, or worse. But you mustn't talk. I will go for the Healers."

He shook his head weakly. "No Healers."

She stared at him. "But you're hurt. Your arm is still bleeding, and I don't know how to make it stop."

He smiled faintly. "It's bound tight. Nothing more to be done. No Healers. Stay with me."

"But . . ." Surely he did not mean it.

"Please." He gripped her arm.

"All right." She did not understand, but how could she leave him? She gave him some more water.

He coughed and groaned. A little fresh blood oozed onto the bandage. "Is she still there?"

Alis nodded.

"I want to speak to her."

Edge crouched down beside him.

With an effort, he turned his head toward her. "Why were you waiting for me?"

"I wasn't," Edge said. "I wanted to speak to Alis. I've news for her. But it was too late when I got here. I meant to sit on your doorstep till morning but I fell asleep. I'm sorry I hurt you." Her voice trembled suddenly. "I didn't mean to. I was dreaming I was still in the city.

Then—I don't know—I thought you were attacking me. I . . ."

He shook his head slightly. "It doesn't matter." He coughed again, wincing at the pain. Then he said, "You must get away. Come daybreak there'll be no escaping. Help me to my bed first."

With some difficulty and many pauses for him to breathe, they got him up the narrow stairs and into the front chamber. Once more the blood oozed through the bandage, and the sweat broke out on his forehead. He was breathing raggedly again, gasping as if he could not get all the air he needed. At last he was propped up on the pillows of the bed. When he could speak he said, "Now you must go before it is too late."

Edge said nervously, "Shouldn't I wait until the moon goes down? I might be seen."

He shook his head. "Once this is known, there'll be a search. You must be as far away as possible."

He closed his eyes as if he had no more strength to speak. Alis and Edge waited. After a while he said in a weaker voice, "Alis, there is money in the cabinet below, you know where. Give her half of it, and some respectable clothes. If she takes a wagon and is dressed better, she'll be less noticed."

He leaned back exhausted and waved them away.

Still dazed with shock, Alis found clothes for Edge and made up a parcel of bread and cheese for her to take with her. The money was little enough but she gave her half as Galin had instructed, putting it on the table so that she did not have to touch Edge's hand. She shrank from her; she could not help it. Edge said desperately, "Don't, Alis. It wasn't my fault. He shouldn't have woken me like that."

Alis cried out in protest, "He couldn't have known. What if he dies?"

Edge clenched her fists. "He won't! I'll go and then you can get help. But Alis, did they catch you? How do you come to be married to him?"

"The boy Luke I told you about—I heard that he was dead. So I came back here."

Edge nodded. "Better here than life on the streets. But this man, your husband"—she looked incredulous—"how can you care about someone like him?"

How could she explain? She had hated Galin often enough and wished him gone, but never like this. "He's a good man, kind. Even though you've hurt him badly—killed him maybe—he didn't want you caught, did he?"

Edge flinched. "No—he didn't. There's not many men like that; most of them are worse than dogs. Jojo was all right, though, and Dancer, too." She looked at her right hand and shuddered suddenly. "I hope he doesn't die. I never wanted to kill anyone."

Edge sat staring at the table, looking pale and sick. Alis watched her. The sour-metal odor of blood seemed to hang in the air. Surely it could not be true that Galin lay bleeding upstairs. And what was Edge doing in Freeborne?

Alis forced herself to speak. "Come, put on these clothes and tell me the news you came to give me."

Slowly Edge reached out a hand for the first item. She began to wrap herself in the dark garments Alis had found for her, saying as she did so, "Jojo and I left the city. Things are bad there. Mute's dead and Weasel lost an eye in a fight—he's nastier than ever. I mean to try life over the sea if I can, but it's no good for Jojo. He has pains in his head, forgets things. He's not fit for a long sea journey, I don't reckon. And he said he wanted to see his parents so I was bringing him."

"Is Joel with you?"

Edge shook her head. "Don't know where he is. He just disappeared one morning. We'd slept the night in a barn and I went off to see if I could find us something to eat. When I got back he was gone. He'd gotten like that."

"Didn't you look for him?"

Edge shrugged wearily. "Didn't know where to look. I waited a bit in case he came back. Nothing else I could do."

"How did you know I was here?"

"Chance. We'd had a lift on a cart with a couple of farm wives and they were gossiping about how the Minister in Freeborne had married a girl less than half his age. They even knew your name. Jojo was asleep. I told him later but you can't be sure what he'll remember. When he disappeared, I thought I'd come and tell you, so you'd know what had happened to us."

The little clock chimed a half hour. "I'll go now." She hesitated, then said pleadingly, "I didn't mean to. It was bad luck." She gestured to the room above, where Galin lay. "He'll be all right if you get help."

Alis's stomach heaved at the remembrance of the terrible wound. With an effort she suppressed the thought. Now she must get Edge safely away and then persuade Galin to let her go for the Healers.

"You must keep the shawl over your head," she said. "You will be noticed otherwise. Hide your knife well, and go as quickly as you can. I hope you will be safe."

She opened the door and looked out. No one. The moon was low in the sky. On the threshold Edge stopped, saying in a low voice, "You were all right, good to me—you and Jojo. That's why I came."

Then she shouldered her little bundle, drew the shawl up over her hair, and began to walk away. From the back she looked like any respectable daughter of the Book. Soon the shadows swallowed her up and there was only the sound of her footsteps dying away in the distance.

Alis went inside and shut the door. She wanted to weep but there was no time. She must look to her husband.

He was leaning back on the pillows with his eyes shut. The lamp-light caught the gleam of wet blood on the bandage. As she moved toward him he opened his eyes.

"Is she gone?" His voice was a whisper.

She nodded.

"Good." He patted the bed feebly with his good hand. "Now come and sit by me. We must give her time to get away."

"Galin." She felt her voice tremble. "Surely I must get some help for you?"

He shook his head slightly, as if even that were an effort. "Not yet."

"But you are still bleeding. And I do not know how to staunch the flow." She was suddenly terrified. He would die.

He turned his head to look at her and motioned toward the cup of water. She gave him a drink. It seemed to revive him, though when he spoke his voice was very weak.

"We must wait. Even if I speak in her defense, she may hang if she is caught, for this attack will have to be reported to the Great

Council. I have blighted one young life. I will not be guilty a second time. Now listen. We must think what we are to say, when they ask how it happened."

She had not thought of this but of course there would be questions asked. What could they say? Her mind was empty. Haltingly, with many pauses to catch his breath, Galin outlined a plan. They must keep as close to the truth as possible. That way they would be less likely to make mistakes. He would say—or she must say if he could no longer speak—that he had been attacked by a man whom he had caught trying to open the front door. It would put them off the scent and it was more likely anyway. And she must say she had woken near dawn and come down to look for him, expecting to find him asleep in the chair, having come home late. And then, wondering what had detained him all night, she had gone to the door thinking that perhaps he was, even then, nearing home. The rest was simple. She had found him on the doorstep, brought him in, bandaged the wound, and helped him to bed. Then she had summoned aid.

He was silent for a while; she thought he had fainted or fallen asleep, but after a few moments he spoke again. "Alis."

His voice was very feeble now. She leaned close to hear him.

"I should not have married you. I am sorry. But we thought we were doing right, your mother and I. When the Book named you, it seemed it must be the Maker's will. I do not believe that any longer. But you will be free now."

His voice trailed away; the effort had exhausted him. His skin had a waxen sheen, as if he were dead already. She felt sick with terror. If she did not fetch the Healers, he would surely die, but if she did, the searchers would find Edge on the road and bring her in to be questioned. Respectable girls did not wander about in the dark, and what account could she give of herself? Galin had said she might hang.

"Alis." He had opened his eyes again and was watching her. "Do not trouble yourself so. Stay by me if you will—I would not be alone—but put your head down and rest a little. There is nothing to be done yet."

She woke with a jerk, feeling stiff and cold. There was light in the room. Was it day already? In terror she started up, but it was only the oil lamp, still burning, and smoking a little for the wick needed trimming. Galin lay back against the pillows, his face tense with pain, but his eyes flickered when she stood up and he tried to speak. She gave him some water to drink and he said, very low and hoarse, "Open the shutters. It must be near dawn now."

She did as she was told and saw that the moon was quite gone. Soon it would grow light. She readied herself to go.

"Remember," he said with a hint of a smile, though his eyes were sunken as though the flesh had fallen away already, "you must make a great clamor, as if you had just found me. And Alis, when you have fetched the Healers, bring your mother to me. I must speak with her."

He closed his eyes as if he had no more strength.

She let herself out into the cool morning air and then in terror that he would die before she could return, she began to run. She had no need to pretend when she reached the Healers' house: she hammered on the door. They must come. They must come. And wide-eyed with shock but ready to ply their craft, they came. When they were safely in the house, Alis went for her mother.

Hannah was already dressed and was lighting the stove in the kitchen when Alis came in. She looked up in surprise and exclaimed when she saw her daughter's white face. Alis gave her no time for questions.

"Galin is hurt. He has asked for you. You must come at once."

She saw Hannah go pale.

"What has happened?" the older woman asked. "Is he sick?"

"He was attacked, stabbed. He has lost a lot of blood," Alis replied. To her amazement she saw her mother's lips tremble. And then Hannah was flinging on her shawl and there were no more words.

The Healers had rebandaged his arm but there was nothing more they could do. He had lost much blood, they said. He was very weak. Alis would have tended Galin herself but they sent her away, and her mother went to sit with him. In her room Alis lay down upon the bed, but sleep would not come. If she closed her eyes, images from the night before burned on her sight like visions from a nightmare. She had often wished Galin dead, and now she was afraid that she would get what she had wished for.

Toward nightfall one of the Healers came to fetch her. He had been unconscious most of the day but now he had called her name and was struggling to speak. She went in, but he had slipped beyond reach again.

In the morning he was dead.

23

While Galin lay sick, searchers on horseback had scoured the surrounding area for traces of his assailant. But neither the outlying farms nor the inns on the highway had anything to report. No one, it seemed, had been robbed or threatened. The man had appeared from nowhere and disappeared without a trace.

Hannah was bitter now—consumed by her grief for Galin, which she must keep in check. Alis pitied her. She could not forget the way her mother's lips had trembled at the news of the attack, or the look on Hannah's face as she sat white and still at the bedside, holding Galin's dead hand in hers. She wondered whether she could contrive—without mentioning Edge—to comfort her mother with the fact that Joel had meant to come home. But it might only be an added sorrow, since he had not appeared, so she said nothing.

After the funeral, her parents would have had her return to live with them but she wanted only to be alone in her own house. In the days that followed, she found herself listening for Galin's footsteps, or thinking that she heard his voice. She prepared food and saw that she had made enough for two. He had been a quiet man, and at night she had barely heard him turn over in his bed, but now when she lay sleepless, the silence had a new quality and she wept for him. Once she lay down in the marriage bed she had never shared with him. She wished she might speak to him, just once, to tell him that she was sorry to have brought his death upon him, and in so dreadful a way.

But devastated and bewildered though she was by what had happened, Alis knew she must look to the future. Though she longed to know if Luke were still with Ellen's friends, she did not dare try to get a message to him at first. But the delay preyed on her mind: Ellen might have been driven away, and no one else would know where Luke had gone. In the end she sent a letter to Ellen at the farm, telling her what had happened. She did not mention Luke: the letter might fall into the wrong hands.

Elzbet's baby gurgled in Alis's lap, sticking out its tongue and kicking vigorously. Its mother smiled proudly.

"She's beautiful, don't you think? And so strong. Martin says she'll be the first girl blacksmith!"

Alis, grateful for Elzbet's efforts to raise her spirits, made an effort to smile and agreed that the baby was both beautiful and strong. And indeed the baby was engaging—so long as it did not cry or soil itself. Then it was strong smelling, and very far from beautiful. Elzbet was laughing.

"Come, I will take her. Your face gives you away. What you will do if ever you have one of your own, I cannot think."

They were making bread and had just taken the loaves from the oven when the prayer-house bell began to ring. They paused to listen, looking at each other in surprise. It was mid-morning: there was no prayer meeting or other activity to be signaled at such a time. But the bell went on and on. Elzbet held the baby close to her and said anxiously, "It is a summons. What can have happened, do you think?"

Alis shook her head. A general summons meant something serious—fire or danger perhaps—and was very rare.

They joined the crowd of people making their way to the prayer house, exchanging subdued greetings with neighbors, all wondering what had happened. Perhaps there was news of the man who had attacked the Minister so brutally.

Elzbet and Alis went inside and found themselves seats on the benches. Thomas and some of her town's Elders were there watching the people as they entered but there was no sign of Hannah, and the three central places at the table where the Minister, Hannah, and her current deputy usually sat were vacant. Alis looked round for her father. She could not see him either, but he might be out at one of the farms.

When at length the bell ceased to ring and the last stragglers were seated, Thomas raised his hand for silence. Alis felt her heart beat faster. Why was Thomas taking charge? And where was her mother? If there was trouble it should be the Senior Elder who addressed the people. The door behind the Elders' table opened and three men came in. They were strangers, dressed in dark, formal clothes and bringing with them an air of authority that seemed to subdue even Thomas. Two of them sat down, leaving one empty place in the center of the table, but the third man—not very tall, broad-shouldered, with cropped gray hair and strong, hard features—came forward to stand beside Thomas. He gestured slightly with his hand and Thomas stepped respectfully back. Then the newcomer spoke, his voice clear and rich in the hushed hall.

"People of the Community of Freeborne, the Great Council has heard of your trouble and of the sudden and terrible death of your Minister. It seems that no one has yet been apprehended for the attack, a state of things not satisfactory in so momentous a matter. We are here, therefore, to inquire into the circumstances of the Minister's death and especially into the part that may have been played in it by a person against whom an accusation has been laid. Where is the woman who was the Minister's wife? Is she here?"

For a moment Alis did not move. What could they know? What was she to be accused of? She must take care not to give anything away. This was Thomas's doing, she had no doubt. He hated her because she had sided with Mistress Elizabeth over the whipping in Two Rivers, and she had challenged his beating of Peter, too. Had he somehow found out about Edge? Well, he must be faced down. She would not let him destroy her. Elzbet was gripping her hand and looking up at her in horror. Gently, she disengaged herself and stood up. "I am here."

The stranger looked at her carefully as if committing her features to memory. "You are Mistress Alis?"

"I am."

He paused a moment, still observing her closely. "Mistress Alis, I must tell you that an accusation has been laid against you by Master Thomas of Two Rivers, that you yourself made the attack upon your husband that resulted in his death."

There was a gasp from the crowd. For a moment Alis did not think she could have heard him right. "You think *I* killed Galin?"

He shook his head. "I think nothing, Mistress Alis. I only tell you that an accusation has been made and it must be tested. And because it is so serious a charge, you must be held as a prisoner until the proceedings are complete."

"A prisoner!" What did he mean? There was no prison in Freeborne.

"Do not fear. You will be well treated and have every means for preparing your defense. But you must see that in such a case it is not fit that the accused person should be free to steal away perhaps, or to suborn the witnesses."

At once her temper rose. She was to be locked up while Thomas was free to do and say what he pleased. Contempt for them banished her fear briefly. Scornfully she asked, "And is my accuser also to be held as a prisoner, so that he may not suborn the witnesses?"

Again he shook his head. "Mistress Alis, you do yourself no good by speaking in such a way. You must come with us to the place where you are to be held. You may name whomever you wish to assist you in your defense."

He seemed to notice Elzbet for the first time and nodding toward her said, "Your friend may accompany you if she wishes and fetch for you such things as are necessary."

Already Alis could feel her courage ebbing away, but Elzbet took her hand again and squeezed it hard. Alis lifted her head. She would not let them see that she was afraid.

The Great Council Judges were lodged in the Community guesthouse, and Alis was to be held there also. She was put into a room at the back, and one of the carpenters came shamefacedly to attach bars to the window. A woman hired from an inn on the highway was to wait on her as far as was necessary, bringing her food and drink, as well as water to wash in, and doing whatever else is needful for someone who is kept in one room. She was a huge, brawny, silent creature who cared only for the pay she was getting and was more than willing to act as jailer if she were paid well to do it. Alis would get neither help nor companionship from her.

Elzbet brought some clothes and the other things she needed. Alis asked about her parents. Why had they not come to the prayer house with everyone else? Did they know what had happened? Elzbet could not tell her, but she would find out and come back on the morrow, she said. She had permission to visit, only the woman, the jailer, must be there all the time. When the time came for her friend to go, Alis clung to her, whispering in terror, "If Thomas has his way they will hang me."

Elzbet embraced her. "Don't be afraid, Alis. No one could believe such a monstrous lie. Thomas has overreached himself this time, you'll see. I must go, for the baby will need feeding. I will come to you here every day."

Soon after she had gone, Master Seth, the temporary Minister, arrived bringing Alis's parents. They had been taken aside beforehand, they said, so that they might not have to hear the news in public among their neighbors. Alis flung her arms about Hannah crying, "It is not true. It is not true. I did not kill him."

Her mother returned her embrace. "Of course not, daughter. You need not tell us so. We know it, and we must take counsel together to determine how you are to refute this wicked accusation. Master Thomas means you ill because he thinks you opposed him in the matter of the whipping, I suppose. Truly he dwells in darkness. Well, you must tell the Judges the truth and trust to the Maker for justice."

They spoke at length of what should be done, and gave her what comfort they could. Alis listened to all they said but her heart misgave her. She dared not name anyone to help her defend herself, for she knew she could not speak the truth. She had told the story that she and Galin had agreed upon and she would have to keep to it.

24

The three Judges sat at the Elders' table facing the packed benches, and beside them was a small, dry man with a voice that scratched like a quill on parchment, who was there to keep the record. On either side, facing each other, two more tables: one for Alis and one for Thomas, her accuser. The chief of the Judges was the man with the cropped gray hair—Master William—who had spoken to the people on the day that she had been accused. Now he stood up, and at once the benches fell silent. His voice rang out in the stillness.

"People of Freeborne, we are here today to test the accusation of Master Thomas against Mistress Alis, that she attacked her husband, Minister Galin, with a knife, causing his death. She who is accused, he who is her accuser, and all who wish or are asked to testify, must take an oath before the Maker to speak truly in all things pertaining to this grave matter. Let accuser and accused be the first to swear."

Thomas spoke the oath soberly as if he knew how momentous

a thing he was undertaking. He was respectful, too, in his manner toward the Judges. Alis thought fearfully that he meant to make a good impression, and that these men from far away could not know what he was really like. Her own voice trembled as she spoke the words; her heart was hammering with fright and she could feel her legs shaking.

William was still on his feet, watching carefully. Now he said to Thomas, "You have sworn to speak truly. And have a care, Master Thomas—the Maker hears you and will judge you. As you fear to be cast away into the darkness forever, weigh well your words." He paused. "Now make your charge."

Thomas bowed his head slightly toward the Judges and said simply, "I charge that Mistress Alis attacked Minister Galin with a knife and so caused his death."

William turned to Alis. "You have sworn to speak truly. Remember also, Mistress Alis, that the Maker hears you and will judge you. As you fear to be cast away into darkness forever, do not be tempted to lie." As he had done for Thomas, he paused. "Now answer this charge."

She did not hesitate. "It is false."

He nodded his head and turned again to Thomas. "Master Thomas, you have made a grave accusation and must give good reason for it, bringing witnesses if you can, to bear out the truth of what you say. And Mistress Alis"—he turned toward her—"you must turn away the accusation and bring witnesses on your own side if you are able." He looked out at the crowd. "Any person of this Community who is called as a witness must speak before us. And any who is not called but has knowledge that bears upon this case must offer it up. Now let us hear what grounds Master Thomas has. You may sit, Mistress Alis."

Thankfully, she obeyed him. Then Thomas began to speak. "I am from the Community of Two Rivers and was a reforming Elder there. I came to Freeborne with my wife on a visit to her sister, and we were given permission to remain. I had known Mistress Alis before, and the manner of her husband's death seemed most strange to me. I was much troubled in spirit concerning it, as you shall hear. I request that the Judges hear the testimony of the Healer, Mistress Clara, who attended Minister Galin on the night he was attacked."

Mistress Clara did not look at Alis as she came to the witness stand. She was a thin, sad-faced woman, much loved for the gift she had of easing pain with her hands. Her little boy had died of the fever but still she went quietly from house to house, bringing what relief she could, and making no account of her loss it seemed, except that she was quieter and gentler than ever. When she had sworn the oath, Thomas asked her to say what had happened when Alis had come to summon the Healers. She described how she had been woken by the frantic knocking on the door and Alis's desperate pleas for them to come at once. Her husband had been attacked; she had found him on the doorstep. He was terribly hurt. He would die if they did not come to save him.

One of the Judges leaned forward to ask whether Alis had seemed genuine in her distress.

"Yes indeed," Clara said. "There was no doubt of it. She was half out of her mind, all wild and staring. But for the news she brought, we would have kept her there but his need was greater, so we went to him."

"And what did you find?"

Clara described the terrible wound and how they had dressed it again, though this had barely staunched the bleeding. There was little they could do, for Minister Galin had lost much blood and was greatly weakened.

The Judge leaned back again and nodded to Thomas to resume his questioning.

"Mistress Clara, you have much experience as a Healer, have you not? Had you ever seen such a wound before?"

Clara nodded. "Yes indeed, Master Thomas, for sometimes at harvest there will be injuries when the great scythes are used. And those who work leather, too, use sharp knives, and it is all too easy to cut flesh to the bone if one is careless."

Thomas nodded. "But there was something unusual about this wound, was there not? Something that prompted you to seek counsel?"

For the first time Clara looked at Alis. It was a troubled look and Alis knew there was trouble to come.

The Healer went on in her soft voice. "Mistress Alis told us that she had found her husband on the doorstep and that she did not know how long he had lain there. And indeed it was clear to see from the wound that he had been hurt some time—some hours—before we came to him. But . . ."

She looked again at Alis, her face sorrowful. But there was no help for it. She turned, not to Thomas, but to William. "You must understand that a wound left untended looks different from one that is dressed immediately. If there is a great deep cut such that the edges draw back, as this was, it will be plain to see whether it has been left. And it was not so with the Minister. His was a cut some hours old, but it had been bound up straightaway. We did not understand how this could have been. Who had dressed the wound if not Mistress Alis? But if it was she, why had she not come at once to fetch us? We might have saved his life, for he must have bled much in the hours between."

There was a shocked murmur from the crowd. Despair seized Alis. They had not dreamed, she and Galin, that their story would be so easily discredited. Thomas's eyes were gleaming and his lips curled in a smile he could not suppress. No wonder he looked pleased, she thought in terror. How was she to explain the delay? William was looking earnestly at the Healer.

"Mistress Clara, are you quite sure of this? Your evidence might help to hang a woman. It would be an ill thing for you to speak with more certainty than you feel."

She made a piteous sound but she nodded her head. It was anguish to her to speak what might bring someone to the gallows but she was sure. She and the other Healers had discussed it.

"Why did you tell this to Master Thomas and not your own Elders? Was he zealous to search out the matter?"

She looked briefly at Thomas and then back at William. "Perhaps we did wrong, but the Senior Elder is Mistress Alis's mother and we hardly thought the matter could rightly be put before her. At first we did not know what to do but Master Thomas came to us in private, saying that he was troubled by the strangeness of the Minister's death and asking our opinion. Knowing that he was an Elder in his own Community, we thought we might properly unburden ourselves to him."

William thanked her soberly and Thomas resumed his questioning. Had the Minister spoken at all, either when the Healers first attended him or later?

Clara said sadly, "He was too feeble, though he was conscious at first, and he tried to speak when Mistress Alis told us what he had said—that he had been attacked by a man on the doorstep. Most of the time after that he was unconscious, but late in the day he came round, and asked for Mistress Alis."

Thomas interrupted her. "Did he ask for her? What were his words exactly, if you please, Mistress Clara?"

She paused an instant, as if to recall more clearly, and then said, "He opened his eyes and said Alis quite clearly—that was all. He wanted to say more, you could see. He tried, but then he was gone again, poor soul."

"It is possible, is it not," Thomas asked her, "that when he tried to speak the first time, the Minister wished to contradict Mistress Alis's account of the attack, and to tell you that his wife was his assailant?"

Her eyes widened in horror. "Oh, no! No, I am sure he did not!" She clasped her hands together and then said falteringly, "But it is possible . . . I suppose it is possible. He was distressed, certainly." There were tears in her eyes.

Thomas went on, "And when Minister Galin spoke his wife's

name later in the day, might he not again have been attempting to accuse her, rather than asking for her?"

Poor Clara! She was an honest woman. She could not deny that it might have been so. Thomas thanked her.

"If I may sum up what you have told us, Mistress Clara: Minister Galin's wound had been dressed immediately, presumably by his wife, but it was some hours before you were called. He was too weak by then to report what had happened himself, but he was in distress and tried to speak while Mistress Alis was telling you. After that, he once uttered his wife's name and wished to say more but was not able. Have I your testimony correct?"

She nodded, still wide-eyed with shock. Thomas smiled, and Alis was reminded of the first time she had seen that smile. Now she knew why it had so terrified his wife. William turned to Alis. Did she wish to question the witness? She shook her head and Clara went back to her place among the crowd.

Thomas looked at William. "With your permission, Master William, I would like to ask Mistress Alis to explain, if she will, how it came about that the Healers were not called at once to the Minister so that his life might be saved. Was it"—his voice was suddenly louder—"that, having struck the blow, she found she had not killed him and hoped that if she waited he would die of his injury?"

"No!" Alis was on her feet. "It is a wicked lie."

But what could she say without betraying Edge?

"He . . . he bade me wait, my husband. He said that the person who attacked him had done so in fright, woken from sleep suddenly, lying on the doorstep. Galin pitied h— the man, and would have it that we must give him time to escape before I went for help."

Even as she spoke she knew how false it sounded. Thomas looked scornful and Master William was frowning at her. "It is hard to believe such an explanation. Why should Minister Galin put his own life at risk for the sake of a stranger and, moreover, one who had attacked him? The man *was* a stranger, was he not?"

Thomas said viciously, "Perhaps he was no stranger to *her* but an accomplice—paid to strike the blow for her."

At once William turned on him. "I am conducting this trial, Master Thomas, and you will not intervene when I ask a question. When you are to speak, I will give you leave. Until then, be silent." Thomas's lips tightened but he remained quiet. William continued to stare at him for a few seconds as if daring him to disobey. Then he returned his gaze to Alis. "Mistress Alis, if you please, continue."

A little comforted by the rebuke to Thomas, Alis said, "My husband did not say he knew the man, only that he pitied him and would not bring him to the gallows if he could help it. And I neither struck the blow myself nor got another to do it for me."

William was watching her closely. "And you are sure there is nothing you can tell us that might help us identify this man you say your husband spoke of?"

She stared back at him. He might not care for Thomas but he was no friend to her. He belonged with those who had said she must marry Galin. She would not give Edge up to him. "There is nothing."

He looked at her thoughtfully but he said no more.

It was already midday. Alis was taken to a room behind the hall, and food and drink were brought to her. She drank gratefully but her stomach rebelled against the idea of eating.

The dry little man who kept the record—Master Aaron—came in.

Seeing the untouched food, he shook his head. "You would do well to eat, Mistress. I doubt not that Master Thomas has more to say against you and you will need all your strength."

He did not say how badly he thought she had done so far, but she knew.

25

When she had been summoned again, Alis braved a quick look at the crowded prayer house to see where her parents were sitting. For a moment, neither Hannah nor her father seemed to be there; then she caught sight of them right at the back, sitting side by side, not speaking to anyone. Her mother was looking straight ahead but her father had his head bowed. Alis looked away.

Now the proceedings were beginning again. A wave of fear swept over her as Thomas got to his feet. But contempt and loathing came to her aid. Sarah was at the front, pale and sickly, with her eyes fixed on her husband, like a small animal fascinated by a snake. Alis stiffened herself. She would not be like Sarah. She would defy him to the end.

Thomas asked permission to recount the history of his association with Alis.

William nodded. "So long as it bears upon the case in hand, you may do so."

Thomas began. "Two springs ago, after visiting her sister here in Freeborne, my wife returned to Two Rivers. She had been sick and was very low in her spirits. She was accompanied by Mistress Alis, who came, as I thought, to care for her. She will not deny, I am sure, that I welcomed her to my house?"

He paused as if to let Alis confirm this but she did not speak. She must listen to all he said and have a care of her own words. When she remained silent, he shrugged slightly and began again.

"I did not know at that time—nor would it have been proper for Alis, as she then was, to tell me—that it had been ordained that she should marry Minister Galin. But I am sure *she* knew, and she was not inclined to be obedient. Even in our first conversations, she flushed and looked ill pleased when her Minister's name was mentioned. And when I asked her about her own possible marriage—for she said she had a mind to be a midwife—it seemed to me that she spoke reluctantly as if she were hiding something."

Alis watched him in horror. How little she had managed to conceal from him and how clearly he had remembered it all. The three Judges were paying close attention, William leaning forward as if to catch every shift of expression. Now Thomas was speaking of the day of the whipping.

"My wife was troubled in spirit that day, and I was, I admit, discomfited that she felt unable to be at my side, but I would not force her of course, and when our young visitor offered to take her place, I did not refuse."

How cunning he was! If she were to say now how cruelly he had treated Sarah that morning, it would seem only that she exaggerated what he had already confessed. She wondered if she could summon Sarah as a witness against him. Even if she would not speak against him, her terror of her husband would surely be obvious. But the moment was gone.

Now Thomas was explaining that she had gone to the house of the Minister and had remained there.

"This displeased me, for I thought my wife neglected, but the Minister had a grandson of seventeen and no doubt that was of more interest to a thoughtless young girl than tending upon a sick woman. I naturally thought her quite safe under the supervision of the Minister's wife so I let the matter rest. It seems, however, that the young people succeeded in evading whatever watch was put upon them, for the night our prayer house caught fire, the girl disappeared. And though he was questioned and denied it, it was suspected that the boy Luke had played a part, for he was missing until morning. The Elders were much puzzled, however, for the boy was back. They had not run off together and though Alis was suspected of having set the fire, we could not think what reason she would have for such an act."

William was frowning and now he interrupted. "How is it, Master Thomas, that these grave matters were not pursued? Mistress Alis returned to Freeborne, did she not?"

Thomas nodded. "We were at fault perhaps, Master William, but my servant girl, who made the accusation of fire setting, we did not think trustworthy. Also, we learned afterward, that a mad creature—the kept woman of a sinner who had been cast out—had been seen entering the building, so it was thought that she must have started the fire. And, as I say, there was no cause that we could see why Alis should have done so. It was only when Minister Galin was attacked that I began to think again of what had passed. And then I wondered if the fire had been set deliberately, so that she might get away under cover of the confusion and so avoid the marriage that had been arranged for her."

Alis felt her stomach churning. How neatly he had put it all together. But she must defend herself; she must not let him have it all his own way. She raised her hand as she had been instructed to do if she wished to challenge anything that was said, and William nodded to her.

"I want Master Thomas to explain how it is that I returned to Freeborne and married Minister Galin. I came voluntarily and why should I do that if I had succeeded in escaping, as by his account I had?"

Thomas smiled as if her question pleased him. "It is indeed strange, and only Mistress Alis herself can solve that mystery for us, but I will take the liberty to suggest that, wherever she was for all those months, she found life outside the Communities of the Book a good deal less easy than she expected. Moreover, it was thought that there had been something between her and the boy Luke, and who knows what she might have hoped for in returning? Anyone will tell you that it was clear she had no relish of her marriage."

There was a murmur of agreement from the crowded benches: it had been plain to all. Alis saw she had fallen into a trap, and struggled not to lose heart. He was trying to discredit her, but he could not prove that she had killed her husband. William was speaking with the other Judges. He turned to Thomas and looked frowningly at him. The people hushed their muttering.

"Master Thomas—I hope that you have something more than insinuation to offer: it is an easy enough matter to suggest what may deprive a woman of her good name. And you have included the fire, a matter that has never been pursued and never tested. This you should not have done. Keep to matters of fact if you please, and come to the evidence."

Alis looked gratefully at William. His face had a brooding look as if he were not pleased with the way matters were progressing. Perhaps things were not so bad after all.

Thomas was apologizing. With Master William's permission he would call a witness who had something material to say. A nod.

Thomas went on smoothly; he seemed terrifyingly sure of himself. "I wish to take the testimony of the girl, Martha, who was servant to the Minister during his marriage."

There was a flurry from the benches and Martha came forward, smirking nervously, to stand at the lectern that was placed for the witnesses. One of the Judges spoke the words of the oath for her to repeat and she stumbled her way through them. Then Thomas said to her, "Martha, you were in the Minister's household from before his marriage, is that not so?"

She nodded.

"Tell the Judges what it was you told your mother when you came home from your work the day after the wedding ceremony."

Martha looked across at Alis and cleared her throat, but her first words were inaudible. Alis held her breath. Surely Martha could know nothing. William said quite gently, "Martha, you must speak so that we and all the people can hear you, otherwise justice cannot be done. What was it you told your mother?"

This time Martha's voice was loud enough and more. "There was no blood on the sheets."

There was a buzz from the crowd.

William stared at her. "What do you mean, there was no blood on the sheets? You have not been asked about the night of the death but about something you told your mother long before the Minister died. You must answer as you have been asked and if you have anything else to tell, there will be time for it later."

Martha looked frightened and Thomas intervened smoothly. "I think the Judge mistakes the girl's meaning. She is referring to the wedding sheets. Is that not so, Martha?"

Martha nodded and went on more confidently. "My mother told me I'd have to wash the wedding sheets the first day, to take the blood out. It was a sure sign that the marriage was sealed, she said. But there was no blood, and Mistress Alis, she'd lain in the little room at the back—the bed there was made up and I never did it—and the sheets were slept in, you could tell."

William was on his feet, his expression dark. "Why, Master Thomas, this is naught but the gossip of servant girls. You are ill advised to trifle with us, for if we find that you have brought this accusation falsely, your own life may be forfeit."

Alis's spirits soared. Thomas had nothing more against her and he had angered the Judges, too. Elzbet was right: he had overreached himself. But Thomas showed no sign of anxiety. He was apologizing once more. He would justify all, if the Judges would be patient. That the marriage was unconsummated was suggested, though not proved, by what had been said, and this had bearing on what they should hear next. He asked Martha to describe what had happened the day of Luke's visit. The girl was sure of herself now.

She threw Alis a triumphant look and embarked on her account. "The young man was come from Two Rivers to see the Minister, and Mistress Alis fainted. I thought she might be with child, for all that there was no sign that she and the Minister . . . Anyway, Minister Galin, he was called away. He wasn't minded to leave her alone but she would have none of it, saying that she was well again, and he must be about his work, for there was some trouble at Boundary Farm and the child Deborah was in the kitchen, crying. The young man'd gone into the garden to be out of the way, and then he came to the kitchen door to beg a word with the Minister's wife. My work was done and Mistress Alis told me to go home. But I hadn't hardly gone a little way when I remembered the elder-flower cordial—Mistress Alis knows my mother's very partial to it and had promised her some—so I went back to fetch it from the lean-to outside the kitchen door where 'tis kept. Mistress Alis and the young man were in the garden talking and I couldn't help hearing." She paused. "The young man reproached Mistress Alis for her marriage but she pleaded with him and said that she and the Minister never lay together."

There were exclamations of surprise from the people, and Martha paused. She was enjoying herself now. She would pay her mistress back for working her to the bone and threatening to carry tales to her mother!

"Then the young man asked her what she would do if the Minister wanted his rights of her, and she said . . ." Again Martha paused, savoring the sweetness of revenge. She could see Alis's white face. "She said she could use a knife and she'd kill him."

There was instant uproar. In vain William called for quiet, but he could not make himself heard above the noise. People were standing up and shouting out. Some were shaking their fists. Others were staring at Alis as if they could not believe what they had heard.

When at length order was restored, William stood before the crowd and rebuked them, his face black with anger. They must contain themselves. They were not savages. How could justice be secured in such conditions?

He waited as if to see whether anyone would defy him, but they were quiet again. He held them with his gaze for a moment and then turned to Alis. This accusation must be answered, he said. Had the witness spoken the truth? She stared at him desperately: he had been on her side briefly, it seemed. Now he must think her guilty, surely. She could not deny what she had said that day, for Martha had spoken near enough the truth. Swallowing, for her mouth was dry as fever, she said hoarsely, "It is true that I said I would kill my husband if he tried to force me. But he did not."

"Mistress Alis." William's voice rose above the crowd's shocked murmur, silencing it. "You have said that you came back of your own free will to marry Minister Galin. You must have expected to lie with him as married women do. Presumably your mother prepared you for what lay ahead. Did you plan to kill your husband on the wedding night, when he claimed his rights of you?"

She shook her head and William raised his eyebrows. In her mind, she saw again the wide bed with the good linen sheets. She must explain to him.

"I did not think about it beforehand but when . . . when I saw the marriage bed where we must lie together, then I thought . . . I could not. But straightaway he said he would not force me. I had no need to kill him. He was a good man, and no more wanted the marriage than I did. He married me out of obedience, because the Great Council sent the Bookseers and the Book named me, so it was the Maker's will, it seemed."

William looked skeptical. "A strange story. And a strange kind of obedience. For a marriage not sealed is no marriage, as I am sure you know, Mistress Alis, and yet you say Minister Galin married you in obedience to the Maker's will."

Thomas was smiling openly, and frightened though she was, Alis's loathing of him enabled her to speak firmly.

"Master Thomas means to have my life, I know. He hates me. But my husband and I lay apart by mutual agreement. And I did not kill him."

William regarded her coldly and then turned to Thomas. Had he finished with the witness? Thomas nodded. When William asked if she wanted to question Martha, Alis shook her head.

William stepped forward to address the people once more. Her terror rose. Was this the end? "People of Freeborne, we have heard the witnesses called by Master Thomas in this case. She who is accused has called none. If there is any here who knows anything that should be heard before judgment is considered, let him or her come forward now, lest there be error in this grave matter."

Alis held herself stiff against the shaking of her body, clenching her fists and pressing her lips together. Her eyes blurred with tears of fright she was determined not to shed. She must not break down; she must have courage to the end so that Thomas's triumph would not be complete. For a terrible moment she wished passionately that Edge had been caught. She did not look at the crowd crammed onto the benches. There was no one to speak for her.

But someone was moving down the aisle. Her vision still clouded, Alis could not at first make out the figure but as her sight cleared she saw that it was Mistress Elizabeth! Soberly dressed, upright as ever, her gray hair coiled neatly at the nape of the neck. She caught Alis's eye and smiled briefly at her. The girl felt her heart lift. Surely all could not be ill, if Mistress Elizabeth was come.

William was evidently surprised. "Mistress Elizabeth of Two Rivers, is it not? Do you have something you wish to say?"

Elizabeth inclined her head and then smiled at William. "Master William, I crave the Judges' indulgence. I have a young woman from my Community with me whose story should be heard before judgment is given."

William looked at her in silence and she returned his gaze steadily. At length he said slowly, "You have an interest in the matter tried here, do you not? Your grandson Luke has been mentioned somewhat."

Elizabeth's calm expression did not alter. "That is not why I am come. I beg that you will give permission for this witness to testify."

"If her testimony bears upon the death of the Minister Galin, we will do so."

Elizabeth looked for the first time at Thomas, and then back at

William. Her voice was even. "It is not evidence in that matter but it bears upon the trustworthiness of the accuser, and surely that is of moment in so grave a case."

For a long moment William was still. Then he nodded. "Let the young woman take the oath."

26

Alis was trembling in every limb. Could it be Edge come to save her despite what Mistress Elizabeth had said? But it was not Edge who came swiftly down between the benches, clutching a tiny, wailing bundle. It was a girl with lank brown hair and a sallow, bitter face: Lilith. Alis heard Thomas's sharp intake of breath, and then Lilith had reached the Elders' table and was confronting the Judges. Her voice was high and angry.

"Let me take the oath."

William said sharply, "Young woman, Mistress Elizabeth vouches for you but beware: a person is on trial for her life here. If you have something to say in the matter, you shall take the oath and say it. If not, get you gone. We do not deal in petty grievances. You must take those to your Elders."

Lilith laughed shrilly and the baby, which had fallen silent, set up again its feeble cry. The girl crushed it to her fiercely, saying at the same time, "I cannot go to my Elders for it is one of them who has sinned against me and that one is here today." She turned abruptly and flung out a hand toward Thomas.

He had recovered from his surprise and put on his blandest look. "Master William, I must beg pardon for this intrusion. This is a former servant of mine, whom I was forced to dismiss. No doubt she seeks—"

Furiously she interrupted him. "It is a wicked lie." Turning to William, she said, "He bears witness against the Minister's wife for the death of her husband, does he not?"

William nodded. "It is true. Do you have anything to tell us of the matter?"

She tossed her hair back out of her eyes and gave Alis a savage look. "I know nothing of that and I care nothing for her."

"Then?"

"But I tell you *he* is a liar and worse. His word cannot be taken. I would not save her but I would bring him down, for he has set my life at naught. I can come by no work now through his doing, and yet he would have left me to beg rather than raise his hand to help me, though my trouble is all of his making."

She was panting in her rage and Thomas stepped forward speaking calmly, though his face was pinched and pale suddenly. "Come, girl, this is no place for such displays. We have solemn business to conduct. Go and wait. When I am done here I will come to you, and if you are in need, I will relieve you."

He went to take her by the arm but she hissed at him with such ferocity that he froze in the act. "Do not touch me. You would have left me to starve, me and my baby. I tell you that it is your child and you must support us both."

At once a great babble broke out. Alis was forgotten briefly, for here was new wonder. When he could make himself heard at last, William said to her, "You shall speak no further until you have taken the oath. Come now."

When it was done, he spoke again. "You say that Master Thomas is the father of your babe. It is easy to claim and hard to prove, the fathering of a child. Have you any tokens of his knowing you, or any witness to say that he showed you such favor as men do in these instances?"

Thomas broke in scornfully. "She is lying. I dismissed her because she was sluttish in her behavior and I would not have such a one in the house who—"

William's voice cut in coldly. "Let the girl answer the question. You will have your chance to speak by and by."

Thomas flushed and then the color receded, leaving him paler than before. Lilith was looking at him oddly. "I need no tokens and no witness. The child is his."

William said patiently, "It is hard, I know, for a woman in such a case but there must be proof."

To Alis's amazement, Lilith smiled, saying to William, "You are the Judge. Will it serve for proof if his wife herself says the child is his?"

There were exclamations of surprise from the listeners. William looked at her with narrowed eyes. "What trick is this? No wife would do such a thing unless she meant to be free of her husband, and if such were the case her word would mean nothing. This will not do."

Lilith was calm now, and she was not dismayed by the Judge's answer. "Will you let me show her my baby and hear what she says? Then you will have proof to satisfy you, I promise."

The hall was utterly silent, awaiting his answer. Finally he nodded. Thomas was on his feet at once. "Master William, I must protest. My wife is in poor health."

The Judge looked at him a moment and he subsided. "Accusations must be put to the test surely, Master Thomas? That is why we are here today. Let your wife come up."

Sarah was helped to her feet by the women beside her, and one of them took her arm to assist her onto the dais. At William's command a chair was brought for her. Alis could see that she could barely stand unsupported. Her frightened eyes sought her husband's: his look was murderous.

When she was seated, William said to Lilith, "Now show Mistress Sarah the child and let us have your proof, if such it be."

Lilith knelt down by Sarah and placed the baby in her lap. Then she began to unwind the wrappings about the upper part of its body. Alis's view of the child was blocked by Lilith's kneeling figure. The people were so still they seemed scarcely to be breathing. Suddenly, Sarah gave a great cry and stood up. The child slid from her lap and Lilith hardly caught it before it fell. Sarah turned to face her husband, howling at him, "It *is* yours! It *is* yours! Liar! Adulterer! What have you done?"

Thomas started forward with his fist raised but William was there, blocking his path. Lilith was standing before the crowd holding up the child. Even those at the back could see the rough crescent of purple that marked the skin on the left side of the chest. Everyone was speaking at once and Sarah had collapsed; one of the women was bending over her. William struggled to silence the noise until once more the baby's thin cry was audible. Then he spoke to Sarah and she looked up at him, her face already blotched with tears.

"Mistress Sarah, do you say that the child is your husband's?"

She did not answer. He repeated his question, adding gently, "I beg you, Mistress Sarah, to give us your answer. Your husband has laid a serious accusation against another person. If his honesty is in question, we must know of it."

She made an effort to suppress her sobs and said clearly enough, "The child is his. He has such a mark also. It is just the same." And she bowed her head once more and wept.

Then Thomas spoke. His voice was angry but he had himself under control again. "I admit that the child is mine. I was tempted and I fell. But that does not change anything. Have you forgotten the great matter that we came here to prove? The Minister of Freeborne was murdered, and his wife murdered him. She must hang for it."

Lilith had swaddled the baby anew, and now she broke in, "I daresay she did murder her husband—she wanted Master Luke for her own and he wanted her. And I do not care if she hangs: I hate her. But if I was a great Judge, I would not trust the word of Master Thomas. He meant her harm because she went to Mistress Elizabeth's house and took her side."

At this, the third Judge, who had not yet spoken, moved abruptly in his seat. "Be mindful of what you say, girl. To mean harm is not to do it. We must have only facts here."

Lilith's expression grew darker. "He meant her harm, I say. I told him it was the mad woman, Iri—whose man was whipped and cast out—that fired our prayer house that night. I saw her at the doorway with her tinderbox. The girl Alis had gone in before. The next day Alis was missing, and Master Luke quarreled with me, saying that Master Thomas had accused her of the fire because of me. He hated me, he said, and would have no more to do with me."

She rubbed her sleeve across her eyes and her voice was flat with despair. "I did not care what happened to me after that, so I let Master Thomas do what he wanted, which I had always refused before." She broke off as if it were beyond bearing.

William was looking at her compassionately. "You say you let him. He did not force you then?"

She hesitated, and Alis saw Thomas clench his fists. Then Lilith said wearily, "I thought to please him. There was none else to care for me."

William said quietly, "What did you do when you knew you were with child?"

Lilith shot a poisonous look at Thomas. "I was afraid to tell him, for I knew he would say it was not his. But soon I could not hide the swelling of my belly anymore and he turned me out, and I found that he had given me a bad name everywhere. I thought Mistress Elizabeth might aid me, though she and the Minister were gone from their house to Mistress Ellen's farm. So I went there and Mistress Ellen said I could bide with the old dairy wife in her cottage. I was to have bed and board, and help with the child's coming, too, if I would serve the old woman while I was able."

William turned to Mistress Elizabeth, saying courteously, "You will confirm all this, Mistress Elizabeth."

Before she could answer, Thomas interjected angrily, "Mistress Elizabeth is not under oath."

William gave him a look of such scorn that he flinched for all his boldness. But Elizabeth got stiffly to her feet saying, "Let me take the oath, Master William, then there can be no doubt in the matter."

She came up on the dais and it was soon done. William ordered that a chair be brought for her. Alis was comforted to have her so near.

When she was seated, William said to her, "Now Mistress Elizabeth, will you confirm that this girl, Lilith, has spoken the truth?"

She nodded. "Yes indeed. She came to the farm and was taken in, as she says."

"And did she tell you all that she has told us here?"

Elizabeth glanced at Lilith. "Not at first, for she was very fearful, but when she knew we would listen with open hearts, then she spoke freely."

"Did you believe her?"

Elizabeth met Thomas's black look steadily. "I did."

William's face was thoughtful. "Why did you not raise this matter in your own Community? A sinning Elder is not above the rule of the Book."

"We had no voice in Two Rivers anymore, my husband and I. Soon afterward, we left there, for we were almost in fear for our lives. And even had it not been so, how could it be proven that the child in her belly was his? Or even that he had lain with her? Only later, when the babe was born with the mark upon it, could the truth be seen."

William turned back to Lilith. "Did you have any further dealings with Master Thomas? Or do you know anything more that bears upon the matter tried here?"

The girl nodded reluctantly. "The Minister and Mistress Elizabeth were gone away, and Mistress Ellen went with them to care for the Minister on the journey because he was so sick. I stayed with the old woman, as I told you. But she did not need me all the time and the child was restless within me, so I would walk about the farm for ease of my pains. One day, I saw her—Alis. She was on the back porch of the farmhouse and I knew what she had come for."

She stopped but Elizabeth said gently, "Remember Lilith, only the truth."

The girl's mouth twisted in a bitter line but she went on. "She thought I did not know her, but I knew her well enough and what she wanted, so I told her Master Luke had died and she went away again."

The third Judge leaned forward as if he would intervene again, but William gestured to him to remain silent and Lilith continued.

"Later, when I was near my time, Master Luke came back, saying he had been to Freeborne. *His* Alis"—she spat out the words venomously—"had married the Minister there because of my lie, and now they would never be together, him and her. He was so angry, I was afraid of him. I told Master Thomas about it, for I thought to win his favor again."

"You returned to Master Thomas?" William's voice was sharp with disbelief.

Lilith nodded. "He hated her. I knew he would be glad to hear ill of her. And so I thought he might take me back, and my child would not be fatherless."

There was a murmur from the crowd, and William said, "Yet he did not take you back. How was it then?"

Once more, Lilith gave Thomas a savage look. "He seemed pleased at what I told him. He walked up and down, and bid me be silent that he might think. Then he said he would go to Freeborne. I begged him to take me also, and our child when it should come, but he grew angry and turned me away as he had before, saying he would have me whipped and driven out. He did not care if we starved."

There was silence for a moment. Then a voice from the crowd, a woman's voice, shouted, "Hang him," and the cry was taken up by others. But William was ready for them, threatening that he would send away those who called out, and they were quiet again.

William was looking coldly at Thomas. "Well, Master Thomas. Will you deny any of this?"

Thomas gave no answer and William went on. "It seems you are an adulterer and a liar. You would deny the child that you have fathered and let its mother beg for bread. You accused Mistress Alis of setting fire to the prayer house in Two Rivers, though this young woman had told you of the mad wife with the tinderbox. What else have you done, I wonder, in your desire to bring Mistress Alis down?"

There was a sullen ferocity in Thomas's expression that was fearful to see; the dark handsome face was ugly with hate. When he spoke it was with no pretense at politeness. His voice was low and savage.

"Whatever I have done, the case against Mistress Alis stands. No one knows how far it had gone between her and the boy Luke, but she withheld from Minister Galin his rights as a husband. She admits she threatened to kill him with a knife, and he was attacked with a knife. She delayed in sending for the Healers, and the delay helped him to his death. Try me for my sins if you will, but let her hang first."

Alis held her breath. He would not give up even now. He meant for her to die. And he was right, too, that the case against her was unaltered by what had been revealed. She looked at Mistress Elizabeth, but she was watching William with an anxious face.

He looked sternly at Thomas. "Master Thomas, you will hold yourself at our disposal. This matter of the girl and her child must be attended to, and there is the accusation of fire-setting to be gone into also." He turned to Alis. "Mistress Alis, is there anything else you wish to say? If there is something you have forgotten, something that you might add to your testimony, you must speak now, before it is too late. Bethink you. We will give you time."

She stared at him. It was as if he willed her to speak. But there was nothing she could say without betraying Edge, and that she would not do. She shook her head.

He frowned, and when he spoke it was clear he was both troubled and angry. "The Judges will consult together before judgment is given. But I tell you, I do not like the way this matter has gone. I would have the truth, and I do not think we have heard it."

Perhaps he spoke of Thomas when he said this, but he looked at Alis and she quailed before his look.

❖   ❖   ❖

The Judges withdrew and Alis was taken to a room behind the hall where she must wait until they were ready to give judgment. She could not control her trembling. It was some comfort to know that Mistress Elizabeth was nearby, and Lilith's story had shown Thomas for a sinner and a liar. But surely he had defeated her all the same and she would hang.

The woman from the inn was on guard outside the door, and Master Aaron sat with her. Sick with terror, she asked him if Elzbet might come and be with her, and her parents. He said he would fetch them and went out, locking the door behind him.

They all came together. Her mother was stiff and white-faced; her father looked at Alis so sorrowfully that her courage failed her, and she wept. She did not want to die, and she was afraid. Why could they not save her? They soothed her as best they could, and though they could not take away the fear of death, their love comforted her. She thought her mother struggled to conceal her horror, and feared Hannah thought her guilty after all, though she spoke comfort to her daughter, telling her that all was not lost. She must trust the Maker. They would all pray for His help.

Time passed. Food and drink was brought. Elzbet went away to tend to the baby and came back again. The Judges were still deliberating. Her parents sat, one on each side of her. Alis rested her head on her father's shoulder, and her mother held her hand, stroking it gently from time to time. They did not speak much. Once she said, "I did not kill him, I promise you."

And her father replied, "Of course not. Your mother and I know that well."

He sounded faintly surprised that she should feel the need to say it, and her mother nodded. Alis was comforted a little.

The sky outside darkened and still there was no word. Then suddenly the door opened and she jumped. Was the time come? But it was Master William. His expression was dark, though he spoke courteously enough, asking her parents and Elzbet to leave so that he might have a few words alone with Alis.

When they were gone, William gestured to her to be seated. He did not speak at once but went over to the window and stood there with his back to her. Heart beating and mouth dry, Alis waited.

At last, he turned and looked at her. His face was in shadow and his voice somber. "Mistress Alis, your time runs short. Do you still say that you are innocent?"

She could not speak, but she nodded her head.

He went on as if she had not responded. "If you must hang, it would be better to confess yourself first, rather than be cast into darkness. The Maker is merciful."

She understood him: he wanted to be sure. It made her angry, and that gave her strength to speak. "Master William, I know that you would have my word, that you might hang me with a clear conscience, but I tell you, I did not attack my husband nor did I do anything to bring him to his death. And if the Maker is merciful He will not cast me into darkness, for He must know the truth even if you do not."

His lips tightened. "If I do not, it is because you will not tell me."

Was it not enough that she must be condemned in a few hours? Why was he tormenting her? Angrily she said, "Would you have me lie? I have told you that I did not kill my husband."

For a moment he was silent, then he said very softly, "But you know who did."

She gasped in shock.

"Mistress Alis . . ."

Her head was spinning. He knew! Edge's name was on her lips. She could save herself. She heard her voice cry out to him, "Go! Go! I will tell you nothing."

Giddiness overcame her and she slid from her chair.

When she came round he was gone, and she was lying on the floor. The woman who guarded her was kneeling over her, splashing her face with water from a bucket. Alis sat up wearily. She felt empty— tired to her bones.

It was dark now and someone came to light a lamp. Then they sent for her.

The people were talking softly among themselves when Alis was brought back in but they ceased at once and a terrible silence fell. Then the door behind the Elders' table opened and the three Judges entered to take their places. William did not sit down. He was not a tall man, but to Alis he seemed immense as he stood there, not looking at her but directing his gaze at the people massed on the benches. He began to speak.

"People of the Community of Freeborne, we have considered all that had been said and it is clear to us that the evidence is heavy against the accused. Her own account is in all respects unsatisfactory and there is nothing to support it. We have no choice therefore but to pass sentence of death upon her."

There was a gasp from the crowd. Alis felt herself go dizzy. She gripped the edge of the table. Master William was still speaking.

"Nevertheless, I am not satisfied with these proceedings. Her accuser is her enemy and not one whose word is to be trusted. And though it is true that the accused herself has confirmed much that points to her guilt, she continues to declare her innocence. So this much I will do. I will have the hanging delayed and we will institute further searches for the man who is supposed to have committed the crime. If at the end of two months he is not found—the sentence will be carried out."

27

Still confined to the prison room in the guesthouse, Alis waited, swinging between terrified despair and irrational hope. Although the weather grew chilly, she insisted on the shutters being open at all times. If they were closed she thought she would choke to death, so trapped did she feel. The window looked out on a lane that led to one of the farms. She watched the scene for hours, though there was little enough to see, only a farm cart, and the people coming and going. They never looked up.

Sometimes she tried to pray but she felt that her words disappeared into a void.

She was allowed some visitors: her father and mother; Elzbet with the baby. Mistress Elizabeth had gone back to Two Rivers with Lilith, but she had come every day until her departure, putting aside her grief for her husband, whose frail heart had given out at last. She blamed herself for letting Alis stay in her household and bringing

Thomas's wrath upon her. She had not thought him so far gone in wickedness.

Minister Seth spent time with her also, doing his spiritual duty. Close up, the skin of his face and scalp looked scorched; it flaked and peeled as though he had been too long in the sun. He meant well, no doubt, speaking to her of the Maker's mercy, trying to ease her terror of dying. But Alis saw that he thought her guilty and that he hoped for a confession, so she closed her mind to all he said.

Luke, she knew from his grandmother, had returned to Ellen's. He was helping on the farm, for two of her men had gone elsewhere, frightened away by her willingness to stand up to the Elders. Alis longed to see him, but of course she could not. She must not even mention him, for it might confirm the suspicion that she had sought her husband's death so that she could be with another man.

In the midst of it all, Alis's parents brought the news that Joel had returned to Freeborne. He was very sick they said, and not fit to visit her. She tried to be glad for their sakes, but Joel's homecoming did not seem real to her. Fear was her only reality now.

She found herself wishing that Edge would be caught. Then she was horrified and tried to stifle the thought, but it would not go away. It was *not* right that she should die for another's crime. Afterward she wept for her wickedness in wishing evil on Edge, who had meant no harm to Galin, and who had been her friend. It was no wonder the Maker did not hear her prayers. But she was so afraid of dying.

Then Master William sent for her.

◈ ◈ ◈

When she entered the room, he was seated at a table. On the dark polished surface lay a rolled-up document whose seal was broken. To the right, Minister Seth sat with paper, ink, and a pen before him.

The Judge looked up as she came in. An empty chair faced him and he motioned her to sit. She had not seen him since the day of the verdict. His gray hair had been recently cropped, and his dark face was as stern as ever. He looked at her in silence. Finally he said, "Well, Mistress Alis, I have some news for you." He tapped the document sharply with his forefinger. "We know who attacked your husband."

The blood pulsed in her head. Surely Edge had not been caught. Hope, treacherous but irresistible, sprang to life. He picked up the document and unrolled it.

"There has been a series of thefts on farms many miles to the south. And one unfortunate man who tried to protect his property has a nasty wound in the forearm for his trouble. According to this report, the assailant evaded the farmer's attempt to detain her by slashing at him with a knife that she carried in her hand."

He looked again at the document. "She said, it is claimed here: *I did for the Minister in Freeborne and I'll do for you if you don't get out of the way.* She goes by the name of Edge, it seems—a city girl—and she had in her possession a shawl stitched in the Freeborne pattern."

Alis felt herself go cold. The shawl was hers; she had given it to Edge that night. Fearfully she said, "She has been caught then?"

William frowned. "Unfortunately not."

She willed herself to keep still, not to show relief. He looked at her and said in a voice edged with anger, "And now, Mistress Alis, I will tell you what I think. I think that you knew this girl, that you kept silent to shield her, and that in doing so you condemned your husband to death."

"No!" She almost shouted it. "That is not how it was."

His expression was hard. "Then you had better tell me how it was."

She did not speak. He leaned forward. The light from the window fell upon his face and the pupils of his eyes were tiny slits. Softly he said, "Would you not like to be free? To walk under the sky again, and feel the fresh breeze on your face?"

She turned her head away. She had meant to be like stone before him, but the shameful tears ran down her cheeks. It was cruel of him to torture her so.

When she did not speak he added in a sharper tone, "Do you mean to hang, Mistress? Will you dangle at the end of a rope rather than break your silence? I must know the truth of what happened that night."

She said angrily, feeling the wetness on her face, "Why must you know any more than you do already?"

His voice was tight with anger. "Because I must decide what is to be done with you. And if you will not confess your part in this, I must hang you, however little I wish to. Can you not understand that?"

She was trembling. Perhaps it was a trap. But she would die if she did not speak, and it could make no difference to Edge, who was condemned out of her own mouth.

So, fearfully, she told him how it had been. She said that Edge was someone she had known in her time away, come to say good-bye because she was going over the sea. That she had lashed out in fright, thinking herself attacked. They had tried together to staunch the bleeding of the terrible wound, and Galin had said Edge must be given clothing, money, and time to get away.

When she ceased speaking, William said to her, "There is one thing that puzzles me still. Why should Minster Galin put his life in jeopardy for a girl he did not know and who had so savagely attacked him? I cannot credit it. Did you plead for her because she was your friend?"

"No. I was afraid for him. I did not want him to die. It was terrible." She shuddered, remembering the dreadful gaping wound and how the blood had oozed through the dressings in spite of their efforts. "But he would not let me go for help. He said he had blighted my life and he would not do it to another. He knew she would hang if they caught her."

William frowned. "What did he mean, that he had blighted your life?"

She paused, unsure whether he would believe her, or whether it was safe to speak the words.

"Well?" He sounded impatient.

Nervously she said, "He meant by marrying me. He said it had been wrong."

She held her breath. To voice such a view was to defy the Great Council's edicts. There was a sardonic expression on William's dark face. "I can well imagine that Minister Galin thought so. He was ever a rebel."

Minister Seth's pen was scratching away. William waited until he was done and had sanded the page to dry it. Then he said to Alis,

"You must read this, and if it is a true record of what you have said, you must sign it."

She took it in her hand but the words blurred before her eyes. She said huskily, "I cannot read it."

William took it from her and handed it back to the other man. "Read it aloud, if you please."

When he had finished, William said to her, "You accept this?"

She nodded. He motioned her to take the pen that the Minister had prepared for her, and placed his finger at the foot of the page to show her where she should sign. Then he signed it also and Minister Seth added his name as witness. The Minister went out, leaving Alis alone with William.

She tried to still her trembling. She did not know whether she was saved or not, but she would not weep and plead. She watched him in silence. He stood by the window looking out for a long time. When he turned to her there was a brooding expression on his face.

"Well, Mistress Alis. You have done ill, there is no doubt of that. I do not know that you deserve your life."

He stopped and frowned, as if he were still in doubt. She pressed her hands together. Would he never speak? When at last he did, his voice was somber. "We cannot have such as you among us, but—you may thank the Maker for His mercy, sinner that you are—I will not hang you."

28

She was not to hang but she must leave Freeborne and make a life for herself in the world somehow. There was no place for her in the Communities of the Book. And she did not care. She was angry. They had made her suffer; they had brought her almost to death. Why should she want to stay? There was Elzbet, of course. And it grieved her to bring more sorrow on her parents, but Joel had come back to them. She comforted herself with that.

He had reappeared in Freeborne one cold day—shivering, ragged, and hungry—seeming not to know where he had been or how he had survived in the months since his parting from Edge. At first he complained of headaches and said his memory failed him, but their mother, who had given up her position as an Elder, cared for him devotedly, and he recovered, though he seemed to Alis a changed person. He would not speak of his former life, and what he felt about Edge's part in his sister's troubles she could not tell. When he was well again, he went to work alongside his father in the carpenter's shop, learning the trade. He seemed content.

A week was all she was given, and then she must leave. Her parents, though sorrowful at the prospect of parting, rejoiced that Alis was to live and exercised themselves to think how she might find work and safety. They knew little of life outside the Communities, and she did not contradict them when they made foolish suggestions. She had survived everything, and she was not afraid. She would go back to Will and Jessie. Even if they had no work for her they might know of someone among the local farmers who wanted help in the household. Then she would write to Ellen with word for Luke. She could not ask him to abandon his grandmother, but he must be told her plans, or how would they ever see each other again? She would not let herself think it might never be.

The day approached. Her father's face grew still more melancholy and she tried to comfort him. "I will send to you when I am settled. You shall hear all that I am doing. And you have Joel back, which you did not dream of."

"But we will miss you so, Alis. And perhaps you will marry again, and we shall not be able see our grandchildren."

There was nothing she could say to that. She put her arm around his shoulder and rested her cheek against his.

Her mother, too, though delighting in Joel's return, mourned her daughter's coming departure. "If only that wicked girl had not come here!" Hannah said bitterly. Edge's guilt had been proclaimed in the prayer house upon Alis's release.

Alis swallowed down an angry answer, saying instead, "Then

perhaps Joel would not have found his way back here. It is thanks to her that he was in these parts."

Hannah sighed. "Yes, that is true. And I cannot be sorry to have my son back. But"—her expression darkened—"she killed Galin. I cannot forgive her for that. And you would never have been tried if she had not done it."

Alis had struggled not to reproach her mother but she could not help herself. It seemed so unfair to blame all on Edge. "If you had not married me to him, it would not have happened at all."

Hannah blanched, her face tightening with pain. "Alis, we sought to do the Maker's will as we are bound to do."

"Galin did not think it was the Maker's will. He told me so at the end. He was sorry."

She wanted to say that her mother should be sorry, too, but the words would not come. Hannah abandoned the dishes she was washing and sat down at the table.

"I know it. And perhaps he was right. We . . . spoke of it once, not long before he died, but it was too late then." She looked up at her daughter. "You cannot understand. We were brought up—as I tried to bring you up—to put aside ourselves, our own selfish desires, and do only our duty: the will of the Maker. And sometimes that is very hard. You are my child whom I love, and Galin was my dear friend. Do you think I wished you married to each other when neither of you wanted it?"

Cold light from the opened shutter fell upon her features. The skin of her face had slackened, worn thin. She looked old and tired. Full of remorse, Alis sat down also, saying, "I know you did not. But why should it have been the Maker's will, Mother? What did it do but bring suffering upon us all? I cannot understand it."

Hannah did not reply at once, and then she straightened her back, saying in the familiar tone that brooked no further argument, "I do not know. But there is no virtue in doing what is easy. We must trust that there is purpose in what seems so cruel."

It was the old answer. Alis looked at Hannah's hands resting on the table, noticing for the first time the way the veins stood out on the weathered skin. Her mother would never change.

The last day. Elzbet and Martin defied the rules and came to visit, bringing with them a purse of money collected secretly after Alis's expulsion had been announced.

"My mother arranged it," Elzbet said. "She knew there were some people who would wish to help you."

When it was time to part, the two girls clung to each other.

"You will send word, won't you, Alis?" Elzbet said through her tears. "Perhaps we will join you one day. I should like to bring my children up where there is more freedom."

It was a comforting thought.

Morning. It was not yet fully light; the mist lay thick in the fields and hid the further houses from view. Her father's old mare—hers now—was waiting, harnessed to the cart. At the door of the house, she embraced her parents for the last time, holding back her tears as best she could. Then Joel lifted her box into the cart and she got onto the cross-seat. She took up the reins, clicked her tongue at the horse, and the cart began to move. When she looked back, the stand-ing figures were already becoming hazy. Soon, they were quite gone.

The mist enclosed her. There was nothing but the rattle of the cart's wheels and the soft fall of the mare's hooves on the road. She and the horse might have been the only living things in the world. She let her tears flow freely as they plodded along. Once, she halted, unable to bear it: she would go back, speak to them all again, have a few more minutes with them. Yes, she would do it! She began to pull the horse round.

And stopped. It was no good. Her heart ached to think how long it would be before she could see any of them again, but if ever she did, it could not be in Freeborne. Well, she would not despair. She must make a new life for herself, and she would. Her courage rose, and on she went.

The mist was clearing and she could see the boundary signpost, with its wooden finger pointing the way to the settlement. Beside it stood a figure, roughly dressed, with a bundle and stick. She thought it must be one of the wandering laborers who worked on the farms in the busy seasons. They sometimes came begging in winter and could be threatening, but she had barely time to feel nervous when a familiar voice called her name.

Her heart seemed to stop. It was Luke! He stood before her, thin and unshaven, shaking the moisture from his hair. While she sat there stunned, he swung himself up into the cart saying, "Quickly! Let us go. We must not be seen together so near to Freeborne."

Caught between joy and terror, she obeyed at once, urging the mare into a fast trot.

Alis could not believe that Luke was there, solid beside her in a farmer's jacket, his boots wet with dew. If only she could stop and embrace him. She put her arm through his, drawing close to him. She could barely keep her eye on the road while questions tumbled over themselves in her mind.

"But Luke, how is it that you are here? What are you doing? Does Mistress Elizabeth know?"

He shook his head. He had not seen his grandmother for many weeks, not since she left Two Rivers for Freeborne, hoping to make Thomas acknowledge his sin with Lilith and offer some support for the child.

"She had only been gone a few days when news arrived of your husband's death. Oh, Alis, I was afraid for you. I thought perhaps he had demanded his rights of you and that you had"—he hesitated— "defended yourself as you said you might. I set off at once and came as quickly as I could but I had to walk, for Ellen could not spare a horse and there was no one else to ask. As I got near to Freeborne, I learned that you had been tried for killing your husband and might hang." He shuddered. "Everyone was talking of it, and how your servant girl had listened to our conversation that day. I came into Freeborne—"

"But Luke!" She was horrified. "Someone might have recognized you."

He shrugged. "I had to take the risk, to see where you were locked up. I did not care that you were well guarded—I would have found a way to get you out. But it was said that Master William believed in your innocence and would not hang you if your husband's attacker could be found. I did not want to bring further suspicion on you and endanger you when you might, perhaps, be safe after all."

"Dear Luke. I wish I had known that you were close by. It would have been a comfort even if—"

He said firmly, "I would have saved you."

She did not see how, but she did not wish to hurt his feelings, so she said, "What would you have done?"

He was silent for a while, then he said quietly, "I would have gone to Master William and told him that it was I who had attacked your husband. I would have died myself, rather than let you hang."

She gave a gasp of horror and clung closer to him. He said with a note of triumph in his voice, "He would have believed me, I am sure. Who had better reason than I did? And it fit with what that girl said."

Appalled, she stopped him. "Don't, Luke! It's too horrible to think of."

"I meant to do it, but the very day I came into Freeborne, there was news that some girl had been accused in your place and you were to be cast out instead of being hanged."

"What did you do then?"

"I went to see your friend, Elzbet. You'd told her our story, I knew. It was a task to convince her who I was at first. She hid me until yesterday, so that I might know which way you were going and join you on the road."

"But she said nothing," Alis cried. "Not even when we were saying good-bye. Why did she not tell me?"

"She meant to, if she could speak to you alone. But not if there was anyone else there, for fear that you would exclaim and give yourself away. She was not sure about your mother, whether she would think she must stop me."

"I do not think she would have interfered," Alis said slowly. "But she is fierce for right, even when she must sacrifice those she loves. Perhaps it was best."

Her heart was heavy at the thought of her mother. She leaned against him and was silent.

After a while, he said gently, "Do not be sad, Alis. We are together now and we thought it could never be."

She smiled at him. "I am happy, truly. But I wish I had not brought so much trouble and sorrow to others—Galin, my parents, and there was poor Ethan, too, who was so good to us. I wish I knew what had happened to him."

"Well, I can tell you that," Luke said. "He came back to Two Rivers only a little before I left, and I spoke with him. He had stayed in the city, working there, searching, and hoping to hear word of you. But at last he gave up and went back to his old trade. He was very thankful to know that you were alive. He blamed himself for what had happened."

"Oh, Luke! I am so glad to have news of him. It has grieved me always that he had been hurt because of me. I feared he might have died of his injury."

She felt that a burden had been lifted from her.

The mist was gone and they could see the newly plowed fields with the crows stalking the furrows. At midday they stopped to share the food that Hannah had packed for her daughter only that morning.

Luke ate hungrily. She watched him with pleasure, noting the curve of his cheek and the glossiness of his dark hair, longer now than when she had first known him. How beautiful he was. She reached out to stroke his arm, feeling the hard muscle under his shirt. Then she took his hand. "Luke, when you heard that I had been found guilty, did you think I had killed my husband?"

He said slowly, "I was not sure, but I did not think so. I thought that if you had done it, you would have said so."

"And if I had—killed Galin, I mean—what would you have felt?"

"That you had been driven to it. And that I would rather you had killed him than let him lie with you. He had no right."

She stroked his hand. "You would not have turned away from me because of it? You are sure?"

He gripped both her hands. "Of course, I am sure. I am glad you did not kill your husband, but it would have made no difference. Alis, you must believe me."

"What about your grandmother? How can you leave her?"

"She will understand, I hope. When my grandfather died, she said to me that I must make my own life and not be tied to her. And the people we stayed with when my grandfather was ill, Ellen's friends, they wanted her to make her home with them. When I can, I will send word to her and tell her all."

She put her arms around him and held him tightly. Then they harnessed the mare again and set off. Mist was already gathering in the hollows and the air was colder. They must look out for a place to sleep that night, and very soon they would have to find somewhere to live for the winter if they were not to freeze or starve to death. But she was full of joy: they could choose their way together, and they would not be parted again.